MATA SARA

MATASARA
(CROOKED EYES)

A novel

By Regis Tove Stella

UPNG PRESS AND BOOKSHOP, 2010

Mata Sara (Crooked Eyes)

Author: Regis Tove Stella
© Copyright 2010

ISBN: 9980-939-68-0

Published by:
UPNG Press and Bookshop

Dedication

**For Maria Nogo who gave so much but
received very little in return.**

Chapter 1

I suddenly felt like my spirit has left my body as the announcement from the cockpit heralded our imminent landing. It was like floating in thin air. I felt like my whole body was going into spasm. The palms of my hands began sweating. I stood up and hurriedly went to use the toilet at the rear of the plane. I could feel the plane descending and it made my legs feel wobbly. I had to steady myself a couple of times. I wanted to pee but it just wasn't coming so after several attempts I came out and went back to my seat. My breathing became heavier and the sweating on my palms continued. I tried looking out the window but the city was covered in thick clouds. I turned nervously and looked back only to see passengers in mixed emotions getting ready to disembark. I fastened my seatbelt and took several deep breaths just to calm my nerves. I checked my passport and the other forms; they were safe in my pocket. I wondered what awaited me here in this new place.

✳✳✳

It was one of those hot summer days when I landed in Sydney. This was not my first time to this big city but what was eventful about this arrival was that I was going to stay here for a long time; longer than the 12 months I first stayed in this country. I was not sure whether my shift to this new place was a forced removal from the place I called home or was one of those journeys that one embarks on as part of one's professional life? What I was sure about was that I was here temporarily until my wounds were healed. Getting the scholarship was my opportunity to get away from everything that I reviled.

I had made arrangements with a *dimdim* (white) woman, Kate who used to teach at the university back home. A former colleague of hers emailed her earlier and asked her if she could wait for me at the airport and also try to find me a place to stay, somewhere closer to the varsity. She willingly obliged and we started to contact each other via email and telephone. She did not reveal much about herself throughout our brief contact. So I did not have much indication of whom I was meeting at the airport. The general information I had about her was from her former colleague who told me that Kate spent her childhood in PNG and that she returned again to teach at the university for four years before she finally left for good.

She had been waiting for about 30 minutes before the flight from Port Moresby was finally announced. I didn't have much luggage and I was one of the first passengers to come out of customs. As soon as I came out to the airport arrival lobby I was confronted by hundreds of eyes, people waiting for their friends and relatives. "I hope Kate is waiting," I thought to myself. I looked around for her but couldn't find her anywhere. I continued to wait. Then I began to panic. I stood there, not exactly knowing what to do or where to go next. After what seemed hours, I heard someone calling my name. When I turned around there she was standing, waving her hand, all smiles! What caught my immediate attention was that she didn't really look like a pure *dimdim*. She looked more Polynesian and she wore a blouse and a *lavalava*, which made her appear peculiar. I thought she looked out of place with her dressing but then again this was a cosmopolitan city and people were entitled to how they dressed.

"Welcome to Sydney," she greeted me, hugging me at the same time. I felt the warmth of her body. I felt good and excited by her feminine touch and affection but I had to break away from her quickly as I could see eyes staring at us from all directions. She let go and looked me up and down for a while before she spoke: "at last we have met in person," and she hugged me again at the same time looking me up and down with a look that could melt any man. I only nodded my head, feeling a little embarrassed and uncomfortable. Then she asked me to follow her. Perhaps sensing that I was rather quiet she asked, "Are you okay?"

"Yes, I am fine," I said rather softly.

"Is that all you've got?"

"Yeah."

"Alright, let's go then; I parked the car over there." I pushed the trolley, following her. We crossed the street to the main car park. There were lots of people and I couldn't believe that Sydney was this big. "How was the flight?" she tried to make conversation with me.

"Pretty smooth."

"How come and the plane was late?" she continued.

"Ask the pilot," I said almost annoyed.

She looked me all over again before continuing to walk toward the car.

"Here we are." She fished the key out and opened the boot of the car. I got my suitcase and put it in.

"Let me get you home quickly," she said as she started the engine. "You must be starving. They don't feed people properly in the plane. Furthermore, you need rest."

It was already evening and the lights that lit up the Sydney sky were beautiful. I sat quietly admiring them. It was indeed a fast city, much bigger and rather impersonal.

"Things are faster here," she started again. I just nodded my head. "It won't take you long before you get the feel of things here though."

"You reckon?"

"You bet," she said smiling.

"How far is it to your place?"

"About 20 minutes if the traffic is not busy."

"That's far."

She looked at me as if to tell me to shut up. I looked away into the traffic and the surroundings. This time she drove without chatting to me. I felt good but homesick nevertheless. It was to be my first night away from the familiar surroundings that I had left behind. I had a mixture of dread and fantasy as we drove along. I wondered what awaited me and how I would cope here.

"We are almost there now," she started again after a while. I didn't say anything. This stretch of the road was not as busy as the one we came on out of the airport. She drove on. After a while I realised that she was slowing down. "I said we are almost home," she emphasised.

"Oh, really?" I answered her; my attention was elsewhere captured by the strangeness of the place, the wide neat streets, the buildings with different architectural styles. Everything that my eyes focused on was different from what I was used to back home. I was totally mesmerised and captivated by the uniqueness of the place. I felt out of place and belittled by what I was seeing. It was a totally different environment.

The car came to a stop in front of a large brick house. Slowly I got out and waited for her to open the boot so I could get my stuff out. Was it taking her a long while to open the boot or was I just panicking?

As soon as she opened the boot, I collected my stuff and followed her to the house. I wondered how it would be like having to stay with a pretty woman. Her legs were revealing and smooth and the way she walked in front of me was very tempting. "Was she deliberately trying to entice me?" I wondered. I felt my legs weakening as I closely followed her and before I knew it I held her for support.

"Are you alright?" she asked me at the same time facing me. I heard her heavy breathing and the smell of her body almost overpowered me. I shook my head, "I am feeling dizzy." She held me and gently pushed me towards the couch. "You'll be fine. Sit down and I'll make you a nice cold drink."

Slowly I regained my composure. For the first time I realised that, the house was indeed big, strange and alienating. At the same time, it was as if prying eyes were monitoring my movements. I thought my legs were about to give way again. I became afraid and felt more of a stranger. The interior of the house however contained things that reminded me of home. After she had shown me my room, which was directly opposite to hers, I went in, put my things down, locked myself in and stretched out on the bed. Although I felt tired and drained I kept on thinking of her, she was beautiful and attractive. After awhile I forced myself not to think of her. The room felt different too. I felt that the room was especially made to accommodate a male like me. It conformed to a certain design and arrangement which only a young male could sense. It wasn't apparent but I felt it. It was almost like a spider's web and if I wasn't careful I could fall into the trap.

My mind traveled back a thousand miles home. I could visualise Deuba standing outside the flat begging me to give her a second chance. I could vividly recall her pleading, going down on her knees, tears falling and wetting the front of the blue T-shirt that she wore. But I was stubborn, suddenly closing the door, my heart and the world behind me. Now at this strange new place, I regret shutting the door and my heart from her. I wanted her now so she could help me make sense of this new place. I was finding it hard to come to terms with this new place. I was lost. I closed my eyes and tried to sleep but my heart and mind refused. I realised that my relocation to this strange place was partly because of her—I was running away from her, from everything to do with her. I sat up, got a writing pad and started writing her a letter. I poured all my emotions and heart into the letter. I was on the fifth page when Kate called me for dinner. Reluctantly I came out and sat down quietly on the table.

She had a concerned look on her face. "Are you alright? Look, if you want to complete your studies you must get used to the fact that you will be here for a long time," she said to me perhaps annoyed at my attitude. I didn't say anything but sat quietly picking at my food. She tried her best to cook me something familiar. In fact in the morning she went to the Indian shop and bought some cassava and other food stuff. She cooked them in coconut cream and it tasted good. As I stole one of my glances (when she was not looking) at her, I realised that she had changed into shorts and a T-shirt. It made her look more attractive and seductive.

"I am just feeling a little homesick that's all," I said quietly after a short while; at the same time eating my food. She realised that I was staring at her and she rewarded me with a smile. "It'll be over in a couple of days. I'll take you to Uni tomorrow and maybe you can meet some of your wantoks there."

"They won't be here for the next couple of weeks," I told her.

"I have seen some of them around," she said. "Could be the old ones who had not gone back home for their holidays." She paused to serve herself some more food. "Then you can check out the flat I got for you. It's close to the university."

I moved closer to her and touched her hand. "Thanks," I said. She glanced back at me, "You are welcome, my dear." At least I felt comforted by the piece of news. "I know you will like the flat." I smiled and pressed her hand again.

"You've been here before haven't you? I mean in Australia."

"I stayed 12 months but it was in another city."

"How did you feel?"

"I felt homesick for a couple of weeks and then I was okay after that."

"You'll pull through. Once you get the feel of things you'll be alright."

"I hope so," I said as I finished my food. I pushed the plate towards her and she looked at me as if to tell me to take it to the kitchen. I felt happy about her reaction; it was my way of teasing her. I gave that smart smile and she took the plates to the kitchen. I got up, moved to the lounge and watched the late night news on television. I waited for her to come and join me but after a while I re-treated to my room and started to write more letters to all the friends I could think of. Writing letters was a way to relieve my loneliness. It was consoling as I poured out my emotions and feelings in the letters. I wondered if Kate was going to come into my room. The more I thought about her the more I wanted her to come. It was like someone had put bait in my room and all I had to do was wait for the right moment.

My first impression of Kate was that she was a *hapkas* and not a pure *dimdim*. There seems to be something strange and mysterious about her. But her mannerism and attitude were that of a *dimdim*. Though she was in her mid-thirties, she looked much younger for her age. She was a woman who could easily attract any man. She has long black hair, a tanned skin (perhaps a result of many years in the tropics), which could be easily mistaken for a Polynesian. She was about 175 centimetres tall and her built was average. She was what you would call a gym fanatic. The combination of these features gave her that eternal youthful look.

She has had a number of long-term relationships (her words) and was once married to another *dimdim*. She was also a flirtatious person (well at least that's how I thought). But I tried my best not to fall into her charms, no matter how much I wanted her. It was also, perhaps something about her charm that camouflaged any traces of her illness from me until the very end when I finally found out.

One thing I found most annoying about her was that she pretended a lot. (Maybe I am wrong about this). She wasn't always herself when it came something to do with PNG. She had this 'know-all' and 'been there' attitude. Then again, it may be that there was something Papua New Guinean about her, something that I didn't know; something that she was concealing from me, something that she didn't want people to know. Rumours had it that she went to work in PNG because of a wounded pride. Like me she also ran away to a new place from a broken relationship. Her husband left her for her best friend. Unable to handle herself, she got a teaching job at the university in PNG. She was there for some years before she returned. I don't know whether this story was true because I have never asked her about it.

After doing the dishes she called me and I came out to join her at the lounge.

"Coffee?" she asked.

"No thanks!"

She went to the kitchen to make herself coffee while I sat quietly for some time, glancing at the room. I noticed that while the scaffolding of the house was done *dimdim* style, the interior décor was more Papua New Guinean. She had carvings and artifacts from PNG, a pandanus mat hanging at one end of the lounge wall, a Highlands bow and some arrows on the other side, two Milne Bay grass skirts, some shell necklaces, a kundu drum and many other assorted items. A mask with some dried leaves was hanging directly over her bedroom door. These things all seemed to be out of place here. They carried other meanings. The house was immaculate and you could tell that there was a feminine touch to the place, except, perhaps for the many papers and books that were scattered all over the lounge. I was about to ask her about the decorations in the house when she ignored my curiosity.

"The place I have found for you is a large flat," she told me as she slowly sipped her coffee. I didn't respond although I was stealing glances at her now and again.

"I paid your bond fee and got the keys a few days ago," she continued.

"Why would I need a large flat?" I asked.

"Perhaps it's better for you to share the place with your wantoks. It will be easier that way, at least initially."

"I don't understand," I said trying to be complicated.

"A city like Sydney can be a monster. Not for you only but for your other wantoks, especially the first timers. Sharing will give you that sense of community." She paused to drink from her cup. "This should stop you from feeling homesick. Staying with wantoks will be good for you."

She paused, then she began again. "By the way, I saw the list of the new PNG students coming here to study. There are very few female students."

"Really?"

She nodded her head. She looked away before speaking again. "It was strange; I had never felt homesick when I went to PNG to do my research initially and later to work at the university there. I only felt scared. There was much that was coming out about your country. Law and order problems. My supervisor didn't want me to go and he even suggested that I change my topic. I gave it a long thought and finally I decided to go."

"You were brave," I said.

"Maybe, I don't know. But I was adamant that I had to pursue and complete what I had embarked on. And in any case that's where I spent my childhood."

"What happened when you arrived?"

"When I arrived at the airport there was someone waiting for me; another Australian. I saw lots of people, many loitering around. They kept staring. I didn't know what they were thinking but my friend told me that it was normal, so I took it on my stride." She paused. "To be honest, I was scared but my friend told me it was alright. We took off to her place and there she told me most things I needed to know. I also found many things strange. Perhaps it was to do with my prolonged exposure to white culture."

"You were quick at adapting."

"If I didn't my whole project would have been a failure. So I told myself not to be afraid."

"That's what Jean Bedford said but all she could do was write about sex with the natives."

"She's a different person and maybe that's how she saw things there," Kate said in a serious tone. "In any case she is a *dimdim* who didn't even set foot in PNG. Most probably she wrote her book from hearsay and what she has read from other books."

"That's always the *dimdims'* excuse!" I said.

"Then why do you bring her into the conversation when you don't like it? I am not a travel writer; I am a serious researcher," Kate told me emphatically.

"Like Malinowski you mean?" I said sarcastically.

"What's gotten into you so suddenly? She threw both hands into the air. Why do you want to accuse me of something that I am not party to? What do you want to prove?" She charged at me like a raging bull. "I had spent half of my life in your country and that makes me one of you guys don't you think?"

I kept quiet for sometime before I began again. "Many outsiders have written about my country out of their private visions," I said trying to talk in an academic fashion. "They just want their friends to believe they are great explorers and discoverers!"

"I don't know about that," she replied in a nonchalant manner.

"But that's what happened in many instances don't you think?" I continued to pursue the subject.

"That argument belongs to the colonial days Perez. Try to think beyond that," she came back hard.

"Not at all, Kate. It's still happening to this day."

"Anyway let's stop this nonsense," she said with finality.

I got up and went to the restroom. I felt bad talking to her like this. When I got back she was smoking and she excused herself.

"I actually spend my early years in Milne Bay," she began again, her voice like a soft captivating melody.

"I didn't know that," I replied with interest.

"They even gave me a local name."

"Really?" I said surprised. I thought things were now falling into place and soon the secret would be revealed.

"My father worked as a missionary over there. I started primary school there and then I was sent to Brisbane to do my high school and university. In between I went back to visit my parents. We finally left the place for good when I was about 20."

"Why did you leave?"

"My father couldn't work well with another white missionary and the local church there. It got so bad that we had to leave. Also my mother was always getting sick. There were rumours that our house girl, a very pretty woman, had done sorcery on my mother because she wanted my father. I think my father liked her too. She treated me like her daughter and I could remember her breast-feeding me, when my mother was not around of course. She had a cute baby about 6 months old and she used to bring her along. I wanted to stay but my parents didn't permit me, so I returned to Australia very angry and didn't want to have anything to do with them. I was the only child too."

"How could you have done that? You were supposed to be that obedient, God-fearing child of missionaries!"

"I know, but I realised there was a lot of bullshit involved. At least I managed to return to PNG to do my research and work at the university after the initial sojourn. When I went back to work in PNG our former house girl (I call her mother) came and stayed with me for several months before she reluctantly left for the village because her husband was very ill. I tried asking her about her relationship with my father and all she did was laugh about it, telling me that was a long time ago." She paused to drink the last dregs of her coffee before continuing. "I have not read Jean Bedford. Would you have a copy of her book?"

I might have a copy somewhere in my bag. Let me go and check," I said at the same time going into my room. I found the book and brought it to her. "Read it and tell me what you think of it," I said, still standing. "Won't you sit down?"

"I think I'll call it a night Kate," I said yawning.

"So soon?" she said looking straight at me. I nodded my head. "Good night then. If you need anything just give me a yell."

I was in an ambivalent mood. I did not go to sleep quickly but continued to write more letters. By the time I stopped it was well past midnight. The traffic on the road was now reduced to a minimum but no matter how hard I tried to sleep I just couldn't. My sleep was constantly disturbed by the strangeness of the place. The smell and everything that my eyes set upon were kind of odd, even the room where I was, was uncharacteristically strange. What I was used to in PNG was different and all this strangeness of the place heightened my anxiety. I tossed and turned and several times Kate called to me to ask if I was alright. It wasn't until the wee hours of the morning when I finally fell into a deep sleep. When I woke up, Kate was already up making breakfast.

"How are you this morning?" she prompted me with a smile that was enchanting.

"I am not feeling too good." She looked intently at me. "I have a feeling that I will hear some bad news from home."

"Oh! What makes you think that?"

"I had a strange dream last night."

"Superstitious again aye?" Kate teased me.

"Mark my word. There are some things that we know that you *dimdims* don't know," I told her. She didn't say anything. She just rolled her eyes. I had my breakfast quietly until she told me it was time for us to leave for Uni. I got my stuff and we went out to the car park. I wondered whom I would be meeting at Uni.

"I'll also take you to the flat and you can check it out yourself."

"Whereabouts is the flat?"

"It's located on 2 Kennedy Lane about 5 minutes walk to the campus," she answered. "I know you will like the flat. Wilmot used to live there before."

"Who is Wilmot?"

"An anthropologist who worked in PNG before. Nice guy. You will get to meet him soon." Since a child, I had always dreaded anthropologists with their long white beards, round-shaped glasses which conjured up an image of a white monster, watching every move ready to pounce upon you. Whenever I saw photos of Father Christmas, I immediately connected them to anthropologists and gradually I also dreaded Father Christmas.

After a few minutes we were on our way to Uni. This time the drive took longer as the traffic was very busy. There were more cars and trucks on the road than in my country, cars of all makes and models, a number of them I was seeing for the first time — strange looking, huge with engine sounds that almost busted my ear drums. Kate told me it would take some 30 minutes to drive to the university. I didn't say anything but just sat there beside her watching the traffic. My mind was elsewhere and I wondered how Deuba was and whether she has recovered from the misery of our broken relationship. I knew that had she known where I was she would have tried to call me. I knew we have hurt each other and it would take some time for our wounds to heal. Kate pointed out certain landmarks but I wasn't really concentrating. My mind was somewhere in between places. The city had changed since the last time I was here. There were many highrise buildings and new buildings were emerging as if out of nowhere.

She drove on, now and again staring at me, but I wasn't talking to her. I didn't want us to have an accident. We just passed a truck that had skidded off the road and had rammed on to the sidewalk. The police and ambulance people were already attending to the driver and to clear the road. This morning there was some rain in this part of the city and the roads were wet and slippery. I prayed silently for our safe passage.

"Here we are. This is the university," I heard Kate as she slowed down. I looked up and saw the big sign. The butterflies in my tummy threatened to fly out but I held on. I mean you know how one feels when coming to a new place. You don't know people and you don't know what you would encounter. Kind of like one who is among buddies and doesn't know which of them would try to kill him first. She drove slowly around until she found a place and parked the car. We got out and walked to the campus.

"See that tall building over there?" Kate said pointing to it.

"Yes," I answered.

"That's where your flat is. After we complete our familiarisation tour of the campus we'll go over and you can see the place."

It was indeed a big campus. Kate showed me the building that housed my school and the other places she thought I should get to know. There weren't many students around. The students who we saw were mostly Asian students who were here attending the English language school before entering university. I realised that this university was much bigger than the one I had been to. Some of the gothic-styled buildings here looked eerie while others looked as if they were in meditation. The quietude that surrounded these buildings gave them that scholarly characteristic. On the other hand my encounter with these buildings gave me that creepy feeling. They made me more panicky, reminding me some-what of what I had just run away from. I was relieved when our tour was over.

✳✳✳

The flat is owned by an Italian guy," Kate told me as we were walking slowly back to the car. "Nice chap too." Kate paused to unlock her car. "You know what he told me?" I shook my head in the negative. "He told me that many real estate agents do not want to deal with black folks. When they come to them, they come up with excuses."

"These Italians can really brag too aye," I said.

"I love their accent though, sounds musical," Kate said laughing. "Don't you think so?"

"I guess so."

Kate drove slowly up a small hill towards 2 Kennedy Lane. "When I told him that the flat was for a PNG friend he started to brag more," Kate continued. "He told me that he had helped many black guys who couldn't be given one by these white real estate guys."

"Is that so?"

"Don't believe every thing people say," she cautioned me. "Listen to what he has to say about himself."

I kept quiet.

"Look, I am not Anglo-Saxon or what ever that garbage is. I am a recent immigrant, well not really recent; I arrived here some 20 years ago. They looked down on me but I worked hard and here I am. I help all kinds of people. I give you this flat now so when your PNG friend comes he will have no problems."

"Oh they have a way to convince people," I said as Kate came to stop outside the block of flats.

"Yes they really do." Pause. "Here we are," Kate, said as we got out.

Although I was looking forward to this new place, for some unknown reasons I also dreaded the place. It was a feeling of thrill and fear that gripped me as soon as we arrived at the flat. Kate unlocked the door and I followed her into the flat. While the flat was indeed attractive, it gave out a strange smell and feel, which I found a little inhospitable and unwelcoming. In PNG the houses were open and you can immediately feel the breeze because of the many windows. This flat was dark and had a ghostly feel. The flat was on the ground level and once inside it's like you have been swallowed by a strange ogre. It reminded me of the biblical story of Jonah in the belly of the huge whale. I had a silly feeling that Kate might have already done something to the place. You know how it is back home when bad people want to do sorcery to you they are the first to visit the place. The flat though was in a good condition, tidy, furnished, with a master bedroom and three other smaller bedrooms, a big lounge and all the extras. It was surrounded by well kept shrubs and a small lawn. I was ambivalent about the place: while I liked the flat, I also felt insecure and frightened for no apparent reason.

"I hope you'll feel comfortable and homely here," Kate said to me. "When you finally meet up with the new PNG students, you can ask three of them if they want to share the place with you."

"It won't be until sometime yet."

"That's alright. Spend the time exploring the city. You won't be bored."

Kate stayed with me for a while, assisting me in rearranging some of the stuff. She made me feel settled by her mere presence but the butterflies in my tummy still threatened to fly out. I had silly thoughts now that we were alone in this new place. Her presence aroused me almost to the extreme. I tried hard to control myself, when she was not looking I stole momentary glances at her. I cursed God for putting me in this awkward situation. After what seemed like hours, Kate asked me a couple of times if I really wanted to stay or go back with her to her place until I was comfortable to stay at the new flat. In the end I knew I had to be strong so I declined her offer.

"Call me if you need anything then," Kate told me as she cuddled me before walking out of the door. I felt my body shake as if malaria had got me suddenly. I wanted to shriek after her but my voice was lost and I fell on the floor until I recovered from this mysterious illness. Perhaps this was a result of me being afraid.

As soon as I recovered I realised that I was on my own again like a castaway on a deserted island. The place was haunting not with ghosts but with the strangeness of an alien place. I regretted leaving in the first place. It was my fault anyway for flirting with Deuba's best friend at the Christmas party. I just don't know why she snapped so quickly. Maybe she felt threatened by a younger woman.

It all started this way. She invited me to her organisation's Christmas party so I tagged along. There were lots of people when the two of us arrived and she introduced me to all her friends. As she was someone senior in the organisation she had to go around meeting and chatting with the other guests. She left me with her best friend, a young lass perhaps in her late 20s. She was sipping wine while I helped myself to beer. Deuba came around several times to see if I was okay and every time her friend would tell her that she was looking after me. As the day swam into night and alcohol started working I began to flirt with the young lass. People were minding their own business. Our flirting continued until we embraced and started kissing and that is when it all happened. She came and pulled me away, and we left the party and that night all hell broke out. She accused me of betraying her trust. She cried all night and I had to take off in the middle of the night to my place.

As soon as Kate left, I tried my best to adjust to the new surrounding; one that I wasn't used to: strange place, strange neighbours, strange smells, strange everything which I need to adjust to if my stay here was going to be successful. The smell from shrubs and the wattles outside almost made me vomit, it was unbearable and it reminded me of the bad smell that emanated from a particular plant at home that people used to kill fish. Even some of the residents acted strangely; so I thought.

The nights were the worst for me. I dreaded each day as the evening began to set in. The strange cityscape had a ghostly grip on me. I felt so alone and every shadow made my goose bumps rise. I continued to write letters to comfort myself and relieve my loneliness.

It wasn't until the second week that things started to happen which I couldn't explain. By this time I had already made friends with a couple of the neighbours. One evening I was reading a book when I sensed a foul smell in the room. I thought it must have been a dead rat or something. I searched the flat but I couldn't find where the smell was coming from. The following morning when I woke up, I realised that my door was slightly open. I knew I had locked my door the night before. My first thought was that the previous tenant had not returned the spare key so he could have used it to gain entry. But nothing was taken from my flat. When I told Kate she dismissed me as being superstitious. But I could tell that she was also afraid. The nervous shifting of her feet and the unnecessary dropping of her keys showed it all. From then on, small incidents started to happen but I never really took any notice of them as I kept myself busy. I also didn't think ghosts would be lurking around in a big city like Sydney.

It wasn't until a week or so later after I was returning from the corner shop one evening when one of the tenants saw me walking and stopped to give me a lift. Then she told me about 2 Kennedy Lane as a haunted place, where strange things and incidents happen. I didn't know whether to believe her but one thing was for sure—she made me really afraid.

Chapter 2

We (that is Kate and myself) first met with the three Uwegu, Reimas and Desimoni (or Desi for short) during registration week. Kate parked the car and we were walking to where the registration was taking place when we spotted these three students sitting on the bench talking quietly amongst themselves. I held Kate's arm, making her stop.

"What is it?" she asked me.

"Those three look like they are my wantoks," I told her pointing to where the three were. She looked closely for some time before she nodded her head. We walked over to them and I greeted them in Tok Pisin. You could see their eyes lighting up as soon as they realised that I was one of them. I shook hands with them and Kate followed suit. But as soon as Kate was about to greet Uwegu she suddenly stopped and looked her in the eye for a few moments. Uwegu also looked intently at her then they reluctantly shook hands and looked away quickly. I thought there was a sense of belated recognition, which was quickly followed by some kind of nervousness between the two women. Kate's eyes were almost fierce like a lioness ready to pounce on a prey, while I thought I saw Uwegu tighten the grip on her right hand perhaps ready to punch. I wondered if they knew each other from somewhere. Throughout our meeting the two ladies avoided each other's eyes. In the end Kate talked them into sharing the flat with me. "It will save you a lot of time house hunting," Kate told them. "Some of these real estate people have problems with black students because either they don't pay up or they trash the place up when they get drunk. It's only a minority who does that but that doesn't really matter to some people."

"Some of these agents are real bastards. They just want to look good in front of you," I added in my effort to convince them. They looked scared and Desimoni kept on shifting his left foot while Reimas kept looking away. It wasn't long before the two guys agreed but not Uwegu. It took her a long while to make up her mind. After Desimoni talked with her quietly she finally acquiesced.

We talked some more until Kate informed us that we should be going, Uwegu politely refused to get into Kate's car preferring to walk instead. She asked Desimoni to walk with her and I gave them the directions. I thought I heard Kate say bitch to her but because of the traffic I wasn't sure whether it was meant for Uwegu or the other woman driver who almost collided with us as she overtook us. I wondered why Uwegu was acting strangely but I never got around to asking her. It could be the effect of the new place. The two arrived some 5 minutes later.

Although we came from the same country we didn't come from the same place. That in itself was a challenge for us. I was the only one who was here to do my postgraduate studies while the three of them were here to do their under-graduate studies. So they looked upon me as their big brother.

"Are you happy about sharing the place with these three?" Kate asked me quietly when the three were out of earshot. "We are all wantoks so we will be able to cope."

"She has grown to be a pretty woman," Kate made reference to Uwegu.

"Yeah, she is pretty alright." Pause. "Do you know her?"

"I don't think so," Kate replied avoiding my eyes. "I hope she will be able to cope with you three guys," Kate continued.

"I think she will."

"Let me give you a little of advice. Be careful with her. You are here to study. She could be your spider's web," Kate told me emphatically. You could tell that she didn't like Uwegu and she was a bit jealous that I would be sharing the place with a pretty young woman. It reminded me again of the relationship that I had opted out of because Deuba was jealous of me flirting with her best friend.

I wondered what it would be like sharing the house with the three guys. This would be my first time to share with strangers and I was a little apprehensive about it. Perhaps I was just paranoid, I don't know. Indeed I have never shared a place with a female who wasn't a relative. This would be an experience! The more I thought about all this, the more Uwegu's pretty face came into my vision. Perhaps she will be my anchor, I told myself.

"You be careful with that lady," Kate said again as she was leaving.

"Don't worry, I can take care of myself," I said provocatively. Man, you could see the expression on her face. She was unbelievably jealous as if I had run away with her daughter or something. But she never uttered a word.

✳✳✳

A few days later I was sitting alone at the lounge when Uwegu came out of her room and joined me. Desimoni and Reimas were elsewhere. I felt awkward and uncomfortable being alone with her. For the first time I realised that she was incredibly pretty. The moment she looked at me, I felt I was being undressed. She came and sat beside me eating an apple. I switched on the television and we sat watching. "How did you come to know her?" Uwegu asked after awhile. Her voice was magical and soothing like a bird cooing from a treetop. I looked at her for a while, not knowing how to answer her. I hesitated. "She used to work at the university back home. She was there for four years."

"Oh I see." There was a long pause. "She looks very much like Mrs. Powell, one of my former tutors at university."

"No, her name is Kate Nolan." There was a long pause again before she answered me. "She looks familiar but I can't really place her. She looks like Mrs. Powell but then again memories are often faulty." She was quiet for a while before she started again. "I don't like her though; there is something evil about her." I stared at Uwegu trying to understand what she was saying. "I feel someone has placed something in this flat."

"I don't get you," I said, at the same time looking straight at her.

"I haven't been sleeping well; like I have been tormented by spirits or something. I had a strange experience last night," Uwegu told me. "I don't like that woman to come here anymore. She is a witch. I know she isn't a true *dimdim* woman. I hate her and this place is full of her evil spirit."

"What's the matter? What are you talking about?"

"I am talking about your friend. She tried to strangle me last night." I thought that Uwegu was only feeling disoriented and homesick.

"Kate was never here last night," I said still confused.

"She was here and whose shoes are those then?"

I looked at the pair of shoes and indeed they were Kate's. "She must have forgotten them when she came yesterday," I tried to justify the presence of the pair of shoes.

"You knew all along that she was a witch and you knew she was not a pure *dimdim,* and yet you never told us the truth!" Uwegu was visibly upset by now.

"Of course she is a *dimdim* woman, what are you talking about?"

"No she is not. White women don't fly in the night. Only our women do. I think I know who she really is."

"She is not your Mrs. Powell or whoever your former tutor was. Don't be irrational; you must have had a terrible nightmare that's all."

"I swear she came in and tried to kill me. I know she knows who I am and she wants to settle old scores."

By now I was totally confused. *Do the two women know each other? Was there something between the two women that we did not know*? I have also heard about women flying in the night but I could not make out this one. I asked her to calm down and I made her a cup of tea. After she calmed down she apologised to me. "I can't help being superstitious. It's my upbringing and culture," She said quietly to me. "Can you see the bruise marks on my neck?" I moved closer to her and touched her neck. My hands were almost trembling. She had bruises but I didn't know what caused them.

"Something must have caused the bruises," I told her. She didn't say anything perhaps she didn't want to pursue something that I didn't believe in, or maybe she didn't want to upset me.

"Tell me, do you know Kate?" Is there something between you and Kate that we don't know?" She shrugged her shoulders.

"I am just confused I supposed." She stopped and for a while before she spoke again. "There was this *dimdim* woman, Mrs. Powell who taught me at university. She was a party animal and almost every weekend students went to her flat to have fun. I occasionally went to her place. But my sister went almost every weekend and she was very close to Mrs. Powell. Sometimes in the middle of the night Mrs. Powell would come for her. At the same time my sister was going around with a student from another province. There were rumours that he was also going around with Mrs. Powell. One evening I went to Mrs. Powell's flat to look for my sister as I had to pass a message to her from home. The place was empty. I thought she must have gone out. As I was about to turn back I thought I would just peep in at her bedroom. When I looked in I was surprised to see two naked figures on the floor. I stood there shocked beyond belief. It was Mrs. Powell. I couldn't recognize the other person at first. It was only when the person stood up to go to the toilet that I realised it was my own sister. I felt disgusted, angry and I almost vomited. I got so upset and quietly left the place."

It was a revelation I did not expect. "Where is this Mrs. Powell now?"

"I think she came back here after people found out. It was later on that I discovered that she wasn't a pure *dimdim*."

"What makes you think that Kate is Mrs. Powell?" I asked her.

"She looks very much like her. But then again many people tend to look alike these days." She paused for a long while before she changed the topic. "Which part of PNG are you from again?"

"I thought I told you already."

"Have you? I must have forgotten. You know when it's your first time you get nervous and you don't really listen to what people tell you," she replied. "Sometimes I am like that. The other day when we first met I wasn't really listening to what you people were saying. My mind was elsewhere."

"I am actually from Madang."

"I thought you were from New Ireland."

"Do I look like it?"

"You do actually. You are much darker and very tall for someone from Madang."

"People change; there are a lot of intermarriages taking place. Did you say you were from Milne Bay?" I asked her in return.

"You can tell, can't you?"

"Yeah, I suppose." I paused for a while. "That's where Kate grew up. Her father was a missionary. I am not sure which part of Milne Bay exactly."

"I don't want to talk about that woman," Uwegu told me.

"Okay, never mind." I stopped for a while. What work did you do back home?" I asked after awhile.

"After completing my diploma in accounting I joined the Central Bank and worked for two years before I got this scholarship. It was good to get away from home for a while too, I reckon. And you?" She asked.

"I worked as a tutor at the university in Port Moresby before getting this scholarship."

"No wonder you know that evil woman," she said with a strong dislike. She paused for a while as she discarded the rubbish from the apple she was eating. "You know, I don't like egocentric people. People who think they are it!" I thought she was making herself clear before anything else. "I mean, at the place I used to work at, my immediate boss was such a pig! He played big and was always bossy. Oh man, he used to get on me if I was late in completing a project and all that. He has a master's degree from some lousy uni in America; I can't remember which one now. When I got this scholarship, I told myself, I'll show this smart ass that I can also make it big time!"

"You are ambitious," I told her.

"If you're not, you may just as well forget it and go stay in the village," she replied smiling. *This woman is different*, I thought. *She is no easy prey*. "Do you have a family?" I asked her.

"Married you mean? I am not married although I have a child and she is with my folks back at home. My boyfriend took off with another woman."

"I am sorry," I said.

"It's alright. Sometimes we try to carve this earth with crooked eyes. I hope we can enjoy it here while we can. I mean work hard in school and have some fun too."

"Yeah," I managed to say.

"So are you married?" she asked me head on.

"No, but I have had a number of relationships. Most of them failed, dying natural deaths," I told her at the same time laughing. Her question quickly brought back memories of the broken relationship that I had left behind. This morning I received a letter from Deuba but I dreaded opening the letter.

"That sounds sad but at the same time poetic," she said smiling. "Maybe you can improve on it this time round."

"You think so?"

"It's worth trying. Nothing is impossible."

As we conversed I studied her closely, stealing quick looks now and again. You couldn't really tell whether she was from Milne Bay. She wasn't your typical Milne Bay girl.

"So is your kid joining you here?" I asked her.

"I don't think so. It will be a disturbance. She'll be okay with my folks. I rang them last night and we talked for about 30 minutes."

"She must be missing you."

"Oh yes, but I told her not to worry. I miss her too but we have to get on."

"So where is your sister now, I mean the one you caught with Mrs. Powell?"

"After I got cross with her for sleeping with Mrs. Powell, she refused to listen to me and we drifted apart. She continued seeing her until others found out and rumours started spreading. Her boyfriend dumped her for another girl. She withdrew from studies and worked for a mining company. It was during one of her field breaks that she was involved in a fatal car accident." She broke down and I waited for her to recover. "I am sorry Perez; I am a very emotional person."

"It's alright," I told her squeezing her arm.

When Uwegu left me along I finally opened the letter Deuba had written me. It read in part, *"I know you aren't expecting a letter from me because of what had happened. I know you blame me for everything. But sometimes it takes one to be a man to admit that he is also to be blamed. I've always tried my best to please you, to do what I am supposed to do. I have always respected you; there was not once that I have betrayed you. Now I must try and survive life without you. If you look closely at yourself, you will realise that often times you are selfish, you are self-centred, you only think about yourself and you forget that you are standing tall because of people around you. You don't have time for people like me, all your time has been budgeted for other things."*

I stopped reading and put the letter aside. Was I really selfish? I asked myself. Maybe Deuba was looking at things from another perspective. Maybe I was quick at blaming other people when I am supposed to look at myself. I kept thinking about the relationship until I reassured myself that it was too late and that we have other paths to follow.

Chapter 3

Kennedy Lane where we established our little community was a dead end lane. When one drives up the lane, there is a false sense of it leading to other places. When cars speed on Kennedy Lane, residents know they are strangers. When you see cars driving in low gear, then they are either residents or people who are familiar with the place. What made our lane famous was the rumour about the place as being haunted. This rumour deterred many people from venturing into Kennedy Lane or living here.

When I first heard of the place as haunted I didn't tell them (although unexplained things were happening, and Uwegu since moving in has had paranormal experiences). I kept it to myself. It was only after a while that I mentioned the story of the haunted block of flats to Reimas as we were walking back from Uni one day. After I told him, I realised that Reimas began coming home early and rarely ventured out in the night on his own. One evening as we sat around, Reimas asked me to tell them the story. I did not want to frighten them but after they all insisted I had no choice but to tell them the story.

"The story about the haunted block of flats at number 2 Kennedy Lane is as old as the lane itself," I began.

"Who told you the story?" Uwegu asked.

"One of the residents. I lived on my own here before you guys came and joined me. One evening as I was returning from the corner shop just down the road, a car came and stopped beside me. Somehow the *dimdim* woman was driving home when she recognised me and stopped to give me a lift. I was reluctant at first but she urged me on. I finally succumbed to her rather maternal urging.

"If I were you, I'd rather not walk home at this time of the night," she told me as soon as I shut the door and the car was in motion. I stared at her in puzzlement for a rather long while before I asked what she meant. I mean, I know Sydney is one of the biggest cities in the world and it also has a high rate of crime. However I was young and I didn't feel threatened by all these things. In fact a week or so before my encounter with this woman, I went to the rescue of another resident, a postgraduate Chinese student, who was about to be mugged by two guys as he was entering Kennedy Lane. I was on one of my evening errands when I heard him call out for help. The call he made was chilling. It was a sound made by a helpless man at the moment of confrontation in which he knew he faced an uncertain fate. I ran and saw him trying to fend off the two attackers. I picked up a piece of wood and whacked one of them on the head. He was the more aggressive of the two. As soon as his accomplice saw what happened he tried to run across the street. I ran after him and tackled him to the ground. By this time a couple of the neighbours (one Indian and one a *dimdim*) were already on the scene. They helped me apprehend the two guys and handed them to the Marouba police.

"I know you are capable of looking after yourself. But this has nothing to do with flexing muscles," the woman captured my attention again. A couple of guys were loitering at the roadside and she had to slow down and tell them to get out of the way.

"When did you move to Kennedy Lane?" the woman driver asked me. I tried looking straight at her face, but her eyes were hidden by the glasses she was wearing.

"A couple of weeks ago."

"Oh, I see. So you are new to the place then?"

"You could say that," I answered.

"Then you would not have heard about number 2 Kennedy Lane as haunted?"

"Haunted? How do you mean?" I was startled. "I mean haunted. Strange things happen, things that can't be explained, paranormal."

"Do you believe in that?" She looked intently at me. I knew I had caught her off guard. A *dimdim*, at that. I wanted to laugh but I held back.

"Don't play smart with me young man." There was a short pause as she slowed down, ready to turn into Kennedy Lane. "Don't you believe in ghosts, dark forces?" She asked again.

"I don't know. Give me something substantial," I pestered her just to see her reaction.

She came to a stop in front of Number 2. I opened the door and got out. Before I could thank her, she drove off. "Ask your neighbours," I heard her call out. I wanted to swear at her but upon second thought I didn't.

The two, Reimas and Desimoni, were now huddled together and you could tell that they were afraid. Uwegu was different she seemed to be the brave one among them.

"Go on," Uwegu urged me, looking at the other two for support.

"There was no one around and it was late in the evening. I was looking over my shoulders all the time as I entered the dark entrance," I continued. "For the first time since I moved into this flat I felt scared. I mean, we come from a culture where the belief in ghosts and spirits is part of our daily existence. Upon arrival at my door I quickly fished my key out. The bloody thing was slow in coming out. My goose bumps stood. I could feel something strange in the air. Quickly I went in, seeking refuge in the sanctuary of this flat. I looked around to see if anything was amiss but everything seemed in place as I had left them. I checked the bathroom but it was normal. I sat on the couch and thought about what the *dimdim* woman had told me. My head was a little heavy and I got up and switched on the jug to make coffee. The night was quiet but I could hear music and laughter from the other flats directly above me. The other student from India (you will meet him soon) whose flat is next to ours wasn't home.

"Gupta (the Indian guy's name) has been a resident at number 2 Kennedy Lane for about 8 years. I was meaning to go straight to him and ask him about what the woman had told me. As his lights were off, I presumed he was out. Somehow I fell asleep on the couch and didn't wake up until the next morning. When I woke up, I realised that my door was slightly ajar and I shuddered with trepidation. However my things weren't disturbed. My mind worked full speed trying to figure out things. I was pretty sure someone had entered the place that night because I remembered locking the door behind me. Did someone have a spare key to this flat? I recalled a woman who was murdered in her flat back home. The murderer used a spare key to gain entry. When the victim returned from work, the murderer was already inside the flat, and as she was talking on the phone the guy started stabbing her."

The three of them sat very quietly listening to my story. They sat together on the couch (the only one) we bought from the Salvation Army shop. The two guys sat on each side of the couch while Uwegu placed herself between them. I sat facing them on another chair. It was cold and it was difficult for us to go out. So we sat around telling stories. In fact back home ghost stories were part of everyday life for us. People would sit around the fire in the evenings and they would tell stories of strange happenings. You would see kids huddled together listening to such stories. Tonight was no different, except that we were in a strange place. The four of us came from different parts, but what brought us together here to be under one house was perhaps the need for community and fellowship. Here we were like a family in a boat in the middle of the ocean, constantly being tossed by rough seas. Our lifeline was the stories we told each other, the letters and phone calls we made and received from home, our fellowship and the need to adapt in a strange landscape.

Most of the time it was the three of them who told stories. I was always listening despite their urging for me to tell them some of my experiences. I have never succumbed to their requests; many times I looked for excuses to get away. This time, it was cold so I couldn't escape to the library. The stories they told were mostly about incidents that took place at home in the islands. I don't know why most of the stories we told each other were about home. Perhaps it was because we were living in an unfamiliar place.

What made Reimas and Desimoni more afraid was that we were on our own and the fact that this place was surrounded by thick shrubs. It was one of the flats that you couldn't see from the street because of shrubs that surrounded it. But at the same time the location of the place gave us a good view of parts of the city. From the elevated courtyard, you could see planes landing at Kingsford Smith International Airport. And in the first few weeks after we moved in, you would often find Reimas and Desimoni standing here looking at the planes landing and taking off. You could also tell what airlines the planes belonged to and one day the two of them surprised Uwegu and me when they called out to us and showed us an Air Niugini plane landing.

There was another thing about 2 Kennedy Lane and its immediate surrounding: in this suburb you would hardly find any black people. Within the block where we were, there were only an Indian guy Gupta, a family from Asia (we didn't know which country, although Uwegu was sure they were from China), a couple from New Zealand and a few eastern European university students. It was mostly a *dimdim* middle class suburb.

They all kept quiet and I continued with the story I was telling them. "The next evening (I slept the whole day); I went out seeking my neighbour Gupta," I continued after a short pause. "Gupta was smoking outside when I emerged.

"You look terrible," Gupta said when he saw me.

"That's not the way to greet your neighbour," I replied.

"Wanna smoke?"

"Okay," I said just to please him.

He pulled out one from the packet and offered it to me. I sat beside him on the pavement. After lighting it, it took me a long while to exhale the smoke. The longer I kept the smoke inside me, the more I felt calm. Once I exhaled it, it was like exhaling everything that was bothering me.

"A strange thing happened to me last night," I started.

"Continue," Gupta urged me.

"When I got home, I locked my door after me but this morning when I woke up my door was unlocked."

"That is indeed strange. Are you sure you locked it after you entered?"

"I am very sure." Gupta paused for a long while and his eyes surveyed the surrounding. I know he was thinking of what to say to me next.

The sudden ringing of the phone surprised us. Uwegu in particular was jolted by the sudden ringing and she almost jumped up. I stared at her and all I could see was the fear in her eyes.

"Aren't you going to answer that phone?" I asked them.

"We don't get that many phone calls except her," Desimoni replied looking at Uwegu.

She did not say anything, and only stared at me. "I don't want to answer that phone it sounds eerie. The other two guys gave faint smiles.

"What?" she asked, looking at them sternly. "Continue with the story."

"Anyway, all Gupta said to me in his Indian accent was, "Mate, strange things happen here all the time."

"Is that all you can tell me?" I tried getting him to talk. "Sue reckons this place is haunted."

"Who is Sue?"

"A *dimdim* woman who picked me up last evening and told me the story."

"I don't know of a Sue who lives here," Gupta told me.

"Anyway she is white, Gupta. If she can believe it, then there is really something here at 2 Kennedy Lane," I persisted.

"That's a lot of rubbish," Gupta said.

"He must be a strange Indian. Indians are generally mystic, they believe in the paranormal," Uwegu said sarcastically.

"A brown man in a white skin bro," Reimas added. "How could he dismiss it that easily?"

I waited for them to finish all the bad mouthing they had to say about Gupta, only to be disturbed by the phone again. We looked at each other but no one wanted to answer it so we left it till it rang out. Uwegu, unsettled by the phone call came and sat next to me. I could see the goose bumps on her hands but I did not say anything.

"Go on with the story," Desimoni urged me.

"Anyway, while I was still with Gupta, another neighbour came out to return a vacuum cleaner to Gupta. Somehow he saw that I was troubled.

"Something bothering you, pal?"

"Nah," I lied.

"Thanks for letting me borrow the vacuum cleaner Gupta," the neighbour said to him.

"That's alright," Gupta replied at the same time taking hold of the vacuum cleaner.

We got into chatting about the current events until I told them that I was thinking of moving to another place. The neighbour displayed a slack interest but when I told him about the strange happenings he became animated.

"Which flat are you in?" he asked.

"I am in flat 21."

"That's where the alleged murder was twelve years ago, wasn't it Gupta?"

"Search me," said Gupta. "I wasn't even here."

"It has to be Gupta. I am quite sure of it. Who can we ask?" He looked around. "Never mind. But I am pretty sure the alleged murder took place in that flat."

"You sure, because that's the flat I am in," I asked for some kind of confirmation.

"It might have been another one. It's been a long time. How many 12 years? It was all over the papers. It was the first alleged murder to have taken place at this block of apartments."

"They never found out who did it," the neighbour added. "Whether it was a real murder, we really don't know."

"But how could the police not find the murderer. Our police are supposed to be one of the best in the world," Gupta said.

"I think because the alleged murderer wasn't human at all," came in the neighbour. "This place is an old burial ground for the local aboriginal tribe. And there was this eccentric old man who had all sorts of artifacts and strange curios from New Guinea." Although I didn't know whom to believe, I felt my spine creep.

"Not long after, everyone had left Gupta and me, we saw another neighbour of ours and we called him over.

"Which flat was it where the alleged murder took place?" I asked him.

"One of these flats, I think it's flat 22."

"Which one?" I asked him again.

"Oh, God I am not sure. Don't pester me with it now," he said.

"I need to know of the exact flat," I urged him almost angrily. "It was number 22 though and not number 21?"

"Might have been. I forgot. It was ages ago. Why are you so steamed up about it anyway?"

"I am in flat 21 and something strange happened to me last night."

"It's a toss between 22 and 21. Go to the library and check the old newspapers."

Not reassured I asked Gupta to come with me to the flat. The place was dark and I half expected to see a spectral face loom at me. As we entered, Gupta suddenly said; "I knew there was something funny about this flat."

"Damn! Can't you talk about something else," I almost screamed at him. He looked at me surprised.

"You asked me to come along with you."

"Look man, I am sorry. I am just pissed off about the place. Something strange has happened to me. Someone should tell me straight."

"That's alright. Let me smell out the murder with my Indian sixth sense," he said with a cheeky smile. I saw him dip his hand into his pocket and come up with a small object which he held in his hand, chanting a mantra or something.

"So you are a mystic," I said after awhile.

He signaled me to be quiet. Then he continued with his chanting. After doing that he came and sat down beside me. I could see that he was also scared. I got up and tiptoed across the dark flat to turn on the lights. I found the switch but nothing happened when I switched it on. Gupta gave a little scream.

"Blackout," I told him.

"But my lights are on," he said. "This flat is mad enough for anything." I found that we were both whispering. On second thought I realised that I had switched off the main when I was replacing a bulb. I went to it and turned it on. Then there was light.

"I hope it is flat 22 and not my flat."

"I do hope so too. I wouldn't like to think of you as good as alone in this flat with a corpse. They never rest you know, when there's been violence done."

After a while Gupta left for his place and I was alone again. I turned on all the lights. There was a funny smell and I checked the flat for a dead rat. I searched the cupboards but to no avail.

"One thing about Kennedy Lane is that you feel there is something there, some invisible beings that are forever watching your movements. The feeling is more apparent when it is very quiet in the night.

The following night I was reading a rather thick Stephen King novel when all of a sudden my goose bumps stood. Then the hairs at the back of my head stood. When I looked at the clock it was 1.30 am in the morning.

It was one of those quiet nights when there was hardly anyone around. I had this spooky feeling that someone was watching me. I pushed back my chair and stood up, walked quietly to the window and peeped out. I heard footsteps walking away. There was no shadow although the lights outside were on. Quickly I went to my bedroom and sat on the bed. When I looked up I saw a firefly on the ceiling. I shivered and switched on the lights. Suddenly my phone rang. I hesitated, praying that someone must have got a wrong number. It rang several times. When I finally picked it up I heard heavy breathing and a few seconds later the line went dead.

The next day I ritually cleansed the flat.

"Did anything happen to you after that?" Uwegu asked.

"Strange things continued to happen. Has anything strange happened to you guys since you moved in here?"

"Yes, all the time." Uwegu said. "Someone tried to strangle me a few nights ago. It was a woman." The two guys all looked at her.

"What do you mean?" Desimoni asked her surprised.

"I mean a woman came into my room and tried to kill me. I struggled and managed to push her off. Someone who has something against us or rather me has done something to this flat." She looked at me. Did you find this flat on your own or did that *dimdim* woman find it for you?"

"Kate reserved the place before I arrived," I told her.

"I know she did something to this place."

"Oh gawd! This is getting on my nerves," I said. "But the alleged murder happened some 12 years ago. How could you blame her?"

"Regardless of the alleged murder someone did something to this flat," Uwegu insisted.

I wanted to tell them that a few nights ago someone came into my room and made love to me. When I woke up I was totally naked and my clothes were all over the room. But I didn't want to embarrass myself in front of them.

There was a prolonged silence before Uwegu broke it again. "But it is very true, human beings are spirits and when people die their spirits remain, roaming the places they used to go to when they were alive. At my place, women actually fly in the night to visit their relatives and family or to kill an enemy." I stared at her not knowing whether to believe her or not.

"She is right Perez. Women fly at night at our place," Desimoni added.

"I have a bad feeling about that woman who got us to live in this flat," Uwegu said. "She seems to be bizarre and weird. Almost every night I see her in my dreams. What is she after?" I didn't say anything.

"Do you know her though?" I asked. She shook her head in the negative.

"Then you should not blame her," I said. She gave me that non-believing look.

We continued telling stories about home. The main subject that night was on ghosts. Desimoni told us about the first time he saw a ghost. It was back in the village during one of his school holidays. He went to the beach with his aunt to collect shells in the evening when they saw a woman walking towards them. They thought it was another aunt from the next village. When the woman got closer, she disappeared. The two quickly went home and upon arrival were told that a relative in the next village had just died.

"Were you frightened bro?" Reimas asked him.

"And what do you think? I was so frightened I practically held to my aunt until we arrived at our house."

What I realised was that whenever we told stories about home, it became our mooring. The stories provided some kind of connection between each one of us and between us and our homes. They also provided a kind of refuge for all of us. Strange though it may be, but whenever one told a story whose setting was elsewhere no one really bothered to listen. Stories about home brought us together as we tried to make sense of some of the things we thought strange and different.

I didn't say anything more. I got carried away thinking about the unexplained incidents that happened to me when I first moved into 2 Kennedy Lane and the fact that we might be living in a flat where a murder once took place. I wondered about what Uwegu had said about Kate; that it could have been her who had placed some kind of sorcery or magic at the flat. When I came back to my senses I became conscious that what I was dreading was more of a surreal kind of a thing.

The following day I had a call from Gupta telling me that the alleged murder took place in flat 22 and not the one we are staying at. It was indeed a relief. When I asked him how he knew, he told me that he has just read it in one of the old newspapers in the library. I sat down and thought about the whole story and I became conscious of the fact that having been transplanted to another culture, we still carried our cultural baggage. It was something that was difficult to dispose of no matter how much we tried. Then I remembered Uwegu's story about someone trying to strangle her and I got more confused.

Chapter 4

Since Uwegu accused Kate of trying to strangle her I tried my best to find out why the two women might not like each other. Uwegu wasn't saying much about it and Kate had not returned to see us since she left for her place. Whether the two women knew each other I did not know. Everything to do with them was shrouded in mystery. I was preoccupied with this when I unlocked the door and entered the flat one afternoon at about 2.00 pm. I thought no one was home because the place was quiet. The quietude brought loneliness and my mind wandered back home. I wondered what my folks were doing. Then the thought of Deuba flooded my mind, almost bringing tears. Not long after, I heard a rustle outside and when I peeked out there was Uwegu sitting quietly. Her head was bowed and her books were on the neatly cut lawn. She seemed to be crying and her body language also showed it. I watched her quietly for sometime. Awhile later she lifted her head and started humming a tune. I felt sorry for her. It was then that I called out to her, surprising her. She quickly wiped what I suspected to be tears and came to me.

"Are you okay?" I asked her as soon as we were inside.

"I am not feeling too well, I keep on thinking about that *dimdim* woman and I am sure she is out to get me," she told me in a timid way.

"But why would she want to harm you?" I said looking at her. "Unless both of you know each other and there is something bad that happened between you two."

"I don't know but strange things keep on happening to me and in my dreams I keep on seeing her trying to harm me," Uwegu continued.

"Unless you are not telling me the truth I can't help you and besides you do not have any evidence." She kept quiet for a long while and I waited for her to say something.

"Perhaps it's the loneliness that is driving me crazy," she replied with some humour. She touched my hand, "honestly Perez, the story you told us had given me ideas."

"What ideas?" I asked her.

"That someone might have concocted the story to frighten us in order to break us apart. Someone who wants either you or me or either of the two boys. People can go to the extremes when they want something real bad. I have been thinking. This story about the haunted apartments could have been made up by someone who doesn't want us here amongst them." She looked me in the eyes. "You said that Sue told you about it yet Sue does not live here. This is strange."

"It could be definitely haunted or it could just be the strangeness of the place, that's all," I told her.

"Perez, you know how it is back home when people want to frighten or stop children from going to certain places or from doing certain things they make up ghost stories," Uwegu told me. I nodded my head in agreement. There was logic in what Uwegu was saying and for all I knew she could be right too.

Loneliness, homesickness together with the strangeness of the place affected us deeply especially in the first few weeks since we moved in. It was almost unbearable. Most of the time the three guys were busy writing letters and almost everyday they would go to the Post Office to post their letters. Even the phone bill skyrocketed, so I had to get Telstra to temporarily terminate the IDD until our bills were paid. I tried my best to make them feel at home requesting them to come with me for bus rides and all that. Desimoni was the worst of the three. He sat for hours writing. I once read his unfinished letter which told about how he was going around with a *dimdim* girl and how she would take him to all the interesting places and all that. In another letter he wrote about playing rugby and how the *dimdims* envy him every time he played. I knew it was not true but what would you expect when everyday they were writing letters home. When there are no more stories to tell they only have to invent and write about fictitious events.

Although this was her first time to come overseas, it didn't take long for Uwegu to make friends. Perhaps it was because she was a woman, I don't know. I just know that it is easier for women to make friends than guys. One thing I knew was that Uwegu has had some experience unlike Reimas and Desimoni who were just fresh from secondary school. Uwegu was 26 years old (a few years younger than me). If you look closely at Uwegu you will notice that she cared a lot about her looks. She mostly wore jeans or long pants but when she wore shorts you could see her sexy legs. She was unbelievably attractive. A mixture of charm, beauty and an independent free spirit was how you could describe her. She was also brave and could speak her mind without hesitation. When you chat with her you get to know her feminine side. Uwegu was about 5 feet, 6 inches tall, with a copper brown skin that was smooth as a liver. While she also had a sporty look, she did not play any sports, at least not that I knew of.

What I didn't like about her though was her habit sometimes of not letting us know when she didn't come home quickly. This made me worried. But whenever I tell her to be careful and vigilant she would dismiss my concern with that 'not to worry' look.

"Hey, I am a big girl; I can do what I want," Uwegu told me one evening after I tried to talk to her about her coming home late.

"Uwegu, recently there has been a spate of crime here," I tried to reason with her. "That's why we are concerned about you. What would your parents say if you happen to be involved in an accident?"

"I have always been independent and I can fend for myself," was all she could say when I tried to advise her.

"At least you should let us know where you are and when you are coming home." We have a phone here," Desimoni supported me.

"Listen, I appreciate your concerns but I know what I am doing. I am only sharing this flat with you but I am independent like everyone else here. How I look after myself here is none of your business."

I knew Uwegu was not in a good mood that evening when I tried to counsel her. There is another thing that I learnt that evening; that she can stand her ground if she wished. Perhaps it's that work experience part that moulded her into a strong woman. Sometimes whenever any one of the two guys get on her, I would just keep quiet and mind my own business despite the fact that I was the oldest, a postgraduate student at that. As soon as I knew they were getting on her I would retreat to my room. It's not that I was afraid but I didn't want to impose myself on people who I thought capable of making their own decisions. I know that Uwegu was a capable woman but you know what boys are like. They sometimes like to treat Uwegu as their mother or something. In the end it is Uwegu who puts the two guys at their place and the two would quietly retreat into their shells. I was more concerned about her welfare. Recently there has been a spate of race-motivated crimes in the city targeted especially at the growing Asian population. I have never encountered any incidents like this. Perhaps it is because I don't roam around too much.

The suburb where Kennedy Lane was located was populated by mostly middle class white folks. These are mainly elderly *dimdim* residents and our immediate neighbours were generally quiet and peaceful. However there is a certain house whose tenant often troubled Uwegu. On our way to campus we would pass this house whose occupant was a grumpy old man who looked like an alcoholic. Whenever we passed him he never uttered a word to us although we would greet him. He would only stare at us as if we were lepers or something. It didn't trouble me one bit but it did trouble Uwegu. Uwegu was bad, always complaining about him even after we have past him.

"What's wrong with this man? Can't he greet us? Talk about neighbourhood!" Uwegu said one morning.

"Don't let it bother you Uwegu," I told her. She gawked at me as if I had said something awful, then she shook her head.

"You know what he thinks of us?" she told me straight.

"Nope!" I tried to play it down.

"Bloody pigs, that's what he thinks of us."

"Don't put words in his mouth. You are just being hysterical," I tried to reason with her.

"Hysterical? I am not. He hates us that's what."

"Why would he? We have not done anything bad to him," I fired back.

"Because we are black, that's why!" she came out forcefully.

I looked intently at her as we crossed the street and made our way to the main Uni entrance.

"Believe me, I know," she said. "Don't think silence means nothing."

Instantly an ugly vision of racism clouded my mind. I knew I have always tried to deny racism a space in my mind but today Uwegu made it resurface. I realised that all this time I have tried to pretend that I was like everyone else. I pretended to pull at the collar of my shirt when in fact I was looking at the colour of my skin. Indeed I was different. All this time I thought Uwegu was naïve but indeed I was mistaken. I disliked her for opening old wounds.

"What have you got to say?" Uwegu asked, staring at me with fire in her eyes that I have never seen before. My susceptibility seems to fill the space in between us.

"I think you are right," I said quietly.

"Perez, I am sorry to have talked to you like this," Uwegu apologised. "But I have experienced it from way back in PNG."

"All we have to do is avoid it," I said. "This is not our place."

"I don't know Perez but it stinks," said Uwegu. "If we own up to it, then at least people can be aware of it."

In my mind I knew that I was trying to sweep the problem under the carpet. I don't know whether it was because of fear or something else.

We arrived at the main library and I stopped. "What are you doing at lunch? Why don't you meet me at the Rhine's Coffee Shop," she asked me. I didn't answer quickly. She kept on looking at me straight in my eyes.

"Alright then."

"Thanks, I'll catch up with you at 12.00 then," she said departing quickly for her class.

As I walked to the building, which housed the Sociology School, I kept thinking about what Uwegu has just said. Since coming to Sydney I have never cared much about discrimination. Australia was supposed to be a great country, with its arms outstretched inviting people of every colour, religion and creed to its shores. I have walked freely along its streets without anyone harassing me. Perhaps I was too naïve, I told myself. But the whole conversation with Uwegu disturbed me. How could I not see racism's ugly tentacles?

I entered the building and went to the School's postgraduate office. No one was in yet and I was the first one. I settled into my desk and turned on the computer to check my emails. Most of the emails I had in my inbox were junks or 'forwards' sent by friends. I continued to think about what Uwegu has just told me and I wondered whether Reimas and Desimoni have also experienced it since their arrival.

Another letter was on my table and it was from my cousin in Port Moresby. The letter was mostly about Deuba. He told me that she had been promoted and that her girlfriend whom I flirted with had left her employment and married an old *dimdim*.

The letter also told about what Deuba has been saying about me. That I have always mistreated her throughout the relationship, that I was a woman basher. She told people about finding things that gave me away, things that were not supposed to be in the house. How the phone would ring and how when she went to answer it, they would hang up on her. How a few times some woman called her a bitch. The letter was embarrassing and had depicted me badly. I got upset, quickly tore it into pieces and threw the pieces into the wastebasket. I vowed never to have anything to do with her again.

✳✳✳

One of the things I noticed about Reimas and Desimoni was that they were young and inexperienced. They sometimes did strange things that you don't expect. The first time they arrived, they would congregate at the lounge and listen to local music in between telling stories about home. Some stories would be repeated numerous times. Perhaps this was because they have never stayed on their own before. Most of their conversation was conducted in Tok Pisin. Desimoni was particularly bad with his spoken English and many times he spoke to us in either Pidgin or his version of English. Reimas was okay and he was catching on fast. He was mostly into *dimdim* food and the latest fashion in clothes and so forth. Most of this he copied from television advertisements.

The funny thing about the two guys is that often they argued with each other, and Uwegu and I found it amusing. One time they almost came to blows but Uwegu separated them. Uwegu often scolded them but they always try to put her down because she was a woman, I think. But as soon as they found out that she was tough and strong they never again bothered her. The first time was terrible for Uwegu because Reimas and Desimoni often got on her when she tried to advise them. A number of times, Uwegu came to me sulking because one of the guys called her a bitch. I got on the two guys and they got upset.

"*Em meri nating*, we don't want to listen to her bro," Reimas said to me.

"She is too bossy," Desimoni came in. "We aren't kids. We are here on our own accords."

"But you act like kids sometimes," I told them. "Here everyone is equal. Respect one another so we can live together and get along well," I advised them.

"She can't mind her own business," Desimoni said quietly.

"I'll talk to her about it," I told them.

I know I can get along with Uwegu very well, perhaps because I was a postgraduate student. But I made sure that I was fair with everyone, not that I poked my nose in everyone's business. I kept to myself and only got involved when they asked me or when there was a real problem.

Two things perhaps held us together in this house; one was the fact that we came from the same country. And therefore we were a community unto ourselves and second what strengthened our group was the ever-present threat from outside. Being wantoks ensured that we maintained our group and being a minority meant that we keep together against threats. Of course there were often times our group was threatened from within — ourselves. I tried my best to hold the group together. Uwegu threatened to move out several times because she could not stand the two guys but I managed to persuade her to stay. At other times the two guys threatened to go away but I would do the same with them. I knew they wouldn't do it on their own, at least not as yet. Eventually they would return to us — me! I don't know whether Uwegu would if she happened to leave, perhaps not. She did have quite a number of friends.

I was so preoccupied with all these random thoughts that when I looked at my watch it was lunchtime so I went to the place where Uwegu said for us to meet. It wasn't crowded because it is located at the edge of the campus. I went in and sat down. Uwegu wasn't in yet. I got myself a cup of coffee and a sandwich and sat down to eat. About 10 minutes later Uwegu rushed in, sweating with her books.

"Sorry to keep you waiting Perez," she apologised. "The lecture ended ten minutes late."

"That's alright. Sit down and I'll get you something to eat. What would you like to have?"

"No, let me buy your lunch," she insisted.

"It's alright, allow me," I said.

"In my culture, when someone asks you to have lunch with her, she buys. So I will buy our lunch. What would you like?"

"But I have already bought my lunch," I said.

"Not to worry I will buy you another sandwich," she said at the same time walking towards the counter. I could not stop her.

For the first few minutes we ate silently although the place was animated with students chatting and laughing. Sitting on the other side, was one of the guys I shared the office with. He sat alone reading a paper. Maybe he was waiting for someone. I tried waving to him but he didn't see me so I gave up.

"I like the sandwich here," Uwegu finally broke the silence that engulfed us. "Yes, it's tasty," I mumbled. "They have the original recipe." I smiled.

We ate in silence again.

"You know what happened to me this morning after we parted?" Uwegu disturbed the silence again. I looked at her hard.

"Some guys in a car swore at me and called me a black bitch," she told me, her eyes fierce like a wild animal.

"Really?" I replied surprised.

"They do that all the time," said a Muslim woman who was all veiled up next to us. We looked at her. "They bad mouth me all the time but I don't give a damn. I belong to this country; I was born here," the veiled Muslim student continued. It was as if we had pricked open a boil that threatened to burst. She stood up and came to Uwegu and pressed her hand. "Don't worry about them, they are cowards!" Then she withdrew her hand, waved to us and left. We looked at each other.

"So what did you do?" I asked Uwegu.

"What could I do?" I pretended not to hear them. There were a number of people crossing the street and they all heard it and knew that it was meant for me. I did not tell you, a month ago a group of white drunken youths tried to block my way as I was crossing to the train station. Luckily the guard came and they all took off. I should have waited for Reimas. We would have clobbered them. Oh, I felt so terrible and lonely. I know I am not in my own country but one would have thought this is a civilised nation. You heard what that Muslim student had said. It's an ongoing thing," Uwegu said.

"What can I say? This is something beyond our control," I tried to reassure Uwegu. "We have to try and live above it."

"I hate it," said Uwegu strongly. "I want to be treated like any other *dimdim*. Has the word respect lost its meaning completely here? I am not here for good. I mean I am only a bird of passage. I am only here to study and then I am going back home. I am not here to steal a piece of their country!"

The incident has indeed left her with a bitter and stormy memory and I felt sorry for her.

"It makes you feel homesick you know! Just at the time when you feel that you are settling in, you get this kind of treatment and it exposes your helplessness. For me it is worse because I can't do anything about it," Uwegu continued.

I sat there listening to her, taking it all quietly, eating my lunch slowly as if this was going to be the last.

"I hope it's not just their way of admiring your beauty. Did you hear the exact words?" I asked her.

"No, but I could tell they were bad mouthing me," said Uwegu. "Some men don't respect beauty. Some men who look at me have the most contemptible urges. Disgusting morons!"

"You are talking about that exotic thing again," I said, trying to make it a joke. "These people can be beasts. They like to play God!" she said in a strong voice.

Suddenly, her anguish and anger made my temper rise. "The fucking *dimdims* act as if they own the place!" I surprised Uwegu with my sudden outburst and she looked at me for a long while.

"True, this country belongs to the black guys. Shame on them!" Uwegu added.

"You know what they did to the black guys? They isolated them into the desert and settlements and they are killing them slowly with alcohol. How many of them are living next to us?"

"They say that Redfern is terrible," said Uwegu.

"I haven't been there. But they say it's a dangerous place."

"It has become dangerous because the poor guys want to defend themselves from these *dimdim* beasts," Uwegu said swallowing the last bit of her sandwich.

"Redfern is a nightmare for the cops."

"But they are only defending themselves, these black fellas," Uwegu cut in.

"I know," I managed to say. "This place belongs to the Aborigines. These white people came later."

"Cowards."

"Have you finished?" I asked her after some time.

"Yes, thank you," Uwegu answered.

"Let's go then," I said.

We stood up and walked outside. The sun was shining bright and all around us you could see students chatting, or going off to classes.

"Reimas didn't make it as he had promised," I said quietly. "I asked him to come and we would have lunch together."

"Don't believe those two guys, they never keep to their promises," Uwegu told me.

"At least if he had come I would have bought him lunch."

Then Uwegu pointed to a group of Muslim students, two were veiled. "You see those people there? They are also treated badly by these *dimdims*. They cop it almost everyday. Look how these *dimdims* stare at you every time you are at a public place."

"For some, it's a way of admiring your beauty and charm," I said. "Especially if you are different." She stared at me for a long time and I could read the seriousness on her face.

"You have not come across what I am talking about Perez. When you do, you will understand what it means to be discriminated against," she said with finality. I was quietly glad that she was giving the matter a conclusion.

As I walked towards my office I thought about Uwegu's bad experience and wondered what it was all about? I wanted to dismiss it as paranoia but then again I wanted to believe her.

✳✳✳

The first thing I did when I got home was to check whether Uwegu was home. I saw her shoes outside her door and I knew she was home. The story she told me sharpened my anxiety and curiosity. Inside Reimas's room I heard music playing. The two were chatting quietly inside. I opened my door and went in and slept on my bed, my mind still preoccupied with what Uwegu had told me.

Later, when I came out I saw Uwegu sitting in the lounge looking at the map of PNG. She has rearranged the place and got out some of the items she brought from home and now our lounge was decorated with objects from home.

"This is to get our minds away from those racist pigs!" Uwegu told me.

"That's nice," I said pointing to the hangings on the wall. "It looks more homely. Where did you get those things from?"

"Bits and pieces from home," Uwegu said.

"It looks more like home to me now," I said admiring her skills in decorating the place.

"Reimas and Desimoni helped me put them up. A piece of New Guinea in a strange place."

"Yeah, home away from home," I said.

Chapter 5

The bad-mouthing and racist comments that Uwegu had recently encountered were still fresh in my memory. It kept on resurfacing and I found it difficult to ignore it. One thing for sure was that I got intimidated. I began to distrust every *dimdim* that gazed at me. Reimas was different, he was developing a confrontational attitude and I advised him to tone it down. Desimoni told me that the other day Reimas swore at a group of *dimdims* who refused to make way for him and he almost manhandled one of them. They threatened to report him to the police. When the bus came he showed them his finger and the bus drove off.

"That's not good and he mustn't do it again," I told Desimoni. "He will only be creating problems for himself."

"*Tru ya*. These *dimdims* have gangs *ya* and they could do something nasty to him," Desimoni replied.

"Or even to us," I added. "When he wakes up I will talk to him," I told Desimoni.

Not long after, Reimas came out but by this time we have moved on to another topic. He came and sat next to Uwegu who was peeling potatoes. We continued talking until we were disturbed by a knock on the door. We wondered who it was because all of us were home. It was around 5.30 pm. I asked one of the guys to go and see who it was. Reimas got up and went to open the door. Then we heard him talking with a woman. All we heard was, "neighbourhood watch meeting." When Reimas returned he was holding a piece of paper. He told us that the *dimdim* woman was handing out notices of a neighbourhood watch meeting for tomorrow as there has been an increase in crime in the neighbourhood. He showed us the notice. Uwegu was the first to get it off him. I watched her closely as she read it. She looked up, squeezed the paper and threw it in the wastebasket. "Why bother with them," she murmured. "They can all go to hell for all I care!" We looked at her but she was already back to cooking.

"Bro, these *dimdims* don't even talk to us as if we aren't human beings," Reimas said after awhile.

Suddenly Uwegu looked up once again from her cooking. "No joking, the other day I was coming home and saw this elderly couple who live two houses from us. Because they were looking at me, I said good afternoon and they didn't even reply. They gave me that glaring stare and I felt ashamed and humiliated."

"Now they want us to be involved in this neighbourhood watch because crime has increased in this suburb just to protect them and their bloody properties bro," Reimas stated. "Especially these so-called Anglo-Saxon *dimdims*. The others are good; they talk to you and are easy to get along with."

"You mean the late arrivals to this country like Italians, Greeks, and those from Eastern Europe. These guys are chatterboxes," Uwegu said.

"Bro, some of these Asians are bloody snobbish too ya. They tend to keep to themselves, especially the Chinese. The others are okay," Reimas added. "One of these days I am going to clobber one of them."

"Reimas don't get too confrontational, you might get into trouble. This is not PNG," I advised him.

"Sorry bro, but how do we get to stop them from harassing us?" They all looked at me for an answer but I did not have one. Uwegu especially stared hard at me. I knew she didn't want me to talk that way to Reimas.

"Because we are a minority here, they think they can do whatever they like with us. But I am sorry I am not a freeloader here," Uwegu uttered. "We have every right to be here; they plundered our country, and stole our resources. We did not kick them out."

"That's true, sis. Part of this country was developed using money stolen from our country by these *dimdims*."

"Well, shame on them, gutless *dimdims*," Uwegu added.

I kept quiet listening to them talking. I could understand their concerns. These could be their first observations upon arrival in this new place. Back home we chat freely with people, even when we don't know them we greet them. We establish strong bonds with those whom we consider our neighbours, even to the extent of treating them as relatives. We call out to neighbours or even passing strangers on the road. We call from our house to the other houses. When someone is ill, we visit them. We like to sing or talk aloud.

"These people keep to themselves as if they are afraid of catching a deadly disease," Uwegu continued.

"Sis, no wonder when people die here, they are not discovered until days later," I heard Reimas said. "You remember that woman whose house is adjacent to the bus stop?"

"Which bus stop?" Desimoni asked.

"Bro, the main one. Wee, there was a woman who lived there alone. I used to see her sometimes. She was in her late 70s I think. She died three weeks ago and they only discovered her corpse last week because of the foul smell. Yet she was part of the neighbourhood watch here!"

"There are many cases of people living alone who die but are not discovered until later. In our place it is different; we live together and watch over each other," said Uwegu.

"*Dimdims* here have a different understanding of neighbourhood, sis," Reimas intoned.

"Really? How do you know that?" Desimoni asked.

"I heard from people that the *dimdim* anthropologist who stayed at our area said the same thing about other *dimdims*," Uwegu supported Reimas.

"Too much reading Malinowski," came in Desimoni.

"What did you say? Let me tell you," she said pointing her finger at Desimoni. "I have never read your bloody Malinowski, whoever that asshole is."

"Stop it you two," I said rather loudly. "Let's understand one thing here. We are here to study and not to be bothered by trivial things. Let's forget about this and talk about something else."

"I am sorry," said Uwegu. Then she disappeared into her room.

"Let me tell you guys something," I said. "Sometimes it's our own fears of other people that make us think they are snobbish and unfriendly. You don't just look at people and judge them by the way they present themselves. At times we are mortified for the wrong reasons."

"Damn if I care, bro. These people are unfriendly because we are different from them," Reimas responded strongly.

"Cut that racist crap Reimas," I told him bluntly.

"It's them not me bro," Reimas argued.

"You don't even know if that is true. People here mind their own business. Did you actually try talking to one?"

"I can just feel it bro, I am not stupid. Back home they crave for our women."

"That shows they aren't racists after all," I said smiling.

"They just wanna screw that's all!" Desimoni came in laughing.

"Cut that rubbish Desimoni. Wee, look at you!" said Uwegu as she came to boil the potatoes she had just peeled.

"It's not crap. Haven't you seen how they mistreat the Aborigines here? These blacks were the first people here; yet they are mistreated by these *dimdims*!"

"Because they are a bunch of alcoholics these Aborigines! All they do is gamble away their lives by drinking."

"It's because the *dimdims* drive them to be alcoholics."

"Let's talk about something else," I said. "Let us not trouble ourselves with other people's business."

"Are we going to this neighbourhood meeting then?" Desimoni asked.

"Bro, I am not going," Reimas said.

Desimoni looked at me and I shook my head in the negative.

"This business is *dimdims'* business and does not concern us. Why should we go?" Uwegu said.

"Bro, if they can keep to themselves, let them protect themselves. *Yumi tu stap ya!*" uttered Reimas.

"What if something happens to us and we need help? Who do we go to?" I asked rhetorically.

"Bro, the cops are there. Just pick up the phone and they'll be here," said Reimas. "*Yumi ol man tu ya*. Bro these *dimdims* are afraid of us. They will never touch us."

"What about me?" asked Uwegu.

"Sis, don't worry we are here for you," said Reimas.

I switched off and picked up the newspaper and started reading it.

"Neighbourhood watch is the *dimdims'* version of wantok system. The point is that it can't really work here," I heard Reimas say.

"True ya. See how we are here among a sea of strange *dimdims* who can't even utter a word of greeting when they see us? We are like rats in some deep hole," Desimoni said.

"Phew some intellectual talk that one," Uwegu teased Desimoni.

Desimoni stared at Uwegu before talking. "It's not. Can't you see that this neighbourhood is buried in a silence that resembles death. You can't even hear anyone talking. Maybe they whisper to each other aye?"

We smiled at Desimoni's metaphor. Indeed it was strange that you don't hear the *dimdim* neighbours talking. All we hear are the vehicles on the road and the occasional laughter from students walking to Uni or returning from Uni. We try to be quiet but it is difficult for us who come from a different culture. "Talking makes us sane," as the saying goes.

No one said anything further. Uwegu instead picked up the *Sydney Morning Herald* and started reading it. It was the Sunday edition. I saw Uwegu reading the fashion section of the newspaper. Then she surprised me.

"Look, did you read this?" she asked, looking up.

"What is it?" I asked her.

"There is this Australian film crew who is going to the Trobriand Islands to do a documentary on the people there."

"They are always after the exotic," I said laughing. "Nothing has changed for these *dimdims*. They just want to make money. It's a big draw card!"

"Bro, how come they don't wanna look at us twice here?" Reimas asked.

"Because we aren't the original; we aren't in the proper context and setting," said Uwegu.

"They want to capture naked breasts and savages. That's what excites these *dimdims*," I said.

"So when are they leaving for the Trobriands?" Desimoni asked Uwegu.

"Next week. The filming will take three weeks."

"Sis, after they leave, we'll see a couple of half *dimdims* again," Reimas cut in.

"That's progress isn't it?" I asked smiling.

"It's rehabilitating the savage," added Uwegu in a joking tone. "A little *dimdim* blood in the native will civilise him."

"Desimoni's dad will be happy because they will give him a little money for filming his subjects," I joked.

"Gees, I didn't realise that. I must contact home quickly so dad can spare me some of those money," Desimoni replied, one of the rare occasions when he joked.

"It's not funny you guys," I said changing into a serious tone. "These *dimdims* are exploiting our people. It is through their eyes that the world sees us, not our own eyes."

"That's true yah. Look how serious crime is committed here everyday yet they don't make big time news back home. For us it is different, every little crime that is committed is big time news here," Reimas added.

"Not all the *dimdims* are like that. Many of them are good," Desimoni came in.

"Of course, people are not all the same. Some are good and some are bad," I said. "Here we are talking about the bad *dimdims*."

"I have not come across a good *dimdim* yet," came in Desimoni. We all looked at him as if he said something bad. "True, I haven't."

"Maybe you aren't opening up," said Uwegu. "Maybe you are not brave enough."

"What about you? It's you who is always passionate about the subject," Desimoni retaliated. Reimas and I kept quiet.

"I have tried to open up to these *dimdims* but every time I do, they ignore me. This is the very reason why I am passionate about this topic."

"You are right, sis. Perhaps I have not tried to open up to these people," said Reimas rather quietly.

"The point can be affirmed in the saying that 'The longest journey in the world is from the lips to the heart,' Uwegu told us.

"Wow! Where did you get that from sis?" Reimas came in.

"It's an old Chinese proverb," Uwegu told him.

"No kidding sis," said Reimas. "Then we can always try to open up to these *dimdims*."

"Just open up to them, especially to the *dimdim* women," Desimoni teased Reimas.

"Are you sure bro?" Reimas asked.

"Of course I am sure."

When Uwegu was out of earshot Desimoni went on. "Didn't you open up to a *dimdim* woman at KX?"

"Oh frikken hell, bro!" said Reimas laughing.

"I bet that was a different kind of opening up," I said quietly. "You were opening up to a corpse."

"That was a commercial transaction," said Desimoni laughing.

"The opening up was purely on economic terms," I added.

"What was that about?" Uwegu asked after returning from her room. The three of us looked at each other.

"Nothing, sis," said Reimas.

"I heard you guys talking," she insisted. We didn't want to tell her so we tried to come up with all sorts of excuses to cover up.

"Let me tell you guys something. I don't feel really at home here." Uwegu paused, coughing. "Where my heart is at ease that is my home."

Chapter 6

Since the time we talked about the *dimdims'* lack of neighbourly attitude towards us, we all felt a little apprehensive. Uwegu unlike us was the only one who didn't want to be put down by all this. It has the opposite effect on her, fueling her to take the dragon head-on (her words). I admired her determination and courage. She told us that she was teaming up with others who suffer from this discrimination and prejudice. I believed her and so did Reimas but Desimoni was ambivalent. I understood where he was coming from given that he was an introverted person, who did not talk much.

Among the four of us I found Desimoni to be the most reserved. He was mostly quiet and the only time he would talk was when you prompted him. It must have been to do with being nervy and unsettled by being in a strange new place. At the same time I was told that he was naturally a quiet person. Above all the talk about *dimdims*, discriminatory attitudes might have added to his despair. Like most of us, perhaps he was a little disturbed by life here in Sydney. While he could handle most situations, he also had his weaknesses and moments of distraction. He was different from Reimas in many ways. While Reimas was quiet in the first few weeks, gradually he began to adapt. He was an extroverted person, adventurous and always willing to explore new things. Desimoni on the other hand was steeped in tradition and could be a little snobbish at times. But overall, he was a happy-go-friendly little fellow. But as the saying goes, 'don't judge the book by its cover.' I knew I must be ready for unexpected surprises.

One of the first things that you notice about him is his size. He wasn't big in figure; in fact he was the smallest among the whole lot of us from PNG. He was about 5 feet 2 inches tall and you would take him for a child sometimes. You would hardly see him in a crowd. His smallness gave him a unique look. He was rather soft-spoken and had a high-pitched voice like a parrot. This also gave him that timid look. He mostly wore shorts, (those six pocket cargo pants were his favourite). The other thing you noticed about him is that he was very much a traditional man; whenever he was sick he went out, collected leaves and roots from many plants and either chewed them or drank their juices. When we tell him to go to the medical clinic he would refuse, saying he knew what he was doing. Once when I was down with fever, he gave me some roots to chew and after awhile I got better. From then on I had a respect for him as someone who was steeped in traditional knowledge.

It was only later that I learnt that he was the son of one of the paramount chiefs back home. Once I knew this, I also became apprehensive about him. Back home, people dreaded the chiefs because they were associated with sorcery and magic. I regretted having him as a flatmate and I became overly cautious about what I did in front of him. Although he was no different from us, there was certain body language that told me otherwise. Certain things have also happened in the flat that seemed unexplainable, a mysterious one of which was the attempted strangling of Uwegu while she was sleeping. As the only son of the chief he was the next heir to the throne once his father died or decides to step down (which was very rare).

"Someone had tried to strangle Uwegu," I told him just trying to get his reaction. He kept quiet for a while. "She must have wronged somebody back home. Now they are trying to get her."

"Or could be someone here in Australia," I said.

"Could be, that *dimdim* woman is a possibility." Every time she is here, I have an unsettled feeling."

"But you can help her can't you?" I continued probing him.

"I am not quiet sure if I can but this seems a women's business," he replied. "What she needs to do is reconcile with whoever she has problems with. She would have a fair idea who that person might be." I continued to prompt him on thinking that he might reveal something but in the end I gave up.

When some students first saw him in the university they thought he was one of those whiz kids; those who are exceptionally brilliant and have gone through the system while they were still kids. A number of people have asked Reimas about him and it kind of gave us (according to Reimas, as he told us later) that air of superiority, that feeling of having a specially gifted person among us. I knew once the cat was let out of the bag, they would mock us (especially Reimas) for elevating someone who wasn't a whiz kid. Nevertheless (as Reimas urged us) we must live on that reputation and as much as possible, Reimas tried to steer Desimoni (without him knowing of course) out of harm's way of not associating with people because they were bound to find out the truth. The poor guy didn't know that he had been elevated into the status of a whiz kid. It was Reimas who did that and it was only later that he told Uwegu and myself about it.

"What if they find out?" Uwegu asked Reimas as soon as he told us about him telling people that Desimoni is a whiz kid.

"Sis, they won't find out soon but if they do I will tell them that he doesn't speak good English but he is a brain box," Reimas told us.

"Does Desimoni know about it?" I asked him.

"Why should he bro?"

"Man, you are getting yourself into a deep shit," Uwegu warned him. "They are bound to find out sooner before you know it."

"Bro, only a few Asian students have asked me about him and maybe one or two *dimdims*," Reimas said.

"What makes them think he is a whiz kid?"

"Because of his stature, I think," I told her.

"If Desi finds out about this he will not like it at all," Uwegu said.

"Sis, I am not conning people, I am only playing along with their assumption," said Reimas. "So what if we have a whiz kid?"

"That is true, this whiz kid thing happens in all cultures," I said.

"But he is misusing it," Uwegu complained. "I don't want to look stupid once people find out about it. They will say *mi wantok blong giaman whiz kid*".

"Sis, calm down, it's nothing big. I have not gained anything from it," said Reimas.

"How about that superiority thing you told us about, saying we will be on par with the *dimdims* because we have a whiz kid?" Uwegu asked.

"Okay sis, maybe I have gained a little bit of respect but nothing more," Reimas countered.

"But you gonna spoil his reputation Reimas. He is a chief's son," Uwegu told him.

"Sis, you are not thinking straight. This is a kind of public relations for him," Reimas hit back.

"You must have planned it all," I said with a smile.

"Do people ask you about the whiz kid thing when you are with Desi?" Uwegu started again.

"Sis, you know they wouldn't do that. They ask me when he isn't with me," Reimas said. "It's mostly the Asians who ask." He paused. "I know they can't approach him directly because they are afraid of him."

"I hope so," came in Uwegu. "I don't want to be part of this conspiracy."

"Sis, it's not a conspiracy."

"It's a way to elevate us to be on par with the *dimdims*," I said, repeating Reimas' earlier statement.

"I hope you are not encouraging him," Uwegu said looking at me sternly. "Mark my word, if you guys fall, you will really fall."

"Don't worry we'll cushion the fall somehow," I said laughing. "I mean Reimas still has some tricks up his sleeve, what you might call plan B."

"Whatever," Uwegu said.

"But Reimas, do you think that whiz kid thing will hold for a long time?" I asked him.

"So long as we can get that bloody shortie guy to avoid those who have been asking about him. And as long as he doesn't know about it."

"I have a feeling you are trying to use him to gain something from it," Uwegu insisted.

"Hey sis, this is not like your U-Vistract pyramid scheme (a money scheme that operated in PNG) and I do not intend to start one up."

"Please don't talk about that U-Vistract thing, I lost a lot of money in it," Uwegu said sadly.

"See how you can be conned easily, even though you were a banker," Reimas told her. "Sis this one is for our reputation, believe me. I don't like them calling us coconuts. Or primitives and uncivilized."

"A fake reputation at that. Please don't include me in it," Uwegu begged Reimas. "Reimas, they are bound to find out, for our sake and reputation, cut the crap."

Just as well we have been talking while Desimoni was not in. He would have been offended if he heard what Reimas had done to him. Or perhaps he would be happy to play along with Reimas. One thing that I was sure about was that these kids were learning fast about how to jump into the bandwagon of a fast moving world.

I thought about Reimas and what he has done to Desimoni and wondered how Desimoni would react when he found out. Would he be mad? Would he do something to Reimas to pay back? "Do you think Desimoni knows how to make sorcery?" I asked Uwegu. She stared at me before she spoke. "Of course, he would know. Why are you asking?"

"Just curious," I replied. She gave me that non-believing look.

"I hope you are not suspecting Desi of something bad," she prompted me. I shrugged my shoulders. "Well, if he knew how to make sorcery, he couldn't possibly bring it here because he couldn't get past Customs at the airport." I was quietly relieved to hear her say that.

We only stopped talking when Desimoni came in. We all looked at him as soon as he opened the door. I felt troubled and fearful towards him. Uwegu giggled at the same time as she got up and left for her room, perhaps to laugh some more before she came out.

"Hey bro, where have you been?" Reimas asked him, smiling.

"I just finished classes," Desimoni said in his high-pitched voice as he threw his bag on the floor and sat down.

"Man I am really dying for *buai ya*".

"I saw you chewing a couple of days ago," I told him.

"I don't know where Reimas got it from."

"Oh, a wantok gave it to me bro," Reimas cut in. "Some people from PNG came and they gave him some *buai*."

"I could do with one right now," said Desimoni sadly.

"You just have to do without it for a while," I told him. "Wait a moment. They actually sell betel nuts and mustard seeds at some of the Indian shops in Newtown."

"Really? Can you show me the place?" Desimoni said excited at the same time.

"Not now, it's late."

Uwegu came out of her room smiling. "Hello Desi, where have you been?" Uwegu asked him again.

"I was at Uni."

"How come and he came home early?" Uwegu asked referring to Reimas.

"Because he ran away from this particular class."

We stared at Reimas wanting to know why he has not attended.

"Bro, I couldn't understand what that frikken guy was saying," Reimas tried to defend himself.

"That's not on Reimas," I said. "We are all here to study not for holidays."

"Sorry bro, it's just this time round that I didn't attend," he said.

"Is that right, Desi?" Uwegu asked him.

"How would I know?" He sits at the back and I am in front. Today I noticed him missing because not many students turned up."

"Yes, you wouldn't know because you are too short to look around bro," Reimas told him perhaps annoyed because Desimoni was telling on him.

"Hey I can notice because there are only four black guys in this class."

"Where are the other two from?" Uwegu asked.

"Fijians," Desimoni said. He paused for a while until he began quietly, "I wonder what my folks are doing back home?"

"I hope you aren't feeling homesick bro," Reimas said.

"I hope it's not about some woman who took your heart away over the Christmas break," Uwegu teased him.

"Come on Uwegu stop teasing him, He is only human like us." I said.

"Bro, these sons of important people are snakes in the grass *tu ya*," Reimas said.

"Keep your comments to yourself," Desimoni said quietly.

"Don't muck about with him, he might do magic on you," Uwegu joked.

Desimoni glared at her, "liar!"

"My foot! You cannot fool me," Uwegu returned. "People are afraid of your family because of your sorcery and magic. What is the use of sorcery and magic Desi? Times have changed." Desimoni made all sorts of noises to try and drown Uwegu's words until she gave up. "If anything happens to me here, I will blame you. Perez and Reimas are my witnesses," Uwegu told him.

"You are been very unfriendly, Uwegu," I tried to intervene.

"Don't meddle in our business, Perez," was all Uwegu could say before she stormed out. Reimas and I could not believe what we had heard. At the same time we did not know what she meant.

"Bro, what was that for?" Reimas asked Desimoni who sat very quietly.

"Don't believe her, she is just confused," Desimoni told us. "It could be to do with a broken relationship with a cousin." I was satisfied that at least Desimoni came up with a reasonable conclusion about Uwegu's outburst.

"Is there any truth in what Uwegu has just said?" I asked Reimas as soon as Desimoni left us.

"I don't know bro. But they come from the same place."

"Never mind," I said.

"I don't understand him sometimes but he is a good lad. When we are alone, he can really crack dirty jokes," Reimas told me.

"Sis are you any relative of his?" Reimas asked Uwegu when she emerged from her room after an hour.

"We are supposed to be distant cousins," Uwegu answered. "But that didn't stop his first cousin from making my aunt pregnant. Talk about that, I heard rumours from my cousin that his father is in the process of finding a girl for him to marry," Uwegu told us.

"That is real news," I said. "We have a future paramount chief among us."

"He hasn't told me anything about it bro."

"Why should he? This is no light matter; it's heavy stuff," I said.

"But it will disturb his studies here. Can't they wait?" Uwegu said. "Hopefully it's someone who has been to school."

"True," I said.

"Bro, let's not talk about it any more." He turned to Uwegu. "Sis, I sent you an email, did you receive it?" Reimas asked her changing the subject of our conversation.

"I haven't been to the computer lab today. I had classes until 3.00 pm," Uwegu replied. "What did you want?"

"Sis, I was just testing my new Hotmail address," Reimas said.

"I hope you don't misuse the thing. Don't start Reimas. I know you guys, when you start you don't stop."

"I hope you don't start sending dirty pictures," I said smiling.

"No bro, I am not like that."

"Please Reimas, promise you don't send me any of those dirty pictures," Uwegu begged him.

"No, I won't sis, I promise you."

"I received one of those disgusting pictures last week. Oh gross, man!" Uwegu said.

"Who sent it to you sis?"

"Someone by the name of Mendana or something. Anyway let's forget it," she said as she got up to go.

"Who could that be?" I quietly asked Reimas after she left.

"It could be Desi bro." I stared at him. "Bro, they come from the same place. Who knows what they had been up to back home. But don't underestimate this kid, bro. He can handle mothers *tu ya!*" But you know something bro? These bastards fuck when they are kids."

"How do you know that?" I asked laughing.

"Bro, I know. If you don't believe me, read Malinowski!"

I couldn't stop laughing. There was something about people like Malinowski and the other *dimdims* that is funny to me. I don't know exactly what.

"What's funny bro?" Reimas asked me.

"How could I ask Malinowski when he is long dead?" I said.

"Well, he has written about Desimoni's area," said Reimas.

"Have you actually read the book?" I asked.

"I learnt it from the lectures, bro, and we were given a copy of one of his chapters."

"Malinowski is a liar," I tried to tell him.

"How do you know that? You are not even studying Anthropology," Reimas told me.

"Ask Desimoni and he will tell you," I said laughing.

"Bro, he is happy with the label, 'islands of free love,'" Reimas told me.

"How could he?" I asked.

"Because it brings tourism dollar, bro," Reimas told me.

"You mean it's the money that matters and not his culture?" I asked.

"Bro, in this world it's the dollar that counts. No dollar, no nothing!"

"Then this world is going crazy," was all I could say.

Chapter 7

The rumour about Desimoni getting married was water under the bridge soon after. Desimoni had not said anything about it and we took it to be just a rumour and that was it. Then again it was something that Desimoni would not tell us about. It was heavy stuff; it was about commitment and taking on big responsibilities for him. Although it was none of my business, I was thinking about it as I walked back to the flat one afternoon. As soon as I entered the flat I saw Uwegu sobbing. "What is the matter?" I asked her at the same time sitting beside her. She didn't talk for a while until I asked her several times. Then she told me that she caught Desimoni spying on her in the shower.

"How did he do that?" I was kind of shocked because I thought Desimoni was not capable of doing that. If it was Reimas, I would have believed.

"He went outside and hid among the shrubs and looked in through the window," Uwegu continued.

"Didn't you shut it and how did you know it was him?"

"I forgot to shut it. I saw him running away when I screamed."

She cried some more and told me that she doesn't want to stay with us anymore.

"Are you sure it was him? There are many *dimdims* here who are peeping toms."

"It was him, I know. He is a pig that Desi. He thinks he is a chief's son and he can do that to me."

"But Uwegu, here you need evidence; that it was really him that you saw," I tried to reason with her.

"Are you calling me a liar?" she said giving me that strong glare.

"No, I am not but it could be a spur of the moment thing Uwegu," I said trying to trivialize the seriousness she was putting on the matter. "You know how guys are. Perhaps he was just teasing you."

"Teasing me? I am a grown up woman Perez. I am 26 and he is what 20?" Uwegu came on me again. "Besides, I have a child. This is my house too."

"Didn't you know that he was in the house?"

"Whether or not he was in is not the point. The point is that I live here too."

She cried some more and I didn't know what to do with her. I was only afraid that she might go and report the matter to the police. I put my hand on her shoulder without saying anything for sometime. She didn't move and I felt good. Then Uwegu spoke again.

"He is a bastard. He saw me naked and now he is gonna make up stories about me."

"I don't think he is going to do that," I said taking my hand off at the same time.

"You too. I know you guys; all you think of is sex!"

"What about me?" I asked her surprised at my inclusion.

"I mean you are all single. If one of you wants to start a relationship with me why don't you ask me?"

I knew she was just confused by the experience.

"I'll talk to him," I said to her.

"I am sorry Perez. I just feel humiliated that's all," she said wiping her tears. She touched my hand, her eyes looking straight at me. It was electrical and I almost pulled her to me.

"That's alright," I whispered. "You have every right to be angry. No one should disgrace you here."

"I saw him when I turned to wipe myself. He has been watching me for quite a long time. He is a devil! This is not the village where we used to play these games. This is another place and we are sharing this place with other people who are not used to such games."

"You mean, this is not the first time?" I asked quite surprised.

"I mean back in the village when we were young, this was considered a game."

"I will talk to him when he comes home then."

I had a bad day at the office. Early that morning I faced the Graduate Progress Committee which monitors the academic progress of graduate students. They drilled me with questions but somehow I managed to show them that I was indeed making progress. Then my colleague (the other graduate student whom I shared the office with) came and wanted me to advise him on how best to deal with a pending personal problem. We had to talk for a couple of hours and I couldn't do much work. Now coming home, I was confronted with another problem.

A while later, I heard Uwegu leave the house and I lay down on my bed and took a nap. I thought about what Uwegu had just told me and I tried to work out what all this was about. I was hoping that Desimoni would come home before Uwegu got back. I didn't have the courage to talk to him while Uwegu was also around. *Was there something between Desimoni and her that we did not know about*? Maybe there is really something about them that I have not discovered. Not long after, I heard a suffocated laughter and I knew it was the two guys. The door opened and I waited for them to settle. I heard them whisper and then one of them giggled. It sounded like Reimas but I couldn't really make it out. After another 5 minutes I came out and they were surprised to see me.

"Bro, we thought you weren't home yet," Reimas said.

"Gees, I didn't get out my shoes. I had a bad day that's why I didn't bother," I replied. "Where are you guys coming from?"

"I was with my mates when Desimoni came across us at the library, bro," Reimas told me. "My mates asked me if I wanted to go and watch rugby on the weekend and I said I'll think about it and get back to them. See, I just bought this *Rugby League Week* from the bookshop."

I sat down on the couch thinking about how I would start. I looked at Desimoni in the eyes. "Desimoni, Uwegu said you spied on her when she was in the shower today," I began.

He gave me a piercing look while Reimas looked intently at him. "Is it true?" I asked. Suddenly Reimas started laughing at the same time poking Desimoni on the side.

"Damn! It's not funny the poor girl was crying when I arrived," I said in a strong voice.

Reimas stopped suddenly realising that I meant what I was saying.

"Daisy lied. I did not spy on her," Desimoni said slowly. "In fact I went outside to hang my towel on the line and that's when I heard her cough or something and when I turned I realised that she did not close the shower window and out of curiosity I took a glance. Then I withdrew and left." There was a long pause before he spoke again. "It's all a mistake. I wasn't spying on her, besides we do it all the time back in the village."

"Who is Daisy?" I asked.

"That's the name we call her back home."

"And why was she crying then if you play this game in your village?" I asked.

"Bro, I hope you are telling the truth?" Reimas teased him.

"She was lying just to get Perez's attention," Desimoni said. "Women are like that. They crave for attention. She'll be okay."

"Listen, if you did spy on her, you must stop it because I don't think she likes it," I told Desimoni. He was very quiet for a while before he said something that surprised us. "She doesn't like it because she is a lesbo."

"Oh man, how can that be bro?" Reimas said with surprise.

"How do you know she is a lesbian?" I asked Desimoni looking hard at him. Quickly I thought about the story Uwegu has told me about her sister and Mrs. Powell and my eyes blinked several times.

"Hey, I just know it. Daisy doesn't like dicks anymore. Dicks are past, history for her. When it didn't work out with the father of her child, she turned her attention to other women. She did it once back in the village with a *dimdim* girl; a daughter of one of the missionaries."

"How do you know that bro?"

"That's my place and people talked. It's a long story and I don't want to dig up something that has already been buried. Can't you see the craving on her face when she sees other girls?"

I stood up and looked at Desimoni. "Whether she has done it in the village before or not, here it is a different place. You must apologize to her when she comes. She is trying to move out and if she does, we'll have to pay a bit more rent amongst the three of us. We don't want to do that."

They kept quiet, perhaps thinking about the need to pay a bit more rent.

"Okay, I'll apologise to her. But I didn't mean to spy on her, you know," Desimoni reiterated.

"But she doesn't like it anymore. What games you played back in the village is best left in the village, alright? What if she reports the matter to the police? You know police here are different from our police back home," I told him in a strong voice.

Desimoni nodded his head in the affirmative. I had a feeling that there was much more to this than what he was telling us. I left the two of them and went inside my room. I thought about what Desimoni has said about Uwegu. I have not seen any thing to suggest that she was a lesbo. If she was, it was a closely guarded secret. Then again Desimoni could only be making up the story to hide something. How did Desimoni know that she was a lesbian? I wanted to go out and ask him to prove it. Damn, what business have I got with her personal life? I questioned myself. I could hear the two guys chatting. Much of the talking this time was being done by Reimas. When I came out some time later Uwegu was not home yet and I began to get worried. I asked the two guys and they said they didn't know where she was.

"Where the hell is this woman?" I asked in frustration.

"Don't worry, she is safe with one of her girlfriends," Desimoni said in a sarcastic way.

"How do you know?"

"I just know."

"I am going to call the police and report her missing."

"No, don't, we might get into trouble," Desimoni quickly begged me. I could see his body language changed so dramatically. He was nervous and I noticed the perspiration on his forehead.

"What are we supposed to do then? Just wait until she comes home? It's bloody late!"

As I was debating whether to call the police the phone rang and I answered it. It was Kate. I told her that we were worried about Uwegu. "What happened to her?" Kate asked. "She isn't home yet," I told her. "She could be with friends. Don't worry she'll be safe," Kate reassured me.

"What are you up to there?" She asked me.

"Busy with studies as usual."

"I hope so too," was all she said and hung up. I was glad the conversation was over.

"Was that Uwegu bro?" Reimas asked after I put down the phone.

"No, that was Kate."

"I know she is safe," I heard Desimoni mumbled.

"You must be crazy over her. That's why you've even gone through the trouble of spying on her when she was in the shower bro," Reimas teased him. "Besides you will be polluting your chiefly status, by fucking with a commoner." There was an ambivalent look on Desimoni's face. He looked as if some bad thing had happened to him. Not long after, I saw him get his towel and he left for the shower. Reimas and I looked at each other but did nor utter a word. It took him an unusually long time to shower. I got myself something to eat while Reimas read a book. Darkness had crept in and wrapped us. After a while Reimas went off to sleep and I waited for Desimoni to emerge from the shower. Finally he emerged. "I am feeling fresh now." I wanted to ask him about Uwegu but I hesitated. I kept on looking at him, not knowing where to start. I got up from the couch and walked to the fridge, opened it and looked for an apple. Then I decided against getting one and came back and sat beside him.

"Are you alright?" he asked me, realising how unsettled I was.

"Yeah." It was the cue I needed to start. "This thing about Uwegu, are you sure about it?"

He kept quiet, his eyes searching the distance. He shifted his left foot and started shaking it in some kind of a shy coordination. I waited. He had a faraway look before his eyes landed on me.

"We come from the same place with Uwegu," he began. "When we were kids we used to play together, you know what I mean. We became very close and we developed a very close bond and people used to tease us. She was however some three years ahead of me at school so she left for an all girls' high school and that's when we lost contact." Then he looked away again and I pitied him. "They caught them a number of times with the *dimdim* girl. I don't know where the *dimdim* girl is now, maybe back here in Australia. This was what drove me away from her." He was quiet for a long time before he spoke. "It was a long time ago."

"It's alright, let bygone days be bygone," I told him squeezing his arm to reassure him of my confidence. Not long after he left me for his room, I sat alone for a long time. Later, I was switching between channels on the television. I wondered if Uwegu and Desimoni had shared some sexual intimacies and I recalled what Reimas has told me, "These guys fuck when they are very young." I almost laughed. Then I heard a door open and then Desimoni appeared. He came and sat down beside me. He held my arm and spoke. "Perez, what happened between Uwegu and me was long time ago. We have gone our own ways until we found ourselves here."

"I hope this is not your fate," I said.

"What do you mean?" he asked me in return.

"I am only joking."

"You just made me miss a heart beat!"

We continued chatting about other things and then he told me about Reimas having been to the brothel at Kings Cross. I was kind of shocked.

"Who told you?"

"He told me himself."

"Man, that guy is fast," I told him. "I mean, I haven't been to a brothel as yet, although I've been to KX a number of times with friends."

"He went with two of his Fijian classmates, Desimoni told me." They were reading the paper when they came across this advertisement of this particular brothel, which specialises in foreign students. Well, they didn't mean to actually go there. They only wanted to go to KX because it is famous and everyone talks about it. You know how curious people are. He said not to tell you but anyway this is his story."

After classes they took off in a bus and got off at KX. One of his friends suggested that they go into a bar and have a few drinks so they did. In the bar Reimas met up with a woman who said she was part PNG and part *dimdim* so they started chatting. The woman apparently knew a bit of Tok Pisin so she convinced Reimas. His two friends got caught up with other Fijians and somehow they lost each other after some time.

Reimas stayed with this chick and not long after, the chick asked him if he wanted to go with her just around the corner. He hesitated but because he was already intoxicated he went along with her. It was one of those buildings at the back of the main street and not long afte, they entered a wretched alleyway into an old unkempt building. They climbed a flight of almost rail-less steps. The place smelled of old dirt and urine. Then she led him past a small office and the woman at the reception greeted them. There was a lone security guard hanging around and he gave a good stare at Reimas. A *dimdim* in a drunken state came out of one of the rooms. He stank of alcohol and sex. Suddenly it dawned on Reimas that this was a brothel. The room was small and decorated with pictures of naked women. There was a double bed and a mattress. On a side table were some creams and toys. The room smelt nice. The woman took off her clothes methodically. It was too much for Reimas. For the first time he saw a fully naked woman and he could not control himself.

"Come to me baby," and she started touching his manhood. "Come on take off your clothes, we don't have that much time." Reimas quickly took off his clothes and the woman steered him into the bed on to her. When Reimas saw the white flesh he went for her like a hungry tiger. In no time it was over for him.

"Oh gosh, that's something," I said. "Hope it wasn't his story that wanted you to spy on Uwegu," I said in a funny kind of a way.

"I don't know about that," Desimoni said.

"He is really a game isn't he?" I said about Reimas.

"He is just curious and trying to feel his way around the place."

"Reimas must not make it a habit though," I advised him.

He looked at me and asked. "Have you tried these *dimdim* women?" I smiled and shook my head in the negative.

"Then you are losing big time Perez."

"What's good about it anyway?" I tried to defend myself.

"Because you will only live in fantasy, every time people talk about KX and the *dimdim* women," Desimoni told me.

"Screwing a decent *dimdim* woman is much more honourable than going to a brothel. If you are a real man, get one who isn't a prostitute," I challenged him.

"You always like a challenge don't you Perez?"

I didn't say anything as I was thinking about Reimas's story.

"Don't tell him I told you about it," Desimoni told me.

"Why?"

"Because he would never trust me again."

"Trust me pal."

He winked at me and then went into the room.

Chapter 8

The intimidation that the city emitted threatened us continuously. At the same time the demands of our studies deterred us from venturing out of our comfort zones. I even had not had the time to take the three of them out and I felt bad about it. Uwegu urged me a number of times to take the two guys out to the city so they can get themselves acquainted. Reimas of course had started going out with his friends but Desimoni hardly ever did. So one Saturday I asked them to go with me to the city. Reimas was quick to agree while Desimoni reluctantly followed us.

We got off the bus and started walking along George Street when Desimoni overheard two *dimdim* girls chatting. One girl was telling the other how she made love to someone she just met that night in a gay bar. Reimas told us to stop and listen but I told him to mind his own business.

"These people don't have no shame at all, bro," Reimas said. "They want the world to listen to their secrets."

"You can do almost anything here without giving a shit what other people will think," I told them.

"They don't give a frikken hell about anybody."

"That's the way they do things here," I told them. "We do ours differently."

"But more quietly and morally," said Desimoni.

"Come on," I said. "Their culture is different from ours."

"You know why people from home come here all the time bro?" Reimas came in. "Because they just want to watch the *dimdims* do it."

"That's part of the attraction I suppose," I said. "See how many people here are with cameras and videos. Many of them just want to catch a glimpse of *dimdim* society."

"Eyes are prying on us as we are walking down this street. So don't scratch your balls because you will be on candid camera!" I teased them after a while.

"Damn I was just doing that a while ago, bro," Reimas said very concerned.

"You've already been captured. This place is always monitored twenty fours hours a day," I told them. "You can't really hide here. Come, I will show you guys something."

I took them closer to the front of a building on the sidewalk and pointed to a camera. "You see this?" I said pointing to the camera. "That's big brother watching."

"I didn't know that," said Desimoni very curiously.

"Even on certain stretches of the road there are hidden cameras watching for traffic offences," I told them. "Many drivers get caught speeding by these hidden cameras."

"The people behind some of these cameras have a feast watching what these cameras record, bro."

"Oh yes, they have fun watching people screwing, stealing, fighting and all sorts of things like that!" Desimoni said.

"This is a voyeur society," I told them.

"What do you mean, bro?" Reimas asked puzzled.

"I mean people are watching us all the time. And people here like to watch although they pretend to mind their own business."

"Bro, you mean like at KX?" I looked at him not getting his point. "Well people go there to watch sex shows. Isn't that watching like what you have been saying?"

"Yes, I suppose you could say that."

"Aah, KX is Reimas's favourite place," Desimoni teased him, laughing at the same time. Reimas gave him that 'don't tell' look and he stopped. I knew his secret about him having been to KX because Desimoni told me about it. I didn't show that 'give away sign' though as I didn't want to make Reimas embarrassed.

"Peep shows are also common here. People here always like to watch. If they are not watching a live sex show like at KX or like behind these hidden cameras they go buy magazines and look at the photos," I told them.

"No wonder some of these *dimdims* don't settle down," Desimoni said.

"They have nothing to lose, bro," Reimas said. "Most of the things they ever want are available at the touch of the button."

It was crowded today as we walked slowly down George Street. Not so long ago this was the street where a Chinese gang murdered a young *dimdim* schoolboy from the country who was here on holidays. It was front-page news in the major newspapers and also television.

As we walked past, two drunken *dimdim* kids came out of a nearby bar and one of them said something to us. I didn't actually hear what he said but they laughed looking at us. Before I knew it, Reimas was already asking them, "What the fuck did you say?" He was indeed angry and was ready for anything.

"We didn't say anything," one of them told him. "Yes, you fucking did. Say it again before I smash your skulls!" By this time Desimoni and I had caught up and the two were so scared that they offered Reimas some money. "I don't fucking need your bloody money, you assholes! Fuck off before we kick the shit out of you!" As he was saying this, Desimoni and I were flexing our muscles and looking at them as if we were going to kill and eat them. You could see terror in their eyes. Before we knew it they took off running for their lives and we started to laugh.

"Did you see how the skinny one ran?" Desimoni said. "He ran like he wanted to pee or something." We laughed as he imitated how he ran.

"Let's move away from here before they report us to the police," I told them.

"But they started it," Reimas said.

"They are white and police will believe them," Desimoni said. We left the place quickly and went. All this time I could see Desimoni look over his shoulders now and again.

"Don't worry, we are way ahead of them," I told them. "They'll get lost in this crowd anyway. Let's continue to the shop where Reimas will buy his stuff. See there are also black people around. This city is a cosmopolitan place."

Reimas told us about a shop on George Street that sold rugby jerseys and he wanted to buy one to send home. I was glad that Uwegu wasn't with us because we would have provoked her and she would have done something. Since that time she told me about her bad experience with some *dimdim* guys, she has not stopped talking about it. Today she was busy so she could not come along.

In the distance Reimas saw one of his mates and waved to him. "That's my mate bro. He is from the West Indies." The guy acknowledged Reimas.

We continued walking until Reimas stopped. "Here's the shop," Reimas told us.

"You go in. We'll wait here for you," I told him. We found a vacant seat nearby and sat down. The street was crowded as usual. We anxiously scouted the place while waiting for Reimas. We saw a gay couple walking hand in hand and I told Desimoni about it.

"This world is getting crazier everyday," Desimoni said. "How can God allow that?"

"The world isn't getting crazier," it's just that every day we are discovering new tastes and new things. We have gays in PNG, except that they are not open about it."

"But it's immoral, they are not human beings," Desimoni retaliated as he kept on staring at the disappearing two gays who had walked past us.

"Don't worry, we have gay priests too! The Pope will accept them soon," I said in a teasing way.

"Being gay is a sickness, I was told," Desimoni told me.

"That's preposterous!" I told him. "It is not a sickness. It's about discovering the complexity of human beings."

"I don't like gays. I hate them!" Desimoni insisted.

"Keep your feelings to yourself," I told him. "This is a different culture."

"You know what I found out recently?" Desimoni started again. "Many people here don't get married because they can get sex from other means." I looked at him hard. He was calm again because there weren't many people where we sat.

"Well, you told us that this was a voyeur society. I am just trying to expand on your point."

"Yes of course," I said. "But they won't tell you that if you ask them. It's happening in KX, you can watch people doing it or you can take part. You can also buy tapes, CDs and books from the adult shops.

"Disgusting aye?" Desimoni said spitting on the ground.

"No, it's what you call an alternative lifestyle."

"Look at those eyes," Desimoni suddenly interrupted, pointing to a woman who stood a couple of metres away from us.

"They are the most beautiful and seductive eyes I have seen so far." I only laughed at him. The woman was actually looking our way and Desimoni couldn't get his eyes off her when Reimas surprised us upon his return.

"*Yupela lukluk long husat?*" Reimas suddenly interrupted us.

"Desimoni thinks that woman with blue eyes is really cute," I told him. "Where is she, bro?"

"On your left."

"Bro, those blue eyes aren't beautiful as black eyes." I stared hard at him.

"Did you buy the thing you went for?" I asked him.

"*Em ya,*" and he showed us the plastic bag that contained the jersey.

"Good, shall we make tracks?"

"Look, she is looking our way."

"Bro, you know what's on her mind?"

"What?"

"She is imagining a black dick bro."

"Oh you devil! Get outa here boy!" I said to him.

"Did you guys see that?" Desimoni asked excitedly.

"Yeah, she responded well to your opening up," I told him. "She is one in a thousand."

"Bro, she is a prostitute. She is waiting for clients. Can't you guys tell?"

Then it dawned on us that indeed she was a prostitute and we walked away from her quickly. Nevertheless for us, this was the first acknowledgement by a *dimdim* woman. I thought about the woman as we continued walking while the other two kept quiet. As we crossed the first traffic lights I showed the others the sign, 'speed cameras used in this area.'

"Man, so it's everywhere, bro," said Reimas. "I have never taken notice of this before."

"That's how they make money too," Desimoni said.

"Oh yeah, these *dimdims* are very creative. If the *dimdim* women are not good enough, they get women from Asian countries, Philippines especially because they think they are exotic and easy. Man, when Bali was still safe these people go there all the time. The South Pacific is a little above their budgets, so many find it hard to come to the islands," I said.

We began chatting again as we walked along. There was a guy who looked like he was from our country but he did not give us that 'know you' look. "He must be from Torres Straits," Reimas said.

"Could be," Desimoni said.

"Some of these guys when they get into the bar they tell everyone that they are from PNG. When they cause trouble people think it is us," Reimas said.

"Why do they want to use our country?" Desimoni asked.

"Because people know that our country is sort of a Wild West kinda place. They see us as troublemakers," I said.

"That's how sometimes we get a bad name; because of other people's doing," Desimoni said.

We arrived at the bus stop and waited for our bus to arrive. As soon as Reimas spoke in Tok Pisin there were glances from the other *dimdims*. There were two Chinese speaking in Cantonese but nobody bothered about them. It was our strange language that made people turn. When the right bus finally came we got on and made our way back home. We sat silently, each one of us preoccupied with his own thoughts. The bus was almost full. Next to me sat an elderly woman with her grandson. They were Greeks, as the woman was speaking to the boy in Greek. They must have been going some place for a visit.

The boy was about 4 and when he looked at me he gave me a shy smile. I returned his smile. I know he was young and innocent.

"That was some experience," said Desimoni. I look intently at him. "I mean about all those cameras that monitor our movements."

"There is no privacy at all, bro," Reimas added.

Chapter 9

Hey guys, guess what?" Uwegu excitedly began after one of her errands in the city. We looked at her but she was taking her time. "We have been invited to a social function."

"By whom?" I asked.

"By the executives of the Wantok Association." We got excited and we bombarded her with questions. "Wow, take it easy, one question at a time," she said equally excited. She moved from her standing position to the chair and sat down. She was like the matriarch commanding courage and confidence. She was in total control and we were like her offspring. "We have been invited to attend a Wantok Association get-together at the Centennial Park," she repeated. "I met up with one of the organisers." Our excitement rested with the fact that we will be meeting up with other wantoks.

"Are we taking anything with us sis?" Reimas asked.

"I don't know, I'll have to ring the woman and find out," Uwegu replied.

"They usually take with them 12 pack," I said.

We looked at Uwegu and she looked away for awhile. "I don't want you guys to get drunk and be disorderly."

"Hey, when did we get drunk and became disorderly, sis?" Reimas got back at her. "I am just warning you. This is Australia."

"I wonder if I would meet someone from my area, bro," Reimas said excitedly. "I heard that there was someone here who comes from my area."

"There will be many from our place though. I know three of them are studying here in Sydney," came in Desimoni at the same time looking at Uwegu. Uwegu nodded her head.

"You will be surprised by who you will meet up with," I told them. "Sydney is such a huge city that we don't know who we will meet up with."

"There are many wantoks here and this will be a good opportunity for us to meet," Uwegu contributed.

"There will be other *dimdims* too at the gathering," I told them.

"This is not their gathering why would they come?" Desimoni questioned.

"Desimoni, there are many *dimdims* who love PNG and have worked and lived there. These are the good *dimdims*," I told him.

"I hope so," was all he could say.

"I hope that Kate won't be there," Uwegu said quietly. "I don't like her. There is something weird about her. This flat is full of her threatening spirit and shadow."

"She could be Yapune, the woman spirit." Desimoni said jokingly. Uwegu looked hard at him and he stopped abruptly.

✳✳✳

Two of the people we first met when we arrived at Centennial Park that Saturday were Kilroy (his village name is Kirori) and Rawiri. In fact they were the first to greet us as we entered Ash Paddock where the gathering was taking place.

"That's them," Uwegu said. "Let's go and join them." I realised that Desimoni was slowing down and his enthusiasm seemed to be ebbing.

"Come on, don't be shy," Uwegu urged him. "These are our wantoks." We looked at her and she nodded her head indicting that we continue walking. She was carrying a container of food that she had prepared. The container was wrapped neatly in a tea towel with a traditional PNG design.

As soon as we arrived Uwegu did the introductions before she went over to where the ladies were. Many of the people were unfamiliar to us. There were several groups and people naturally fell into the group where people they knew were. The three of us joined Kilroy and Rawiri and a few others. The group was not intimidating and we felt comfortable in their company. People were chewing *buai* and talking animatedly. There was an air of jubilation and merriment. A number of the guys were drinking. People came around to shake hands with us and welcome us to the club. Not long after, we fell into the rhythm and we began to exchange yarns and pleasantries. Rawiri told us that he was a student at a college in the city, while Kilroy worked somewhere in the city. He wasn't specific about it though.

When I looked around to check for Uwegu she was already engaged in conversation with the people in the other group. A number of times, I caught her looking our way perhaps to check whether we were okay. She was attractive in her blue jeans and T-shirt. Desimoni was slow in opening up. He remained quiet for sometime until after a few more *buais*.

I saw a woman waving at me. I recognised her. She was Deuba's cousin. She came over and greeted me calling me *tambu* (in-law). I felt awkward because I was no longer in a relationship with Deuba. I wondered if she knew this. She sat beside me and we talked about many things before she finally asked about Deuba. I wondered what to say and it took me a very long time before I spoke.

"We are no longer seeing each other."

"Sorry, I didn't know that," she replied. "How long ago was this?"

"A few weeks before I came here." She remained quiet perhaps thinking what to say next. "She called me sometime ago and told me you were here. She didn't tell me about you guys breaking up." She kept quiet for a while. "Well I guess some things are best kept under wraps," she told me. I smiled at her and nodded my head in agreement.

"I really don't know what happened," I told her.

"She told me that she caught you with another female staff at the Christmas party."

"Well, you know how it is when you have a few drinks and some things get disorderly."

She laughed. "I hope you can resolve things and get together again."

"It's a difficult climb but nothing is impossible," I said.

After a few more exchanges she left and went to Uwegu's group. Local music was playing and it blended well with the gathering.

When I got back to the group Rawiri was already telling them about his first arrival here.

"I've never been away from home until last year when I came here for studies. When the pilot announced that we were landing here in Sydney, I felt my stomach roll and turn. There were other wantoks on the flight but I didn't know any of them and I was too shy to ask. I followed the others and went through immigration and customs and all that. When I came out to the arrival area I saw that people knew where they were heading to except me. I came and stood outside until Kilroy came to my rescue. Man, I was so relieved."

"What would you have done had you not met Kilroy?" Desimoni asked Rawiri.

"I was frightened, man. I think I would have asked around and if worse came to worse, I would have just stayed at the airport lobby until the next morning."

"You could have checked for cheap places to stay the night bro" Reimas asked.

"I thought about that too. I saw these young guys looking up cheap accommodation at one corner of the airport, and there was an information counter which I could have gone to and ask for directions."

"So you were his saviour bro," Reimas told Kilroy.

"I felt sorry for him. I mean this is not our place," Kilroy continued.

Two other guys came and joined our group. One of them was already intoxicated and he started talking about how his people were trying to break away from PNG and all that stuff.

"This is not a political rally mate," someone told him. "It's a social gathering." "Politics is always part of any social gathering, buddy," the guy replied.

"Let's keep it out from this one gathering," another person came in.

"Go to hell then!" the drunken guy said staggering away from our group.

"Land of the Unexpected," Rawiri said smiling.

"In these types of gatherings, you get all sorts of people."

"We should have let him stay and listen to his politics,' someone said.

"He would have bored us," another one remarked.

"Bro, I can't even see any of my wantoks here," Reimas said after awhile. "Maybe I don't have any wantoks here after all."

"There are many PNG people living here in Sydney but not all of them get to hear about these get-togethers," said Rawiri.

"I was hoping to see my wantoks here but it seems none has turned up," Reimas continued.

"Maybe next time," Desimoni said.

People continued to arrive, many were unfamiliar faces. The important thing for us was that we comprise a community in a landscape of *dimdims*. But you could tell that we were like a house constantly being shaken by earthquakes. Some of the people at the gathering seem to be nervous and uncomfortable. You could just tell by their body language. Others were trying to rise above the limits of their shyness. While a few brave ones warmed up to the conviviality.

As the day grew on I noticed that there were quite a number of PNG women married to *dimdim* men but there weren't any PNG men married to *dimdim* women around. Most of these *dimdim* men sat quietly with their wives and kids while one or two *dimdim* guys got around to chat with us. There appeared to be an air of hostility that seemed to be present between us and some of the *dimdims*. Although you couldn't see it, you could feel it. For those *dimdim* men who sat quietly, there was that sense of apprehension. Perhaps they just didn't want to get involve and only came because their wives urged them to. If they wanted to talk, they mostly talked with the other *dimdim* men. I felt sorry for them while the rest of the guys felt frustrated with them. As afternoon drew to an end, a few more people came, mostly young men who were already intoxicated.

After Kilroy or Kirori (whichever name you want to call him) had taken off again, we asked Rawiri about him. According to Rawiri, Kilroy was one of the few Papua New Guinean illegal immigrants. He came to Sydney some 20 years ago to attend TAFE but failed and as he didn't want to go back home, he hung around Sydney, initially staying with friends. Later when he found a job he moved to stay elsewhere. A little later he married a *dimdim* woman but the marriage failed after 2 years. I am not too sure if it was a legal marriage or not. But the woman blamed Kilroy for the break up.

During the short time I met Kilroy, I got the impression that he was a sweet talker and sometimes he has that boastful air around him. I realised that if he could escape the immigration officers then he was damn smart. Or if he can get *dimdim* women just like that, he must be pretty cool. Indeed, Kilroy could be mistaken for an African American; he was tall, slim and sometimes he tries to put on an America accent although he loses it easily once he is drunk.

He was also someone who was open and was very good company. He made us feel at home. He was informal and he wore tight jeans that made him look heavy and outgoing.

Rawiri on the other hand was quiet, even when he drank beer. He looked soft. He has been in the city for one year. He told us that he was studying education and that he wanted to be a teacher when he finished his studies. Rawiri didn't say anything out of the ordinary even though he was getting drunk.

We talked about many things as we drank our beers. Occasionally we laughed at what someone in the other group was doing. Uwegu brought us some food, which we eagerly took. "Don't drink too much," she quietly told us. We nodded our heads. Not long after, Kilroy was back to our group. I scrutinised him closely before I finally asked him why he didn't go home when he flunked his studies.

"What would I do at home?"

"Weren't you worried they might find you out here and deport you?"

"Listen; there are very few PNG guys who you could call illegal immigrants compared to thousands from other countries. They only manage to catch a few hundreds every now and again while the rest become part of the Australian society. Without us, this country will never move forward. Do you think these *dimdims* want to pick fruits, work in the farms and all that? NO! It is people like me who do that kind of work here."

"You must know your way around because they have not caught you yet," I said.

"I use my head all the time. Those who get caught are stupid Asians. Well, to be honest, a number of times I was nearly caught. One day the police raided a car-washing yard where I was working. Luckily I had gone to the shop to buy a packet of cigarettes when they raided. As soon as I came out and saw what was happening I walked calmly to the bus stop, caught a bus and left the place for good."

"Man you were bloody lucky," I told him.

"Indeed I was. You've got to be creative to get around here."

"Listen to this one," Rawiri attracted our attention. "The other time he placed an advertisement in the local papers advertising a new product that could cure impotency. The product was going for $49.95. He actually used my post office box telling people that they have to pay up front before the product can be delivered. He made some $20,000.00 before someone alerted the cops."

"I guess he is different from us because he was brought up by *dimdim* people and he is more at ease with them," Rawiri told us.

"Were you adopted by *dimdims*?" I asked him. "Yes, I was adopted by a white missionary couple who worked in my area for many years and when they finished they brought me with them here. I was only 18 years old when I came here. I went to high school here, did my TAFE and flunked it and ran away from them."

"Good one, bro," Reimas said.

Chapter 10

When we arrived back at the flat after the social get-together at the park, Uwegu told us about how she didn't like the snobbish attitudes of some of the women who were married to the *dimdims*.

"They think they are it! Many of them would not have made it if they did not marry these *dimdims*. It was the way out for them to escape the poverty and misery of their lives. Look at some of their husbands; they are almost the same age as their fathers or even their grandfathers! Ha, I pity them. In any case we are not there to steal their husbands."

"What happened to you?" I asked her.

"I was chatting with this *dimdim* man when his wife came and told him in a rude way they were leaving. I felt embarrassed. I could see the expression on his face he was also embarrassed. It complicates the whole problem about discrimination. I mean poor guy. He is probably in his late fifties. In any case I am not attracted to *dimdim* men."

"It's natural to be jealous, especially when you have a pretty woman like you chatting with her husband," I said.

She gave me that funny look. "This is not PNG; it's about time they get over it," she said.

"I don't know," was all I could say.

The way Uwegu told the story reminded me about an incident that I witnessed when I was a kid, which happened between my grandfather and the *dimdim kiap* (patrol officer) whom people called 'Crooked Masta.' The incident was to leave a deep impression on me. It was funny though, how I had never given the incident a second thought as I went through my primary and secondary education. Perhaps there was nothing to trigger it again and it lay buried in the recesses of my mind until I went to university.

"What happened?" Uwegu asked folding her legs, her eyes focused on me.

"It's not exactly the kind of experience that you would like to go through. It's one that will make you angry," I told her.

"Tell it, I don't care any more about what the *dimdims* think of us. My heart has become rock-hard," Uwegu said in a strong voice. I looked at Desimoni but he did not say anything.

"They can all go to hell for all I care!" Reimas uttered. "Sis, the thing is if we keep quiet about racism, the bastards will continue to mistreat us. We must confront them head on!"

"Yes, they are cowards!" Uwegu supported him.

After they all stopped, I began the story. "I was about 5 when a new *kiap* came, an older *dimdim* in his mid fifties. The story was that he was having an affair with a fifteen-year-old girl from the next village whose father was a bigman. So he spent most of his patrol time in the girl's village. He was always bumping into things. He didn't see properly. During his patrols a native policeman was always holding his hand to guide him. If he was left alone, he wouldn't see properly. The villagers called him 'Crooked Masta.'

"One day, word came that 'Crooked Masta' wanted the villagers to work on a particularly bad section of the road which led to our village. He wanted them to make a detour to avoid the creek that often flooded that section of the road. My grandfather told the policeman that they were willing to build a wooden bridge across the creek because they didn't want to cut the road too close to our burial site. The policeman went back and told 'Crooked Masta' about the villagers' intention to build a wooden bridge. He was furious and informed the policeman to come back and tell the villagers to do what he has ordered them to do. The villagers refused and instead constructed a wooden bridge. This infuriated him. He called my grandfather up and blasted him. My grandfather just hung his head down while 'Crooked Masta' swore and called him names. The villagers were very timid and only watched from a distance. Suddenly he called one of his policemen to put handcuffs on my grandfather and take him to the dark house (prison). Out of nowhere I heard my grandfather scream, "You think you can shape this earth with your crooked eyes? Your head is crooked, that is why you can't understand us!" The *kiap* was extremely furious and he threw his walking stick at my grandfather and it hit him on his forehead. Then he fell down, blood gushing from his head. I ran to my mother and held her tightly with my eyes shut. I was very frightened of the *dimdim kiap*. He started talking rapidly to his policemen. He told the lead policeman to unlock the handcuff. The last word I heard him say was, "bloody *longlong kanaka*" (stupid native). Then he led his policemen out of our village. The last we heard of him was that he had impregnated the girl but had left her for another girl in a different village. Luckily my grandfather wasn't gaoled but he was stripped of his title as the village *luluai* (bigman). When he died, the lump on his forehead where the *kiap* had hit him was still visible. It was a mark that went with him to the grave.

"What is memorable most to me perhaps is how the whole incident terrified me. From that time on, I was always afraid of the *dimdim*, any *dimdim* for that matter up until I went to Uni."

"Shame on him, racist pig! He presented himself as if he were the law unto himself," Uwegu said in an angry tone.

"*Sapos nau bai mi kilim wanpela stret ya*!" Reimas added.

"This is what I don't understand. They use our women for their satisfaction and at the same time they discriminate against us," Uwegu continued.

"What triggered it off at the university bro?" Reimas asked.

"I am not quite sure actually," I said. I thought for a while, trying to remember. "Now I got it," I told them. "I had a bit of confrontation with a *dimdim* lecturer who they said was a World War Two veteran. I was doing my second year and I presented a talk based on a novel written by Beatrice Grimshaw, *White Savage Simon*. After my presentation he told me emphatically that my analysis of the book was not scholarly but full of sentimental crap."

"Then what happened next bro?" Reimas asked. "I felt ashamed because he told me off in front of about 60 students. I never attended his class again and he failed me in the end." I stared into space thinking for a while. "What was good about it though was that, the whole incident also provoked me to see things much more critically."

"Perhaps you weren't sensitive enough until then, bro," said Reimas.

"I think so. But I am happy that the lecturer had me head on that time."

"Some of these lecturers here can be very nasty, bro," Reimas said. "The other day this *dimdim* lecturer really brutalised the Muslim people. I could sense that there was tension among the Muslim students in class. Two women in particular were very upset and I could see their body language, bro."

"Didn't they argue with him?" Desimoni asked.

"Well, Jamal did try to explain to this *dimdim* lecturer but his English wasn't that good and the lecturer couldn't understand him. Or maybe the lecturer wasn't interested in listening to his point of view."

"What about the other students in class?" I asked.

"They just sat there, bro," said Reimas. "But you could see the fury in their eyes."

"Some of these lecturers need to be sensitised about such issues. The students here come from different cultures and backgrounds," Uwegu said.

"Lucky the lecturers in our courses have not talked about PNG, bro," Reimas came in. "If I see that a topic will deal with PNG, I won't attend."

"Come on Reimas, don't be a chicken," Uwegu said.

"Bro, I know one of these days, there will be a lecture on PNG."

"So?"

Reimas shrugged his shoulders, "I don't know. I don't want them to think of me as a primitive, bro."

"I don't think they will think that way," I tried to soften his view. "Besides, the lecturer isn't stupid to forage into that area of analysis."

"But bro, he likes to bring up provocative issues," Reimas pressed on.

"If it comes to that tell him, you are from Vanuatu," Uwegu told him jokingly. "Or Solomon Islands," I added.

"Don't give me ideas, bro," Reimas replied.

"Hey, why don't you listen to your whiz kid," Uwegu said.

Desimoni gave her that stinging glare.

"Don't look at me. Ask Reimas."

"Whiz kid? What's that suppose to mean?" Desimoni asked.

"Hey bro, I told this Asian guy that you were a whiz kid," Reimas tried to explain.

"Why?" Desimoni insisted.

"Because he asked me whether you were a whiz kid," Reimas replied. "You know those guys who are so clever that they start school very early."

"No wonder some of those guys keep on staring at me."

"It's not a bad label though," I said.

"I don't like it Reimas. Don't do it again. I just want to be me!"

We talked some more until Desimoni suggested that we go to Circular Quay the next day. We took up his idea enthusiastically. Desimoni's idea was to take some photographs for us to send home and show to our friends and families. The next day, Sunday, we quickly had an early breakfast and as soon as we were about to depart we realised that Uwegu was missing.

"Where is this girl?" Desimoni asked in an impatient manner. I could see that he was getting impatient.

"She was here a while ago bro," Reimas said at the same time knocking on her door. There was no answer. "She is not in."

"She was talking about ringing her folks last night," I told them.

"Yes, she must have gone to call from the public phone bro. Let's wait, she won't be long," Reimas said.

The expression on Desimoni's face was one of impatience and annoyance. He walked to and from his room a couple of times. "She is always ringing home. Not a day goes by without her calling home," Desimoni said.

"So what? Does that bother you?" I tried to defend Uwegu. "We still have a lot of time. Don't worry."

"I hate the way women carry on. They are always slow," Desimoni persisted. "*Hey, ol meri stap na yumi stap*," came on Reimas.

"Whatever," said Desimoni as he got up.

"Bro but not all *dimdims* are bad, aye," Reimas came in. We looked at him hard because we were talking about something different and all of a sudden he was coming up with this topic.

"No!" I answered.

"But why do they always look down on us, bro?" I shrugged my shoulders. "Because we aren't white. Oh I don't know! Some of these *dimdims* that worked in PNG are good."

"Like that *giaman dimdim*," came in Desimoni sarcastically. I gawked at Desimoni as if he had sworn at me.

"Desimoni, just because Uwegu had said that Kate flew in the night and tried to strangle her doesn't mean that we believe her," I tried to reason with him.

"You are from a different place and you don't know our culture."

"I give up!" was all I could say.

"I think the majority of these *dimdims* are cruel towards black people," Desimoni said.

"What makes you say that?" I asked him.

"I just think they are."

"Not all *dimdims* are like that," I said.

Suddenly the door opened and it made us turn. It was Uwegu returning.

"What?" Uwegu asked as she caught all our eyes staring at her.

"We are waiting for you," Desimoni told her.

"Well, I am here now. Can't you guys have a bit more patience," she said going into her room. "Give me five minutes and I'll be out there."

"So what made you come up with this idea of shooting photos today?" I asked Desimoni.

"It's good to have memories of the places you have been to, don't you think?"

"Bro, if you capture things on camera, people will believe you, even if you con them. It's evidence, bro," Reimas said.

"Or fabricated evidence," I said laughing.

"They are like paths to some destiny," Desimoni added.

"That's true bro."

"I hope you guys don't use the photographs to con people back home," I told them. They burst out laughing.

Not long after, Uwegu came out and we all left for Circular Quay.

"Were you calling home again?" Reimas asked her as we were walking to the bus stop. She nodded her head. "The little girl told me about her father calling her," I overheard Uwegu tell Reimas.

So are you planning to get back with him, sis?" Reimas asked.

"No I am not."

"He could be trying to come back to you," Reimas continued.

"Over my dead body," Uwegu said.

"Sis, fate acts in strange ways."

"Stop it," Uwegu told him. She made Desimoni and me turn.

"What?" Uwegu asked the two of us.

"Nothing," I said to her.

"Hey the bus is here, let's go," I called out to Reimas and Uwegu after a while. We all got in and went to Circular Quay.

✷✷✷

Where do we start?" I asked them as soon as we got off.

"Too many people around, I am feeling uncomfortable," Desimoni said. We all looked at him in disbelief.

"Hey, these people are doing their own things. Don't worry about them. Look, they are mostly tourists like us," Uwegu tried to calm his nerves.

"Reimas go stand over there, and I'll snap you," Uwegu told him.

"Where?" Reimas asked.

"There near that statue. Perez go join him and I'll take a shot of you guys," Uwegu told me.

Reimas and I stood beside the statue while Uwegu took shots of us. I could see Desimoni looking around before photographing us too. He was very nervy and we could see it in his eyes and body language.

We moved on to a different place. There were many Japanese tourists around all speaking in their language and taking photographs. A couple who looked like Pacific Islanders walked past us and we smiled at them.

"That is a good place to take a shot," said Uwegu. "Here, this time Desimoni and Reimas you stand while I take your photographs." I could see Desimoni was hesitant.

"How about standing over there, Desimoni," Uwegu asked him.

"You mean next to those two *dimdim* guys?"

"Yeah. Go on."

He hesitated for a while until Uwegu literally pushed him towards the two *dimdim* guys.

"Excuse us," Uwegu said to the two guys.

"It's alright, you go ahead," one of the *dimdim* guys said to us smiling.

As soon as Desimoni heard that he just went and stood all smiles and Uwegu took his photograph.

"Easy and simple," Uwegu told Desimoni.

"Can one of you get a photograph of all of us please," Uwegu asked one of the *dimdim* guys.

"Sure," answered the *dimdim* guy and Uwegu gave him the camera and we all stood together.

"Say cheese," the *dimdim* guy told us.

"Cheese," we all chorused and he snapped us.

"Thanks," Uwegu told him as she got the camera from him.

"Did you see that?" I said to Desimoni. "Not all the *dimdims* are bad. Most just mind their own business."

Uwegu took some more pictures and we continued looking for interesting locations to take photographs. We spend most of the day at Circular Quay and in the afternoon we returned home, tired.

✳✳✳

"**H**ow come you weren't too forthcoming when we were at Circular Quay?"
I asked Desimoni later.

"Too many eyes were focused at us. It was kind of unnerving for me."

"You shouldn't have bothered about them. You should be yourself."

"I don't know but I still have this tendency of having nerves when I am
among *dimdims*."

"You have been here for quite sometime now. You should be confident by
now."

"But some of these *dimdims tu ya*, when they look at you, their eyes really
penetrate your whole body," said Uwegu.

"Because you are exotic, sis," called Reimas laughing at the same time.

"You and your exotic term," Uwegu called back to him.

"You know the other day, I was reading the newspaper in the Internet and I
read about this *dimdim* guy killed in PNG by some rascals. That's why I am
getting a bit scared. They might want to pay back," Desimoni told me.

"Is that so? This is a civilised country Desimoni. Don't think like that."

"Look at you, bloody native," Reimas came in.

"You are the worse one. When I told you about this news you told me that
we must not go around on our own because the *dimdims* are going to payback,"
Desimoni returned. "And it is him who made me to feel this way."

"Hey, you never know. You have the worse murderers here bro," said
Reimas.

"But why did they kill that *dimdim* man?" Uwegu asked.

"Maybe the killing wasn't intentional. It could be to do with robbery," I told
them.

"It was on the television last week and in the Australian newspapers," said
Desimoni.

"I think it is the journalists who cause trouble for us," said Uwegu softly. "I don't like them. Even when they interview people, they try to force you to admit something that is not true."

"You mean they harass people for the news?"

"Yes," Uwegu came in. "They are bad, they have bad manners."

"But if they can't do that we won't know the truth sis," Reimas said. "I mean people will still be hiding the truth."

"But I don't like it when they make big things out of minor incidents," said Uwegu. "These Australian journalists are fond of that."

"True indeed sis. If they can work normally many of the troubles in the world won't live beyond their means."

"So who was murdered Desimoni?" I asked him.

"This *dimdim* guy. I think one mining executive. He was driving into his house and they shot him. They took his car and everything."

"Poor guy," said Uwegu. "Those who shot him are bloody useless people."

We continued talking about this *dimdim* guy who was killed in PNG until Desimoni brought up the subject of Kilroy.

"Kilroy seems to be different from us. I mean he doesn't seem to care," Desimoni started.

"He can move freely anywhere."

"Because he has been here a very long time," Uwegu came in.

"And he knows the people and places like the palm of his hand."

"Bro, but there is this sense of inauthenticity about him sometimes," Reimas said.

"What do you mean?" I asked.

"Well, he plays that 'know all' guy but sometimes he fakes it," Reimas continued.

"I think he only fakes it when he can't control himself," came in Uwegu.

"Bro, he is very good."

"You guys are very observant," I said.

"But he can really get along fine with us and with the *dimdims*," said Uwegu.

"I like to be with him because of that bro," Reimas said. "I mean, he can cope with everyone."

"That's what makes him different from us," said Uwegu.

"I don't like the way he does it sometimes," came in Desimoni. "He annoys people by some of his jokes."

"Say, he could be a stand up comedian if he wants to, bro," said Reimas.

"Oh man, he is very funny sometimes," Uwegu added.

"Sometimes he can be very nasty too, bro."

"How?" Uwegu asked.

"I mean with the *dimdim* women. He doesn't care," Reimas said. "He can just go up to a woman and start a conversation with her and if the woman responds positively, he can just get her like that!"

"He is a smart ass sometimes," Uwegu said.

"Hey, and what about Rawiri?" I asked.

"Bro, he is a chicken. He hides behind a computer and chats women up," Reimas said. We laughed. "And when he sees these *dimdim* women he will come up with all sorts of weird ideas about them. He can't face them and talk with them though," Reimas continued.

"He has a wild imagination, that one," Uwegu said. "Well all you guys are like that. When you see women you get all crazy in your heads."

"Count me out sis," Reimas said. "Rawiri can be quiet and can be a gentleman at other times. But there are times when he can change colours quickly like a chameleon." He paused for a while as he coughed. "He can be moody too, bro. Last time he wanted to belt the shit out of this *dimdim* guy who was asking him for some coins at the train station. I stopped him."

"Crazy guy," Uwegu said.

"But bro, most of the time he is good."

"You never know, he could be a snake in the grass," I said. I looked at my watch and I told them it was news time.

Uwegu switched on the television and the first news item was about this black guy in America who was beaten by some white policemen. We suddenly stopped talking and glued our eyes to the television. There was footage of him being beaten and it was terrible.

"Man, how can they do that? They are policemen," said Uwegu.

"Because he is a black guy and they are white, sis," Reimas said. "*Gutpela na oli kilim dispela masta long ples ya*," Reimas continued. "I mean look!"

"But that is America, not here," said Uwegu.

"They are all the same, sis," said Reimas. "Bro I think *dimdims* in America are more racist than here," Reimas said looking at me.

"What makes you think that?"

"Because the policemen are thrashing the black guy. They are not supposed to do that."

"I don't know," I said.

"They can even do it in front of the cameras, bro," said Reimas.

"Oh damn if I care," I said. "That's America not here." Uwegu looked hard at me. "It's still the same terrible thing. It's about racism or whatever you want to call it. That is the physical version of it. What I have experienced is the hidden version, which is more traumatic. I don't like it one bit."

The three of us did not say anything, as we did not want to inflame her further. Not long after, the two guys went into their rooms and Uwegu and myself were the only ones left outside.

"Perez, I couldn't understand Desimoni today," Uwegu told me after awhile. I looked at her. "I mean why would he be so nervous when we were out there today?"

"Perhaps it was just a one-off thing," I said. "People are different and they react to different situations in different ways."

"This could be the result of him staying at home most of the time."

"I wouldn't know that," I told her. "You could be right. Perhaps he has not adapted to being with *dimdims*."

"He needs to socialise more with other people."

"How about you? I mean how do you feel with other people?"

"I have become stronger after encountering those white pigs. I can move around freely despite the fact that I have copped nasty comments from them."

"It's not even five months into the year yet," I said. "Give him a little bit more time."

"You could be right. "But one thing I am sure about is that this country can also be mean and unfriendly," Uwegu told me. "You see how these *dimdims* can be brutal and all that. But it is what is not spoken that is the most poisonous and painful. Sometimes these *dimdims* will sit next to you but won't even greet you. You will be like a rejected lover in the agony of an absent phone call."

"That is very poetic Uwegu."

I sat there listening to Uwegu. I realised that she was aware of things here, that she wasn't that ignorant island girl who had just arrived in an alien landscape.

"I want to take Desimoni around the city but he doesn't want to." She paused. "You should be the one taking him around. At least you have been here longer and you are more experienced."

"They have to learn to be independent Uwegu. In order to be independent they have to learn the ropes on their own," I told her, perhaps trying to hide my guilt.

"I wish that Rawiri or that Kilroy guy would come and get him out sometimes," said Uwegu. "The way Desimoni carried on today is bad. *Madi*, my love for him."

Chapter 11

One Friday evening two weeks after we had gone to Circular Quay the three of us were sitting around the lounge, listening to some local music when Uwegu burst in and started complaining about people at home asking her to buy them this and that. No one said anything but she kept on and on about how mean some people were and all that woman talk.

"What do they think I am?" Uwegu continued. "I am not a millionaire. They think because I am on scholarship I must have a lot of money. I can understand if it was my daughter asking me. But it's almost the whole clan who wants this and that." She paused for a while then started again. "I wish I had won that lotto. I only lost by two numbers." She smiled which made Reimas laugh.

"People at home don't realise that we are here as students and not tourists or workers," I managed to chip in.

That was it. It was like putting more fuel into the fire. Uwegu was animated again. Reimas pinched me — telling me not to say any more.

"When I was working, they were always fronting up every fortnight. I got sick of them but what could I do? This is one reason why I got this scholarship thinking I am escaping them. But no!" She paused. "I shouldn't have given them my address."

I could see Desimoni getting annoyed. Uwegu knew that we weren't interested but she kept on; perhaps she wanted us to sympathise with her or perhaps she just wanted to annoy us. Earlier during the day she complained to me about listening to Reimas and Desimoni play the same old songs over and over. I didn't say anything.

"I have some very good CDs but whenever I offer to play them they refuse," she told me.

"I don't know but you know how guys are," I tried to reassure her.

"But we all have different tastes in music don't we?" she replied.

"I suppose so."

"What do you mean you suppose so? Damn, you know that. I bet you don't like it too but you don't tell the two guys because you don't want to upset them."

"Listen, Uwegu this is the first time for these guys to leave their villages and come here; especially Desimoni. It is difficult to adjust quickly. Perhaps that's their way of connecting with home," I tried to explain to her.

She didn't say anything but I knew she was pondering upon what I just said.

"Your case maybe different. You may have adapted very quickly but these two guys are still learning the ropes. When you see them hanging around the courtyard watching the planes land and take off, what does that tell you? When you see them confined to their rooms sleeping, what does that indicate to you?"

"Whatever," she said shrugging her shoulders at the same time.

She leaned against the window and looked into the darkness. A dog was barking nearby and the traffic lights on the main ANZAC Parade seem to blink nervously. There was occasional burst of drunken laughter from the streets.

She got up and went and knocked on Reimas's room. A while later Reimas emerged and came to where Uwegu was. "What is it?"

"Can you come with me tomorrow please?"

"Where to?"

"To the shopping mall, next to the railway station." He didn't say anything for a while.

"Sis, if you pay for my bus fare and lunch I'll come with you," Reimas tried to bargain with her.

"Reimas, we all get the same stipend and we all have expenses to cater for. Damn, you are a difficult kid to lure. It's Saturday and what will you be doing here all day? All you do on weekends is sleep and play the tape or stand on the courtyard and watch the planes land and take off. Just as well I am not your wife!" I burst out laughing which made her turn and look at me sternly.

"How do you know that, sis?" Reimas replied. "If you want me to accompany you, then pay for my bus fare and lunch. It's your trip not mine."

"You are too demanding! Forget it, I'll ask Desi instead.

"Reimas, why don't you want to go with her?" I said quietly. "We are a family here and we have to help each other."

Reimas looked at me and then Uwegu. "Alright. *Mi tok pilai tasol.*" Uwegu displayed a faint smile.

"Thanks Reimas. Don't worry I'll shout you lunch and pay your bus fare," Uwegu assured him.

"What are you gonna buy?" I asked. "My kid sister will be celebrating her 18th birthday in two weeks' time so I have to buy her something nice. She is always very fussy about presents, that girl. If she doesn't like what you give her, she'll sulk for days. She is stubborn. My aunt also wants me to get her a dress. She will be going to this women's fellowship some place outside Port Moresby. Then my brother wants a pair of stockman boots."

"That will cost you a lot of money, sis," Reimas came in.

"You must put your feet down. Don't let them get away with it."

"I know. They are very bad these people. They think we are getting a lot of money here." She was quiet for a short while. "Sometimes it's difficult. I mean they are looking after my daughter so I have to oblige."

"That's black mail, isn't it? I mean they are looking after your child because they are family," I said.

"Times have changed. Nowadays, it is often material love," Uwegu said.

"That is sad. Oh well, people are different and they have different meanings to relationships," I said.

"My family is different, sis," came in Reimas.

"Reimas, I wish my folks were like yours."

"Uwegu get them the things they asked for but tell them that you don't earn much, that you are a student living on a student's allowance," I told her.

"Sometimes that's what you lead them to believe sis," Reimas told her.

She looked at him for a while, then at me. "It's not because of me it's the bloody *dimdims* who taught them about what has value and what hasn't. This is my first time to buy them presents since coming here. I can't resist their requests can I? They are my folks!"

"Then don't complain, sis," Reimas told her.

"You go ahead and buy the presents," I told her. "The world has changed and we must keep abreast with it." I stopped to see how Reimas would react but he was blank. I paused just before getting up. "I am going that way tomorrow but I will be leaving early. I have an 8.30 am appointment."

"That's rather too early for us," Uwegu said.

"I suppose you could meet me at the park at about 9.30 am. By that time, I will have finished my business. I'll wait for you two there," I told Uwegu and Reimas.

"Yeah, that sounds alright," Uwegu said, at the same time looking at Reimas.

I was leaving early because I wanted to pass on Deuba's letter to her cousin (whom I met at the Wantok Association gathering sometime back). She was returning to Port Moresby. This letter contained some money for Deuba. I wanted to repay what I owed her. I didn't want her to harass me.

I wondered though if any of them (Desimoni, Reimas or Uwegu) has read Deuba's letter, which I had forgotten in the lounge. In the letter she told me how she knew about my involvement with a gang who broke into a bank and stole thousands. She said she knew I planned it with them by allowing them to 'steal' my car and use it as a getaway vehicle. Although I was held up and almost got shot for refusing to hand over my car key she didn't believe my story. She told me that if I didn't repay her money, which I borrowed to fix my car, she would tell the cops of my involvement with the gang. She called me a compulsive liar who preyed on vulnerable women like her.

Knowing that her cousin was flying back to PNG that morning, I wanted to leave early to catch up with her and give her Deuba's money, as I was scared that Deuba might report me to the cops.

By 9.30 am the next day, I was sitting in the park looking at the birds as they waited for the food scraps that people were throwing at them. Overlooking the park was a small pond, and ducks were swimming in it and they were making strange noises. Next to me sat a couple, lovers who were busy pecking each other. They were whispering and I hardly heard what they were talking about. I sat waiting for Uwegu and Reimas. Every now and again I would look up to the direction from where they would emerge. As the clock ticked away, I became anxious.

A small child was playing nearby while the mother was eating her food. She called to the child (who was about 2 years old) now and again. The child hadn't seen me yet, as I was shaded by a sculpture of one of the early explorers of this continent. One of the birds flew low and as soon as the child saw it, she chased after it. It was heading my way. The child followed and as soon as she saw me, she was so frightened that she just fell down and cried. The mother thought something terrible had happened to her. Even the couple sitting next to me was surprised at such a reaction. The mother rushed to her.

She looked angrily at me but did not say a word. She pulled up the child, kissed her and left. I could see the child pointing back at me, and the mother said something which I couldn't hear. I felt embarrassed; people were staring at me. I looked different. I got angry at the two of them for not arriving quickly. Then I got angry with myself. If I hadn't suggested meeting here, I wouldn't have been accused of something I was innocent of. At that moment I realised how Uwegu felt when she was insulted by those *dimdims* sometime back. It was painful.

I got up from the seat I was sitting on and walked some distance away. I could feel the accusing eyes watching me as I strolled along, trying to distance myself from them. On my right there were two Aborigines who were drunk to their eye balls; they had bottles wrapped in papers. They smiled at me and one actually called me brother. I returned the gesture and continued on, looking for another seat where I could sit away from prying eyes. For the first time, I remembered what Uwegu had said about the old man who never seemed to greet us whenever we did: that silence cuts more deeply and is much more potent. I found an empty seat and sat down. I waited but there was no sign of them. At 10.30 am I stood up and left the place vowing never to return there again.

I walked past a heap of colourful Bougainvillea plants, which cheered me up. I stood beside them and picked a red flower. *Aren't they beautiful?* I told myself. I remembered my mother planting them around our house. As I stopped to admire the plants a *dimdim* man walking his dog on the pavement passed me, giving me a good stare. Further down two elderly couples were waiting for the bus. It was dole day and many of the senior citizens were going to the banks to get their welfare money. I thought about the guy whom I met in the pub who told me that he fought in Rabaul during the Second World War. Good man.

I could not get my mind away from what happened to me in the park. Although Uwegu has talked to me openly about *dimdims* swearing at her and making nasty comments, I pretended that it wasn't real, that she was imagining it and that it happens only to other people. Now it was my turn to cope it and I found it difficult to understand why it could happen in a cosmopolitan city like Sydney. I know we were different that we did not belong to this country but then again we were not here to steal their place.

It was another 10 minutes before I got onto the bus. The bus was full but I managed to find a vacant seat and squeezed myself in. In the bus I noticed a young woman with an elderly guy. The woman looked like she was in her mid twenties while the man was perhaps in his late 50s or so. She looked like she was from my place except for the hairstyle. She looked at me and turned away quickly. I watched them from the corner of my eyes. She was talking to her husband and looking my way. I pretended to read the newspaper but all this time I was watching them. They were talking about me, perhaps trying to figure out where I was from. Just before my bus stop, they got off. I regretted not chatting to her. In any case she could have been from anywhere.

"Man, what's she doing with that old man I think he is long dead," someone inside me spoke.

"Money man," someone else inside my head replied.

"The guy must have worked in PNG and found this chick. I hope it's love," the two people inside my head were conversing.

"Love is just a term now. It has lost its meaning long ago."

"Then what is it that's holding these two together?"

"Loneliness and old age for the man and money for the woman."

"Bitch! Why can't she be honest with him? They are the types that spoil our names."

When I arrived home, Uwegu and Reimas were not in. As I was tired and cranky, I went into my room to rest. My mind was still focused on the incident that occurred to me at the park. I felt terrible about it. Sometime later, I was disturbed by the two of them chatting outside in the lounge. Reimas was admiring the things that Uwegu had bought. I lay awake on my bed for sometime, my anger having subsided. As soon as they heard me unlocking my door they looked up.

"What happened to you guys?" was my first question.

"We are really sorry, Perez. We were waiting for the bus when one of my friends appeared and asked us to go drop her off at Coogee. As she was new here, we had no choice but to help her. From Coogee we caught the bus that was heading your way but when we saw the time we knew you would have gone already and we headed straight for the mall," Uwegu told me apologetically. "Reimas insisted we stop to check on you but I told him you must have got tired of waiting and left."

"Don't worry," I dismissed the whole episode. I didn't want to tell them what has happened to me in the park, as I did not want to alarm them. I looked at the things on the floor. "Man that's a lot of shopping."

"There was a sale on so I thought why not make use of it," Uwegu told me.

"Are you going to send this entire stuff home?"

"I don't know yet," Uwegu answered.

"You have done well," I said as I put on the jug.

"Bro, we saw a group of people who looked like they were from home," Reimas told me.

"Did you try to talk to them? Check their teeth if they had *buai* stains. I usually identify them that way."

"Oh you idiot. There are others who don't chew that stuff," came in Uwegu.

"That's the quick way to identify them. Otherwise you have to go up and ask them."

"Yes, we should have done that. I am pretty sure they were our wantoks, sis." Uwegu looked at him and shook her head. "Be more civilised Reimas."

You know something, bro?" Reimas said solemnly after a short pause.

"What!"

"When we got off the bus we made across a small park opposite the train station. Uwegu wanted to do a shortcut so she pulled me through that park. Man, would you believe it, bro? I was surprised to see so many homeless and drunken *dimdims* in the park. How could they be homeless? This is a very rich country, bro."

"You know Perez? There were many of them all over the park. Some were still sleeping covered in dirty blankets, others were drinking and they smell horrible," added Uwegu. "Some even called out, 'Brother, sister give us a spare coin.' The unbelievable thing about it all is that they were mostly *dimdims*. There were a few blacks though."

"How can that be, bro?" asked Reimas again.

"There are many reasons why they are like that," I tried to be reasonable and simple. "Many of them are alcoholics and they spent all their welfare cheques on alcohol and therefore can't afford to rent a place. Others are from broken homes."

"It's a pity aye?" said Uwegu as she continued to wrap the things she bought.

"But bro, you don't find this back at home. Everyone has a family," said Reimas.

"The extended family system has long disappeared here."

"No wonder, they are all over the place, bro."

I got up and went to make myself a cup of coffee. "And where could Desimoni be?" I asked.

"He could be in the library with his Indonesian pal, bro," said Reimas.

"So now he is making friends with Indonesians, aye. Is this the Look North Policy?" Uwegu said at the same time smiling.

"Well at least he is trying to connect with other people," I said.

"They are terrorists and murderers," Uwegu said.

"Come on sis you are too judgmental," Reimas countered.

"Judgmental my foot, look what happened in Bali," Uwegu cut in. Reimas looked at me but I did not say anything. I made my coffee and sat down.

"Please hold this end and I'll tape the box," Uwegu requested Reimas.

"It's too bulky, get some things out sis."

"Oh shut up! Just press on it hard. *Yu wanem yu mangi?*" I smiled at Uwegu's expression in Tok Pisin. It sounded a bit funny to me. Reimas looked at me and also smiled.

"What's that look supposed to mean?" she asked Reimas.

"Nothing."

"Okay press hard while I tape the box." Uwegu pulled the tape and stuck it on the box. After awhile Uwegu thanked Reimas and took the box to her room.

"Bro, since I've been here I have seen these *dimdims* doing crazy things," Reimas started again. "But worse still, all they do in their many talk shows is talk about sex and all that taboo subjects. That is disgusting isn't it! Have you ever watched a TV talk show, bro? Man, they'll bring all these people and they will confide and confess and tell their secrets. They even try to fight each other on TV. They fight over men or women and all that crazy stuff. *Ol longlong lain stret yah,*" he added in Tok Pisin.

"But they are different from us. You have to learn to accept it," I tried to tell him.

"And you know what, bro? The other weekend Desimoni and I went to the beach and we saw these *dimdims*. They crowded every part of the beach. Desimoni told me that they were sun bathing or something. We moved on a bit to where people were fishing. One fella when he caught fish, he released it again. Why fish in the first place when you don't want the fish? Aren't they crazy, bro?"

"Everyone does crazy things sometimes. Wait till you stay a bit longer here. You'll find out more strange and bizarre things that happen here."

"You know bro, when I first arrived here these *dimdims* were always giving me that look as if I was from another planet. You could also feel it. It bears down on you and you don't want to hang around any more," Reimas told me.

"I suppose you are right. I don't know how to explain it to you."

"Maybe they are just curious because you are not a *dimdim*."

"So what if I am not, bro?" Reimas came back at me.

"Then you are the other."

The door suddenly opened and Desimoni entered. He greeted us and sat down on the sofa. "Where did you go, bro?" Reimas asked him.

"Went to the library to do some work with a friend of mine."

"You mean that Indonesian friend of yours?" I asked.

"Yes."

"So how did you meet your Indonesian friend?" I asked him.

"We are actually classmates. He has a problem with reading and writing English, so I help him out if I can. He used to work as a teacher back home. When he got the scholarship to study here he resigned his job and came here. He is much older than us of course. Skinny guy like Gupta."

"Bro, this people are so hungry for knowledge, aye?" Reimas came in.

"Not hungry, they want to move up the ladder. When you have many educated people you want to compete for the limited jobs a country can offer."

"I pity the poor guy. He speaks with an almost impenetrable accent. For the greater part I have no idea what he says. He says he can't understand the lecturers. He says they talk too fast," Desimoni told us.

"Bro, some of these lecturers speak in strange accents. There is this Iranian lecturer who I barely understand," said Reimas. "So when I know it is him giving the lecture I usually sit in front so I can hear him properly."

After a while the three of us just sat around watching television. Now and again we would switch to a different channel trying to find what to look at. I laughed when we switched to a channel and up came a talk show program.

Desimoni looked at me and then at Reimas. Quickly I changed the channel to another one. This time Reimas wanted to watch cricket so we all watched. I realised that we all felt a sense of community when we were together. Individually we were like retreating seashells afraid of the outside world. When we go out of the cocoon of our house, we are at the mercy of the outside forces. This is why when we are back in the house we are so happy and free.

Chapter 12

Despite all these prejudices and discriminations that we continued to encounter, there is only one place where we can escape to; to avoid them—our flat. I don't know what Uwegu and the other two guys feel but every time I step into our flat here in Sydney, I feel I am at home in PNG. It is the only secure place for me. Our flat is an island, a piece of PNG in a strange landscape. I am glad that Uwegu was able to give the flat that touch of home. There are also some pictures of village scenes. This decoration of the lounge was what made the flat homely and a place to take refuge when the strangeness of the city gets on your nerves or when you feel lonely and homesick.

We saw our coming here to a strange place as part of a journey out of the upheaval of certain relationships—love relationships, family relationships, cultural relationships and so on. This coming together whilst natural was at the same time strange. Making a landfall in this alien place meant that we all occupied the same nightmare.

The lounge was the center of our community. Many times when we come back from school (very true in the first few weeks), this is where we congregated; it was where we congregated each weekend and anytime when we are able to unite. That's what makes the lounge to me so special a place to be. We also had collections of CDs and tapes by wantok musicians that we played frequently. Indeed, in the first few weeks since the three of them came, they were always into playing local music and sitting around the lounge. I knew it was their way of trying to relieve themselves of homesickness. At times I pitied them although at other times I wish they would adapt quickly and get on with their studies. A number of our wantok students failed and returned home due to the homesickness that prevented them from attending classes. Having me around from the beginning was good because I provided a kind of anchor for them.

Uwegu on the other hand provided that sense of feminine presence, which gave us a real feeling of community.

Ironically, the decoration of the lounge with PNG things at the same time almost became a trap for us. The two guys used to just hang around the lounge and this made them miss a number of their classes (especially in the first few weeks) until I got on them once I realised what was happening. Uwegu did it sometimes but as soon as she made friends she discarded the habit. Reimas and Desimoni were different. They would just sit quietly in the lounge and look at the artifacts or they would quietly tell stories about home. They never would go to their rooms until late in the evening. I observed them for sometime before I told them again what I thought of them. They would talk about this and that and many times they repeated themselves.

A few months later, after I got on them for spending too much time in the house, the next place they frequented was the computer labs. One of them must have discovered the *wantok forum* and the PNG chat site and they would spend hours in the lab. Sometimes they would come home late in the night when Uwegu and I were already fast asleep. Oh, you could see the smile on their faces after they had discovered the marvels of modern technology. I was confused when they called each other different names and I wondered what was happening. But I could see that they were having fun, lots of it too. Uwegu didn't know that the two were now spending their time chatting on the Internet. However, one day Uwegu was in the lab when she saw the two guys talking in Pidgin and giggling. She walked quietly up to them and saw that they were chatting with some people on the net. She stood quietly watching them and then she left. They never found out that she saw them and knew what they were up to. Later during the night Uwegu asked Reimas what they were doing huddled together at the corner of the computer lab and Reimas told her about the chat site.

"Sis, nowadays we are busy chatting in the computer with friends, so we don't have much time for you and big bro."

"Who do you chat with?" Uwegu asked him.

"Sis, it's a PNG chat site and anyone from PNG can go in and chat. It's not for the faint-hearted though; there are a lot of abusive chatters too," Reimas tried to sound sophisticated perhaps wanting to impress Uwegu.

"But who showed you into the chat site?" Uwegu persisted.

"One of our Fijian mates did, sis."

"Who is he?" "A guy who we are doing the same course with. He gave us the website address. There is also a *wantok forum* where people from PNG comment on issues happening back home."

"So were you chatting the other day when I saw you two huddled in the corner of the computer lab?"

"Could have been. You should try and get in. I can give you the address if you like."

"Give it to me tomorrow then."

"Oh sis, you will love it, it's fun. You can meet guys and girls there."

It was Uwegu who told me later what these two guys had been doing lately. So the change from hanging around the house to the computer labs was a way to avoid us. Not that they have left the house completely but they minimised their time there. When they get back sometimes in the afternoons, they congregate in the lounge and do all sorts of silly things. Uwegu often gets on them. Reimas has the tendency to argue back.

When Uwegu told me about what these two guys had been up to, I didn't show any interest. I thought that at least they were adapting to the place. I was happy for them. Then one day, there was a phone call that came to the flat. The two guys were still away at Uni and I was the one who answered. It was a woman's voice asking for "Castro." It was the first time I heard the voice and I asked her to repeat the name again. I told her that she must have the wrong number and she said the guy just gave her that number. I asked where the guy is from and she said he was a Pacific Islander.

Somehow I managed to convince her that either she got the wrong number or someone must have hoodwinked her. Not long after, the phone rang again and the same woman asked for the same name. I told her that Castro doesn't live there and that she definitely got it all wrong. She insisted and I hung up on her. Thereafter the phone continuously rang almost every 15 minutes but I wasn't bothered. The last time the phone rang and when I got to answer it the line went dead. I had a feeling it was the same caller.

I kept quiet about it until several days later; a different voice rang the flat and asked for Santos. I told her that we don't have anyone going by that name. She said, she knew it wasn't the guy's real name but a chat line name and the guy gave it to her in the chat room a few moments ago.

"There is no one here at the moment except me, and I wouldn't be much of a help to you," I told the caller.

"Alright I am sorry to disturb you then," the caller apologised and hung up.

I wondered who might be playing this trick. It hasn't clicked on me that the two guys have been frequenting the chat room lately. Somehow this escaped me. I was alone and Uwegu was still away at Uni, so were the two guys. I knew someone was playing a trick but who that someone was escaped my mind. I wanted Uwegu or the two guys to arrive. Then another call came and it was for Castro. They were trying my patience but I had to answer politely as I thought they were also victims of someone's game. This was yet a different female voice.

"We don't have that kind of name in this household," I told her.

"Are you sure of this?" the caller asked.

"I am very sure as I live here."

"Sorry," was all the caller could say before hanging up.

Not long after, Uwegu arrived and I told her about the funny calls I have been receiving asking for either Castro or Santos. She threw her bag down and sat down looking at me.

"When was this?"

"It started a few nights ago but I didn't mention it to you."

"How did they sound?"

"All the callers were *dimdim* women."

"Someone could be playing some kind of a sick joke," Uwegu told me.

"Did you ask the two guys?"

"No, I didn't. But it's nothing really," I said.

"Wait a minute," Uwegu said. "You better ask the two guys, they have been in the chat room lately."

"That reminds me. One of the women callers said she was given the number when she was in the chat room."

"Try and ask the two guys then. They may know something."

"The thing about the two is that for the last several weeks, they are never home early," I said.

"It could be them giving this number to the women they are chatting with."

"In that case they should be home to get their calls." I paused. "It could be someone else doing it."

"I think it's the two guys," Uwegu said.

"Why?" I asked her.

"I don't know but I just have a feeling it's something to do with them."

We waited for them to come home but it was taking them a long time to arrive. Perhaps they were busy in the library.

"Haven't you seen them in the computer lab?" I asked Uwegu.

"I have not seen them lately," she told me. "It could be that they have changed to another computer lab. They know that I also used the first one that they were going to. What did you say the names were again?"

"Castro and Santos."

"I'll note it down and ask them when they come," Uwegu told me.

"Alright. I'll go in and rest. I am feeling rather tired."

I left her and went into my room and lay down on my bed. I made sure that my small radio in the room was off so I could hear them when they come in. I lay awake for a long time listening to the sounds outside until I faintly heard Uwegu talking to them. This was followed by a burst of laughter from the two guys. I knew that the two guys would know something about the funny calls we have been receiving. Indeed it could have been the two guys who gave the number to the women who called. I didn't want to go out but let Uwegu find out from them. The laughter continued for a while until I couldn't determine anymore what they were talking about. I couldn't hear clearly what Uwegu was telling them about or what they were saying to her. I stayed awake listening to other sounds, both familiar and unfamiliar until I drifted off to a deep sleep.

I was woken up in the middle of the night by the ringing of the phone and not long after, I heard one of the two boys go out. Whoever answered the phone (either Reimas or Desimoni) must have talked with the caller for a long while because I did not hear the person go back into his room. He talked in whispered tones. Then I heard the door to the other room open and the other guy also went out. I smiled to myself at the two guys. Indeed they thought I was fast asleep when in fact I was listening to them, not that I heard what they were talking about. At one stage I could hear the two guys struggling with each other for the handset. I think the other guy also wanted to be given a chance to talk with the caller. As I couldn't hold my eyes steady, I went back to sleep.

The next day Uwegu told me that when she asked them about the two names and how lately we've been receiving strange calls from women they denied it. They said they had not been chatting for the last couple of weeks.

"Did they convince you?" I asked Uwegu.

"I am not too sure myself," she told me. "You should have been the one asking them. I can't tell whether they were lying to me or not."

"But you said they laughed," I tried to corner her.

"Yes they did."

"Isn't that the give away line?"

"It might be that they know someone using this chat name and they were laughing," Uwegu told me.

"You could be right too," I replied. "I mean, there is nothing wrong with people calling here but they should give the real names or tell us about their nicknames so we know who the caller really wants."

"That is true indeed Perez," Uwegu told me.

"Anyway, let's forget all about it but if there are any such phone calls, don't blame me if I say something bad to the caller."

"Go ahead, they have denied it," Uwegu told me.

"Then again I am not that kind of a person who talks bad to people."

"I know."

"What would you do if you receive such calls?" I asked her.

"I am not sure how to handle them," she replied. "I mean I can handle it the first time but I don't know how I can handle subsequent calls. But sometimes I can be bad." I looked at her. "I mean I can be nasty too sometimes."

"Nothing wrong with that," I said.

As we were talking there was a phone call. Uwegu went and answered it and it was some female wanting to talk with Santos or someone of that name.

"You sure you got the right number?" she asked.

"I am sure I have," came the caller.

"We don't have a person living here by that name," Uwegu told her.

"Yes you do," the caller insisted.

"No, we don't."

"Yes you do."

"No, we don't"

"Yes you do."

"No, we don't you white cunt," I heard Uwegu say and then she hung up, taking the receiver off the hook. I was shocked to hear her use that word but I didn't say anything. I just kept quiet.

"Sorry the caller pissed me off," Uwegu said to me.

"Where is she from?" I asked.

"Sounds like a *dimdim* woman."

"Someone has to tell the truth," I said. "I don't want people calling and abusing us here at our own home."

"Please ask the two guys as it's beginning to affect my nerves," Uwegu kind of begged me.

"I will talk to them when they return," I assured her. "If they want to play these games they have to tell us so we are aware. It's like they are disturbing the place we call home."

"They are losers whoever they are," Uwegu ventured on.

"These bloody callers are disturbing our piece of paradise. You know something? This house with the set up and all the decoration reminds me of home. The callers are disturbing our piece of home," I told her.

"Yes, this is where we are supposed to feel at home, to escape from such morons who have no manners at all. I meant it to be that way. It gives us that sense of place and identity."

"It's like they are intruding into our privacy."

"Honestly. Can't they disturb other people?"

Chapter 13

After Uwegu swore at the woman caller we did not have any more of the strange calls. Then one morning a call came which Uwegu answered. It was about 6.00 am. She talked for a long time. After that it did not take her long to leave the flat. When I came out to make my breakfast she was already gone. I didn't think much about it but what bothered me was the fact that the call came through very early. It was unusual for her to get calls that early. It was when she came home that afternoon that I realised that there was something wrong. She seemed upset but I did not bother to ask her. She wasn't usually like this and that was what told me that something was wrong.

Upon arriving home, she just buzzed into the house and straight into her room without uttering a word of greeting. I knew something had happened because it was odd for her not to greet me. Firstly, I thought she was just tired but she never came out again despite the fact that I was making a lot of noise. The two guys were not around and I never told them about Uwegu being upset until later.

I was exhausted and to make things worse I had a strange phone call from a man claiming to be Deuba's husband who threatened to kill me if ever I contacted her again. I was confused by the whole thing. I knew it may have been Deuba who gave him my number or he may have enquired with the International Students Centre. The caller told me never again to write to Deuba. I knew he was referring to the money I sent her as repayment of her money I had borrowed. How he knew about it, I don't know. Perhaps Deuba must have deliberately placed the letter where he could find it. I hung up on him twice and the next time he rang the other postgraduate student got it and the caller told him to tell me that he would kill me. The face of the *dimdim* student changed as if he had seen a ghost—he was shocked beyond belief. I calmed him down by lying to him that the caller was just joking. I couldn't do any more work, as the call was unnerving.

As I was pondering about the strange call I received earlier that day, suddenly the phone rang and it made me panic, thinking it could be the same caller. I didn't want to answer it. I heard Uwegu open her door and I got up to signal to her that if the call was mine tell the caller that I have moved residence. Then I disappeared into my room.

Uwegu was on the phone for a long time. I then knew that the call was not mine. At times I could hear her swearing to whomever she was talking with. At other times she spoke with deep emotion, which made her almost cry. Occasionally I heard her making unintelligible sounds as if she didn't want to hear what the other person on the other end of the phone was saying. Desimoni was already fast asleep and Reimas was out with his *dimdim* mate when the phone call came through. As usual I waited for her to calm down. I mean, I was the more experienced person and she knew that I am always available to give advice wherever I can.

There was something about the phone call late that night that made me suspicious. I had a feeling that it was either from her ex-boyfriend, (her daughter's dad) or someone she was into a relationship with. I mean, you could sometimes tell from the way the person speaks on the phone even though you can't really hear the conversation. The way she spoke on the phone told me that it was to do with a relationship. How do I know? I just know. I really wanted to go out and ask her that night but I hesitated. In fact I got up ready to go out to her but my sixth sense told me not to.

The next couple of days Uwegu kept to herself. She was always out before we got up and coming back late in the evening straight into her room. Reimas wanted to talk to her but in the last minute he decided against it saying, "It's up to her to talk to us." Desimoni also said he was going to talk to her no matter what because they are relatives and both came from the same place. I didn't say anything but let them do what they thought was best. I knew that Desimoni was just saying it as a matter of talking and that he wouldn't do it.

A few days later I saw Uwegu at Uni and she smiled and waved at me as she went past me with her Asian girlfriends. One of the girls just gave me that funny look and walked past. I tried to smile but wasn't good at it and I gave up. I mean, I did smile but it was a fake one. I waved to her but she didn't see me waving. I noticed that she has recovered from whatever was bothering her for the last few days. When I told the two other guys about seeing Uwegu very animated with her Asian friends, they came up with all sorts of reasons.

"You know something, bro?" It could be something to do with that Asian bitch," Reimas said to me.

"What do you mean?" I asked him surprised.

"Well, Desimoni told me that Uwegu was now a lesbo, bro," Reimas continued.

I stared at him for a long time shocked beyond belief. You know that kind of shock that gets you when someone tells you that a close friend has had an accident.

"Ask Desimoni," Reimas told me seeing that I was shocked.

"How does he know that Uwegu is a lesbo?" I asked. "That can't be."

"Bro, I am just thinking aloud. I mean look, you said that you saw her chatting happily with some Asian friends. It could mean something to do with one of those girls."

"It can't be true Reimas," I told him. "I just don't buy it. And who is this girl?"

"Ask Desimoni if you think I am bluffing, bro," Reimas advised. "There is this particular girl called Suniya that she is very close to."

"Where is Desimoni then?"

I thought for a while. "Never mind," I'll ask him when he returns. In the meantime don't ever say that Uwegu is a lesbo to anyone. You could be in serious trouble," I warned him. "But who gave you this idea that Uwegu is doing it with Suniya?" I asked.

"Desimoni told me, bro," Reimas said coyly. "Bro, I have never mentioned this to anyone except you. Well, Desimoni said it because Uwegu didn't respond to his email. Remember Uwegu told us about someone sending her an email?"

Now I realised that this rumour about Uwegu being a lesbo could have been fabricated by Desimoni because Uwegu didn't respond to his email.

"Reimas just because she didn't reply to Desimoni's email, doesn't mean she doesn't like men," I told him. "In any case Desimoni used a different name which Uwegu didn't know. I am sure if he had used his real name, she would have replied.

"Bro, she only responded to the one in which we used a female's name. We conned her."

"Oh my God. How did she respond?" I asked.

"Oh well the usual, that she doesn't know her but she is interested in meeting her. She told this other woman that she likes being with women because women can understand other women's problems and they are not as aggressive as men, that nowadays she is more into women's company than male company."

"I see. It could be nothing. Women are bound to respond to an email from another woman. That's psychology."

"Bro, whether that is true or not, I have a strong feeling she is turning into a lesbo."

"Oh cut the crap, Reimas," I told him. "I don't know where you guys get all these silly ideas from."

"Okay bro, but I won't be surprised," he told me.

"I'll have to find Desimoni and ask him about this."

"So did you go to the rugby game?"

"I went twice with my mates. They even asked me if I wanted to play rugby with them and I told them that I'll think about it."

"Which team do you support?"

"Bro, my team is Roosters. They are just next door to us. Their captain is very good, bro. He is very good in doing zigzag and the *magani* dance. When he has the ball close to the opposition's try line, he always scores."

"You are becoming a rugby fanatic," I said to him. "I hope you are not neglecting your studies."

"No, my school work is fine. Look, I even bought myself a pair of rugby boots and training shorts."

"That's good; you are balancing your life now."

We talked some more and I told him about my suspicion that her problem could have been to do with a relationship back home. I told him that I wanted to come out that night when she was on the phone, but I hesitated and didn't come out. He told me that he came in the early hours of the morning.

"How about Desimoni?" I asked.

"I don't think he heard anything, bro."

"Man, you guys when you sleep, you really sleep," I said. "What if something happens, say a break in or something?"

"That is very true, bro," Reimas said. "I don't know but I am like this, when I sleep, I really sleep."

"I'm not a deep sleeper. Any little noise can wake me up."

"Bro, before I used to sleepwalk when I was at primary school."

"Really? Oh, man that is really funny. Tell me all about it. How did you overcome it?"

"It just stopped, bro."

"Just as well, you could have had an accident," I told him.

"I don't know the cause of it, bro," Reimas told me. "My parents approached a medicine man and he gave me some concoction of leaves and other stuff but it continued until some 6 months later. I don't know whether it stopped by itself or the medicine man stopped it. The other kids used to tease me, calling me 'midnight rider' and other names."

"True. If I were you, I would have punched those kids," I said just trying to make conversation with him.

"I couldn't fight them bro, they were much stronger than me. Now they are all grown up and most of them are married."

"Imagine how quickly we move from our childhood to adulthood."

"When you are a grown up, you have other worries to think about and you don't have time to think about your past, bro," Reimas said.

"That's right. That payback mentality that we have as children goes out with childhood. I mean you don't think about it when you are an adult."

"Bro, when I was a kid and these other kids teased me as 'midnight rider,' I used to really get upset and cranky. I fought a few of the kids but they usually got me in a group. You know two to three guys coming on you at once."

I laughed because the experience was similar. "The only other way to get back at them is to corner one of them when he is alone," I said.

"Bro, I did that once or twice but the bloody kid ran faster than me," Reimas said laughing.

"I usually get something and throw it at the kid to hurt his bloody legs."

"Bro, so you were bad as well."

"Revenge, pal," I told him. "You get some of your powers back when you clobber a kid real good."

There was a rustling noise from Uwegu's room and we turned our eyes towards it only to discover that it was the wind blowing, which made the leaves rub against the window.

"Bro, I thought it was Uwegu," Reimas said.

"Me too," I said. "Did you know that her other name is Daisy?"

"I heard Desimoni call that name. I wonder when she is going to come home, bro?"

"I don't know but for the last few days she's been coming home late."

"I have not seen her lately too," Reimas said.

"She could be just busy with her studies, I said.

Just then Desimoni appeared at the doorway with his school bag. "Here comes the chief's son, bro," Reimas said smiling at Desimoni.

"We thought you were sleeping," I told him.

He laughed. "I sneaked out when Reimas wasn't looking."

"You must have some secret plans, bro," Reimas joked.

"No, I just wanted to be on my own today."

"I know you are up to no good Desimoni," Reimas told him.

"Search me," Desimoni said lifting his two hands up.

"I am not a policeman, bro," Reimas said laughing.

"Well, then let me alone."

"Say, have you seen Uwegu at Uni?" I asked.

"Nope."

"I hope she is alright."

"Hey, don't worry about her. She is okay now that she and her Asian girlfriend are in good terms again," said Desimoni.

"What do you mean? Am I missing out on something here?"

"I mean, she must have had an argument with her Asian lover girl and now they must have reconciled and are in good terms again."

"How do you know that?" I asked. "I don't get you."

Desimoni kept quiet for a while. "I just know it," he said.

"You must have some way of knowing about it," I insisted.

"Bro, this guy has something from the village. He can tell just about anything," Reimas told me.

"He is lying. It's logic. If you can put one and one together then you are into something."

"I hope she can get back to the rhythm of things here and we can be family again. I mean the problem has nothing to do with us. We are just waiting for her to come back to us," I said.

"I think she is shy, bro," Reimas said. "We need to talk to her and get her back with us."

"Why can't Desimoni talk to her? They are wantoks," I suggested.

"Can you talk to her, bro?" You told us you were going to talk to her," Reimas prompted Desimoni.

"I have changed my mind because I think she is the one who needs to get back to us," Desimoni replied. "If she shuts herself from us, then she is the one to open up first."

"That is true, bro," Reimas chipped in his support.

"Okay, we will see if she does that, otherwise I am gonna talk to her," I told the two guys. "She should not act like a stranger in her own house. She also pays rent. Besides, I don't want a small problem to break us apart."

"Well we didn't create her problems," Reimas said. "She created it herself."

"I don't think it's really a problem. She is just shy to speak to us," I told them.

"Bro, I am beginning to feel sorry for her now," said Reimas.

Desimoni looked to the ground before he spoke in that funny high-pitched voice. "I just know it, my gut feeling tells me. Perhaps not a lesbo but something is driving her towards that way of life."

"But you don't have any evidence," I insisted.

"There are different ways of finding out." The *dimdim* way is just one of many ways."

Now he was speaking truly as a man of both worlds. I realised where he was coming from. As a son of one of the paramount chiefs, he was also rigid in tradition.

"But at least you must have seen her doing something?"

"You will see later," Desimoni told me. "For now, let's say nothing happened."

"Alright from now on, let's not say she is a lesbo," I told them.

I knew that deep inside Desimoni was laughing at me, at my *dimdim* way of thinking about things. Reimas just sat there listening to our conversation.

"I wonder when Uwegu is gonna come home, bro?" Reimas repeated.

"She will come," I told him. "She is not a small girl."

"But it's getting late and the place is not safe, bro."

"Let her be. She doesn't worry me," Desimoni said rather softly.

"She is not angry with us," I told them. "She is just feeling bad that's all."

Chapter 14

Finally Uwegu told me what had happened. Although I didn't believe her I had no proof to dismiss her story. She told me that she got a phone call from her cousin who told her that someone from here had been spreading rumours about her being a lesbian. Even her folks have heard about it. I sat there dumbfounded. "Why would someone tell lies about me? Now that people have heard such stories they will despise me. You know how it is back home."

"Who would spread such rumours?" I said. "I mean there are only the three of us here and I don't think anyone of us will do that. Are you suspecting anyone?"

She was quiet for a long time. Then she shrugged her shoulders and looked away. "I am not sure."

"Then don't worry too much about it. A rumour is like a wind, it blows away as quickly as it comes."

"But my name and reputation have been tarnished, Perez."

"Sorry," was all I could say.

"I don't think you understand, Perez. I feel like a whore. It's my reputation we are talking about here."

I sat there listening to her. I wondered if it was Desimoni who had spread the story. It could even be Reimas.

"So why did you keep away from us when you heard about it?"

"I did not trust any one of you and I suspected it might have been one of you guys," she told me.

"I wonder who could it be." I said quietly.

"I'll find out sooner or later," Uwegu told me. "I don't even trust that *dimdim* woman as well."

No sooner had Uwegu recovered from the incident when another episode happened. The week after the June exams, Desimoni left us. One morning he just got up and told us that he was flying home that day and that was it. He never told us whether he was coming back or not. All of us thought that he was just going for holidays. Later Uwegu told me that she didn't think Desi was going to return.

A week later Reimas went with his *dimdim* mate to Melbourne. So I was left with Uwegu. I felt good thinking that at last I can spend some time together with her. To my regret however Uwegu did not spend much time at the flat. I felt down but on the other hand, I was glad that I could concentrate on my work. When Uwegu stayed the night (which was rarely) she was mostly in her room. I hung around the lounge thinking she would come and join me but most often she never did. When she came home at other times she came with her girlfriend who I learnt later was a Malaysian, Suniya, who was doing the same course as Uwegu. At other times Uwegu went and stayed with her. Suniya was petite and quite pretty. Her spoken English was above average and she was quite talkative. Uwegu started bringing her after Reimas had left. She told me that she didn't like the two guys to tease and make fun of them.

"You know how PNG guys are like. They tend to tease a lot," Uwegu told me.

"But why would they tease you?"

"You know, they would ask me if my friend is willing and all that. Or they would say we are lesbians," she tried to reason with me. "You know that rumour I told you about, someone spreading the story that I was a lesbian?" I nodded my head.

"Sometimes these guys don't think. They just throw out what's in their heads," I said. "Don't worry about me though."

"I don't mean you." I smiled. "You wouldn't mind if I bring Suniya and she stayed with me for a night or so?"

"No," I replied.

"Thanks. I'll bring her this afternoon and we can work on our project."

Suniya stayed with Uwegu for two consecutive nights this time round. They told me they were working on a project that was due after the break. I wondered what kind of project it was but I never got around to asking them. Whenever they arrived when I was outside at the lounge, I would see them bring lots of books. They mostly stayed in the room. Oftentimes by the time I returned from my errands, they would already be home. I didn't object to her visits and I thought it was good that she dropped in.

One day I suddenly noticed some strange marks on Uwegu's neck. They looked like love bites but then again I wasn't sure. They would have been scratch marks or insect bites. I noticed it just after Suniya had left. Uwegu wore a high cut skivvy in the morning, which hid her neck. I only noticed it in the afternoon when she changed clothes. Once she caught me looking at the side of her neck, she got up and went to the room. When she returned I could see that she had applied Vaseline on it. The look on her face was one of embarrassment. I made sure I didn't look at her too much.

"How is your project coming along?" I asked her just to let her forget her embarrassment.

"We have completed our first draft. There are four of us in the group but the other two aren't cooperating. They don't always make it when we ask to meet as a group," she said. "The project is being shaped by Suniya and me."

"You could report them to your lecturer," I suggested.

"It's alright; we'll let them go this time."

"Man, you are considerate."

"Sometimes one has to," Uwegu said smiling.

We talked some more about other things before I told Uwegu that I will be away for a few days. She began to worry about being on her own. I told her it was all right and that she would be safe.

"Why don't you ask Suniya to stay with you?"

"I could do that, couldn't I?"

"Of course," I replied. "I mean if you are scared of being on your own, do ask her to come and stay with you."

"I'll do that then. When are you meaning to come back?"

"Two days' time."

She got up and went to call Suniya. I hovered around to hear what they would talk about. I could see her waiting, somewhat impatient. There seemed to be no response from the other end. She put down the receiver.

"She isn't home."

"Try again later." I paused for a while until I asked, "Why are you scared Uwegu?"

"Never been on my own before. Besides you told us that this place is haunted. I am also afraid of that woman who attacked me earlier. I don't want that bitch to find me alone here."

"Do you still believe that it was Kate that tried to strangle you? Why would she do that?"

"Because she is jealous of me. She wants you. Besides she might be trying to settle an old score." She paused for a long time. "Can't she let sleeping dogs lie?"

"But nothing terrible has ever happened to us here except for minor strange disturbances," I told her.

"What happened to me wasn't a minor thing. It's a matter of life and death." She stopped. "Anyway we mustn't take things for granted. In my society, people often killed each other. Besides, I have had strange dreams, people trying to kill me and a couple of times I saw ghosts." I looked at her.

"Are you sure of this?" Why didn't you tell us then?"

"What would you have done? You know nothing about these things."

"You mean it's something from your area that you have been seeing?"

She did not reply. I left her and went to my room. I was confused about what Uwegu had just said and the fact that she has refused to elaborate. I wondered if Kate has another name that I didn't know of.

As soon as I closed my eyes I had a strange dream. I dreamt that as I walked to my room, Uwegu came from behind me and held me back. When I turned around, she kissed me. Then she came on top of me. Took my clothes off and made love to me. "*What's that suppose to mean?*" I asked her trembling with excitement. "*I've always wanted to make love to you,*" she told me. Then she let go and went to her room. I was dumbfounded. I didn't know what to say or how to feel. I just stood there for sometime. It was so strange and yet so sweet. Then I opened my eyes and realised I had been dreaming. I noticed that I was naked which was odd. When I went to bed I was fully clothed. Then there was a knock on my door. I got up and opened my door. It was Uwegu she was standing there smiling.

"Man, I was waiting for you out here."

"What for?"

"Well, Suniya is not home and her friend says she won't be home until tomorrow."

"That's no good," I managed to say. "I have to leave tomorrow afternoon. It's important that I go."

We chatted about other things but my mind was still savouring the dream. I prayed that she would make love to me for real but my prayer went unanswered. Then she moved closer to me and held my arm. "I don't want you to leave me alone; I am scared. Strange things continue to happen to me here. I think it has to do with that *dimdim* woman. I know she did something to this place."

"Why would she do that? And besides, *dimdims* don't do that."

"Perez, I don't think Kate is a true *dimdim*. I am pretty sure of that." She moved closer again. "I have a strong suspicion that she is someone I once knew but my memory is failing me." I stared at her.

Then it happened. Our mouths touched and we kissed. It was so beautiful. As I was fumbling with her clothes the phone suddenly rang disturbing us. I stopped and got off her. We looked at each other but no words came. I felt embarrassed all of a sudden. She got up and picked up the phone. "It's for you," she told me. I got up and went to the phone. As soon as I answered it went dead. "The caller hung up on me," I told Uwegu. She just shrugged her shoulders and went into her room, perhaps ashamed.

After awhile I went and knocked on her door. After several knocks I gave up. I sat there hoping that she would come out but she never did for a long time.

She only came out when the phone rang. I picked the phone up and answered. I laughed when I heard the voice.

"Who is it?" she asked quietly.

"It's Reimas."

"Oh good!" she said her eyes lighting up at the same time. "Come, I'll talk to him." I gave her the phone.

"Where are you?" Uwegu asked him.

"Sis, I am at the Central Station. I am waiting for the bus and I'll be there soon."

"Man, you didn't stay that long," Uwegu said.

"Oh well, at least I have seen Melbourne," Reimas said. "Sis, I forgot my flat key in my room so please don't go anywhere till I arrive."

"We will be here."

"I just met Kilroy a few minutes ago and he said he will be coming over, sis."

"I am scared of him, Reimas."

"True sis, he is bad news, that guy."

"Why do you say that?" "*Em wanpela con artist yah, sis*!" Reimas said.

"Is he? I thought so." Then she looked at me and made a face at me. "Okay we'll see you shortly then," and she put down the phone.

"Reimas says that Kilroy is a con artist," Uwegu said.

"I don't know about that," I said.

"There are many stories about impostors in PNG. I don't know what they get out of it," Uwegu said. "At the university back home we have guys carrying law books pretending to be law students. They even attend classes and use the library. Once you find them out they hide for a while and then resurface again later."

"Some even pretend to be doctors," I added.

"*Nogat sem blong ol ya*!"

We were suddenly disturbed by someone knocking on the door. We hesitated for a moment until I slowly went and opened it. It was Reimas. We all smiled.

"How come you are back early?" Uwegu asked him.

"Sis, I just didn't want to stay that long there."

"And where is your mate?" Uwegu asked.

"He is still in Melbourne, sis. He's coming back next week."

"Did you take some photos?"

"Wait till you see them sis."

"Just as well you came back early. I am going out of town for a couple of days," I told him. "Uwegu was a little scared. Now that you are back, the two of you can stay."

"Where are you going to, bro?"

"The place is about 1 hour from here. We are going with our lecturer. It's part of our fieldwork researching into the early indigenous settlement of Wollongong."

"That should be fun, bro."

"Damn, it's hard work."

"Good for you," said Uwegu giving a teasing look.

Reimas left us and went into his room. He didn't come out again. We sat there chatting about nothing in particular. Her eyes were still moody and then she moved closer to me. As she was about to come onto me, I moved back indicating that Reimas might catch us. "You chicken," she whispered giving me that seductive look.

We sat quietly for a long while only the sounds of our heartbeats were audible. Then Uwegu apologised to me. "Sorry, I don't know how it happened." She paused. "I feel ashamed Perez but we are both unattached so it's not that bad."

"It's alright, don't worry about it. Let's pretend that nothing happened."

"I hope Kilroy doesn't turn up when you aren't here," Uwegu told me.

"He doesn't know I am going. You'll be alright, Reimas is back now."

"That fellow is spooky," she said.

"Did you know that Kilroy was adopted by *dimdim* missionaries?"

"What?"

"Yes, he was adopted and they brought him here. I thought you would know because the *dimdim* missionaries served in your area."

Uwegu sat for a while without speaking. I looked at her but she was in deep thought. "There were a number of missionaries that served in my area. They served there for a long time until just before independence when most of them returned. I mean, I was very young when most of the *dimdim* missionaries left my place."

"Well, one of the *dimdim* couples were Kilroy's adopted parents. They brought him here and he abandoned them."

"But he doesn't show that Christian side of him much does he?"

"Because he had been corrupted by the evils of this city." Uwegu laughed.

"I think his adopted parents have ex-communicated him long time ago."

"They should not have brought him here in the first place."

"I am sure he has his reasons for cutting the ties with them," I said. "There are quite a number of Papua New Guineans who had been adopted by *dimdim* missionaries around here. Some have made it big time others like Kilroy have not."

"I think Kilroy's parents may have adopted two local boys. One of them was the one who was going around with the *dimdim* girl, daughter of the other missionary couple who served in my area. Kilroy's adopted parents and the other missionary couple had a bitter quarrel and since then they were never again in good terms," Uwegu told me. She stopped and thought for a long while then I saw her nodding her head. "Something is beginning to fall into place," she said.

"What are you talking about?" She did not respond. "I could ask Kilroy about it," I said.

"Yes, try and ask him. I don't know whether this *dimdim* girl committed abortion or whether she gave birth to the baby. If she did deliver the baby, I wonder where she would be now?"

Chapter 15

We waited for Desimoni to return from home but he never did. We were into the third week of classes when Uwegu broke the news that Desimoni had decided not to return.

"Why would that be?" I asked.

"I don't know. It could be to do with the rumour we heard earlier. But I think he is stupid to abandon his studies," Uwegu said.

"He is stupid, sis. This is his chance," Reimas added. "Maybe his father has influenced him not to return aye, sis."

"He should not have accepted the scholarship in the first place. There are many deserving people out there," Uwegu continued. "I know who influenced him. It's his father. Gosh, one would think a man of his status would be wise enough to let his son continue."

"But why would his father do that?" I asked.

"He may have found him a woman at last," Uwegu said.

"The least he could have done was to complete his studies here," I said.

"He still has some of his things here. What's gonna happened to them sis?" Reimas asked.

"I don't know," said Uwegu.

"He might get in touch with us again," I said hopefully. "There is another thing that we need to talk about."

"What, bro?"

"Whether we need to take in another flatmate or we chip in a bit more to cover for Desimoni," I told them.

"Man, that's true. Now that he has gone we need to pay a bit more for rent," said Uwegu.

"We have a choice either to chip in to cover it or get another flatmate."

"Let's try getting someone to join us. But I don't know if people are willing to share with us," said Uwegu.

"Unless, of course someone is really desperate for a place to stay," I said.

So we began our discussion on what kind of person we would like to come and share with us. Uwegu wanted another woman and Reimas insisted on a male. I tried my best to remain neutral. We didn't know of any wantoks who would want to come and share with us.

"There aren't that many wantoks whom we can ask to share," I said.

"How about your friend Suniya?" Reimas asked Uwegu.

"I don't know, I'll have to ask her. But I think she is happy where she is."

We continued talking about what we wanted and how we want the advertisement to be written and all that.

"As much as possible, let's try to get a Pacific Islander to share with us," I told them.

"What if there are no Pacific Islanders interested, bro?"

"Then we have to get the next interested person I suppose."

"I wish there was a wantok who was willing to move in with us," said Uwegu.

We talked some more before we begin the advertisement.

"Flatmate wanted to share a four bedroom house with three others, (two guys and one female). Must be a non-smoker, clean and tidy. Able to communicate cross-culturally. Rent is $50.00 weekly. If interested phone 67998701."

Reimas was the one whose task it was to write the advertisement because he was artistic, so Uwegu told me. I wanted to write it but Uwegu told me that my writing was like a crab, almost illegible. I've seen Reimas write a few times and indeed his handwriting was good and he can even draw. Uwegu told me that Reimas won an art competition one time. I just went along with her. Uwegu also said that our advertisement must be eye-catching as there are other people advertising to get people to share with them. We stood around watching Reimas design the advert. He had with him different colours of pens that he used. My job was to get the original and use a colour copier to run a few copies. When he finally finished the work it was indeed artistic except there were traces of slightly exaggerated wordings. When I pointed this out Uwegu said that was for effect and impact. I didn't say anything more as I somehow felt that these two were more artistic than me.

That evening as I was going to the office, they gave me the advertisement so I could get some copies.

"We need about 10 copies, bro," Reimas told me.

"That many?" I asked.

"We need to put them on various notice boards. We need to get the best person. We don't want a drunkard or a criminal," Uwegu came in.

I didn't say anything more but took the advertisement and went to Uni. I got about 11 copies using the colour copier and it turned out good. After doing a bit of work I got the copies and took them home to the two guys. They were waiting. As soon as they saw me they rushed to me to see how it appeared.

"They came out alright," Uwegu told Reimas. "Come and have a look."

"As soon as you guys put them up, you must be here to answer the calls," I told them.

"What do we tell them?" Uwegu asked.

"If they are interested tell them to come around and see the place. Give them the address. Don't forget to tidy up a bit," I said.

"What about you?" Uwegu asked me.

"What do you want me to do?"

"Stay around too. Just in case they confuse us," Uwegu told me.

"Alright."

"What's that cross-cultural communication thing, bro?"

"Well, it means basically that a person who intends to share with us must be able to deal with us, understand where we come from."

"I don't want a *dimdim* to come and share with us," said Reimas.

I looked at Uwegu. She didn't say anything. "We cross them out then?"

"Yes. Our first choice is a Pacific Islander. If there are no Pacific Islanders then an Asian," Uwegu said.

"Which part of Asia?" I asked.

"Indonesia, Burma or Thailand, bro," Reimas said.

"Gees you guys are very selective."

"How about an Indian guy, sis?" Reimas asked.

"Yake!" said Uwegu. We stared at her. "I don't want any Indians to come."

"But Indians have lots of money. We could con one of them to pay a bit more, sis," Reimas said.

"How do you know that?"

"I just know, sis."

"Alright, let's talk sense," I told them. "Tell me when are you going to put up these notices?"

"Early tomorrow morning. Or even tonight when the place is empty bro," said Reimas. He looked at Uwegu and then me.

"Okay two of you go now and put up the notices. Try to put them in different places."

"Aren't you coming with us?" Uwegu asked.

"I'll wait here in case someone calls."

"You mean people are gonna start calling tonight?"

"Hey, you never know. There are desperate students out there who are looking for cheap accommodation. They hang around campus waiting for people to put up notices like this." I paused and looked at them. "Remember; if we don't get anyone interested, we are gonna pay a bit more."

Reimas got the advertisements and both of them went out to put them up. I gave them an excuse because I didn't want to go out in the rain.

I waited but the phone didn't ring. I though about Kate again and the fact that the guys have accused her of not being a pure *dimdim*. Most importantly I thought about the fact that Uwegu has accused her of flying in the night and trying to kill her. I waited for them. I wondered why it was taking them so long.

After another 20 minutes of waiting I heard them laughing outside. I quickly got up, went outside and waited for them. As soon as they saw me they smiled.

"What's that supposed to mean?"

"Guess what?" As we were putting up the last notice, Gupta came along. I was standing on a chair and Reimas was giving me instructions. Gupta came and stood beside me and I didn't notice him. As soon as I finished I gave my hand for support and Gupta held it and I came down. As soon as I turned to say thank you, I screamed because I realised it wasn't Reimas. My spirit almost took off. Gupta also got a fright because of my scream, and he also screamed. When we realised what was happening we started laughing."

"So where is Gupta?"

"We left him on campus. He told us that had we put up the notice last week he would have got his wantok to move in with us. You could have seen the way he was looking at Uwegu. Man, he seems to be in love with her, bro," Reimas said.

"Uwegu, the poor guy is genuine," I teased her.

"I don't want to wear sari all my life," she said laughing.

"But he is rich, sis."

"I don't want to smell curry."

"Cut the crap off, you two," I told them.

"Has anyone called yet, bro?" Reimas asked changing the topic.

"Man, it's too early," Uwegu said.

"Make sure to wake up early and wait for the calls that will come in. I am putting a copy of the notice here so you are familiar with what we have put up."

"Perez, you better be the one to answer the calls. You would know how to handle the callers better, bro," Reimas told me.

"I hate this Desi for putting us in this mess," said Uwegu.

"Very true, sis," Reimas supported her.

"I would need the two of you to write down the details of each call then," I told them. "You will need to write down the name. Just guess from the voice whether the caller is a *dimdim* or Asian or African.

"I dislike sharing a place with Africans," said Uwegu.

"Damn, you seems to be disliking everybody sis. Very soon we will run out of nationalities" Reimas told her.

"Why do you dislike them?"

"I don't know but I just dislike them," Uwegu answered. "They are arrogant and they talk too much."

"You shouldn't be here at all then. You should be on your little island with your own people," Reimas told her in a rather rude manner.

"Hey, I can speak my mind any time here." Reimas did not say anything further.

"But it's true; these Africans here tend to think they are IT!" Uwegu kept quiet again. She stared into the night before she spoke quietly. "I wonder if Desi is truly happy about the decision to give up his studies."

"Maybe he is happy," Reimas said.

We talked some more until I left them outside and I went in. I could hear them making a lot of noise but I was too preoccupied with thinking about Kate again. Somehow I kept thinking about her today. I wanted to call her but when I looked at my watch it was late, so I decided against calling. The next morning, I was awoken by Uwegu knocking on my door. When I looked at my watch it was 7.30 am and I got up.

"Gees you sure sleep like a pregnant woman," she teased me. I pinched her side and she giggled making Reimas turn. She stepped on my left foot giving me that 'stop it look.'

I got my towel and went in to have my bath while they waited. They have already placed a writing pad on the table next to the telephone. I had a strong feeling that we wouldn't be getting anyone to share with us, but I kept quiet about it. By the time I was ready, it was 8.15 am.

I could see Reimas walking nervously. "Hey, Reimas don't let this bother you. It's nothing," Uwegu told him trying to calm him down.

"I don't know, sis. I am always nervous about little things."

"Here's your coffee," Uwegu told me. I took a sip. It was bloody hot. I winked at her and she made a funny face to me. She was not nervous.

"Well guys, soon the phone will be ringing and we will have a field day."

As soon as I said that the phone rang. We all looked at one another. It seems that no one wanted to answer it. I asked Uwegu to answer it. She went and answered it. It was for me.

"Hello," I answered.

"Hey buddy how are you?" It was Kilroy.

"I am alright." I closed the mouthpiece and whispered to them.

"It's Kilroy." They breathed normally again.

"So what's up, mate?"

"I just called to see how you guys are doing. Sorry I couldn't make it the other day."

"That's alright. We are okay and we are just about to go to Uni," I lied to him.

"Did you want anything?"

"No, I just needed to chat with wantoks that's all. Sick and tired of the *dimdims*."

"Weekend will be good, not weekdays."

"I thought so," he said. "Okay I'll let you guys go then. Bye."

"That's Kilroy," I told them smiling.

"Shame on him," Uwegu said. "What's that supposed to mean, sis?" Uwegu did not answer him.

The phone didn't ring again until 9.20 am; I got up and answered it. It was a female. She asked about the vacancy and I told her it was available.

"She is Japanese, isn't she?" Reimas asked. "Yes. The name is Japanese alright." I asked Uwegu to check the room again and see if everything was in order. She went in and checked.

"It's alright. Reimas and I did a very good job tidying the room."

The phone rang again. I answered and this time it was a male. I couldn't place his accent. He didn't sound like a *dimdim* or an Asian. I gave the address and he said he was going to come around. We waited.

"What if we won't get any more calls?" Uwegu asked.

"Then we will have to make a decision which one of the two we will get as our flatmate."

"What if they both reject it, bro?" Reimas asked.

"Then I guess we will have to just chip in a bit more."

Not long after, the phone rang again. I got it. It was for Uwegu.

Uwegu got the phone and soon after, we heard her laughing away. It must have been one of her girlfriends. When she finished she told us that her girlfriend wants to come and check the place up.

"Is it Suniya, sis?"

"No, this is Suniya's friend and you guys haven't met her yet. I met her through Suniya."

"Where is she from sis?"

"She is Javanese from Indonesia."

Then there was a knock on the door. Reimas went and opened it and it was a Japanese woman with her friend. She looked a little frightened upon seeing Reimas and me.

She said "*Moshi moshi,*" at the same time giving us a little bow and told us that she was Yusiko and she rang earlier about the room.

"Please come in and Uwegu will show you around the house." I introduced ourselves and let Uwegu show her around. I signaled to Reimas to follow me to the corner shop.

"We shouldn't leave Uwegu alone. She might get confused, bro," Reimas told me. "Uwegu is a smart woman. She'll do the job," I reassured him.

"She might do a bad job out of it, bro," Reimas said in a concerned manner.

"Calm down, people learn by making mistakes."

"Yes of course, bro," he replied.

"You never know, she might even show Uwegu how to make sushi."

When we returned, Uwegu was laughing away with Yusiko and her friend over a cup of tea. She was telling her about how the Japanese fought in PNG during the Second World War and Yusiko was telling her about her grandfather who was a General in the Japanese Imperial Army who was stationed on Bougainville.

"I like the room," Yusiko told us. "Nice house with good people. You students at Uni; I am student at Uni too." We were nodding our heads in agreement. She stood up. "*Arigato*. I'll call this afternoon." We all shook hands, and she left with her friend.

"Phew, that was it," said Uwegu as she sat down.

"How did it go?"

"She is nice and she said she really likes the place. I told her that we were from PNG and she said she heard a lot about the country because of the war. She is doing history and geography at Uni," Uwegu told us.

"You could have asked her to show you how to make sushi, sis."

"Oh, I hate raw fish."

"I don't think the other guy is coming, bro."

"If Yusiko doesn't get it my friend will," Uwegu said. By this time we were feeling a little tired.

"Let's just wait and see if others are gonna call. If they don't we'll have to decide on the two. Yusiko looks cool bro," Reimas said.

A while later a *dimdim* guy rang about the place and we lied to him that it has been taken already. It was Reimas who told him that.

It was going to lunch time when I called the two and we had a little meeting. "We have to decide which one of the two we are going to take in. Whoever calls first will get the place," I said. "If they don't call again then we will presume that they don't want to take the room and we will have to pay a bit more to cover the $50.00." We talked some more as we waited for any of the two to call.

"It's a pity we didn't have any Pacific Islander call," Uwegu said after a short while.

"Perhaps islanders don't seem to have too much of a problem about housing, sis," Reimas said.

"You think so? Man, they are the worst. Landlords chuck them out every so often," I said.

"Just as well we didn't get a call from any of them," said Uwegu. I smiled at her.

"Who did you say we are taking in?" I asked them again.

"We have decided to take in Uwegu's girlfriend. Oh man, you won't believe it but she is sexy and pretty, bro," Reimas told me. I looked at Uwegu and she nodded her head.

"That's fine with me."

It was indeed a long wait. But no call came from either Yusiko or Uwegu's friend. Somehow I knew that the outcome would be like this.

"No one has called yet, bro," said Reimas as he yawned.

"Can't we give them a call?" Uwegu suggested.

"We don't have Yusiko's contact number," I said.

"That's right," said Uwegu.

"Tell you what, let's forget about them. Next payday, you two pay $16.00 on top of your current rent and I will pay $18.00," I told the two. "This means both of you will be paying $66.00 for your rent."

They stood silent for a while.

"That's okay bro," said Reimas. "That's not a big increase."

"Besides, we don't want someone from another place to disturb us. Let us stay as we are," I told them. "It's much better to be on our own than to have problems."

Chapter 16

My brief encounter with Uwegu had not developed into anything serious no matter how much I hoped. Uwegu too has not given me any further signs. Perhaps she was afraid of falling in love with me because it would get Reimas out of our orbit. Falling in love with Uwegu would also have its own consequences. I was hoping for an impossible miracle, I told myself. Despite this she was always in my mind. Perhaps thinking of her was one way to forget Deuba. Or was I using her as a substitute for a lost distant relationship? I wasn't sure what to make of it. Perhaps I wasn't making enough effort to entice her into my charm.

Since Deuba's so-called husband rang I had not received any more letters from her. I wanted to consult a clairvoyant to see what my chances of getting back with Deuba would be but in the end I gave up. I had a feeling that Deuba may have severed the thin link that held what little hope I had for the survival of our relationship. I sat there idling away. Uwegu and Reimas were not in. My thoughts wandered everywhere. Then all of a sudden, I heard something right outside Uwegu's bedroom. I thought it was a cat and I didn't bother. Then suddenly my goose bumps stood and I quietly tiptoed to the window and peeked out. I was shocked. Squatting outside Uwegu's bedroom was a skinny woman burying something in the ground. I blinked my eyes twice just trying to get a clear view who the woman might be. I thought it could be the wife of the landlord. It was all strange. It was only when she stood up that I realised it was Kate. I wondered what she was doing just then. Then there was soft knocking. Suddenly I felt afraid of her. I don't know why I suddenly began to feel this way towards her. There was something weird about her, something I could not pin down. It was like a sudden apparition of a bad spirit.

I hesitated then after a couple more knocks I slowly got up and opened the door and there she was trying to smile at me. She was much thinner and looked so feeble, almost unrecognisable. She looked more like a witch. I stood there holding the door ready to shut it anytime. I nervously invited her in. I stared at her and for the first time I saw a vulnerable Kate, talking helplessly. I sat muted, not knowing what to say next. Her vulnerability seems to fill the place around her. I sat quietly not knowing what to do. She looked tired and her face displayed traces of tiredness. Indeed she wasn't her normal self although she tried to hide it from me. It was obvious to me that whatever sicknes she had, it must have affected her badly. I knew what I was seeing could just be the tip of an iceberg. The rest was hidden by the loose fitting clothes that she wore, which hid the deeper traces of her pain and worries.

In her vulnerability, I could look right into her bones. They were literally decaying right in front of my eyes and her body was disintegrating like ice cubes. I could tell that whatever illness she had was no ordinary one — I could feel the power of the illness, weakening me as it radiated around her. *Or was it an evil power*? All of a sudden the words of Uwegu came back to me. They did not come in complete sentences but in fragments leaving gaps in between. Just as well Uwegu was not in. I didn't want to be seen as a pretender or even a traitor by her.

"Are you alright?" I finally asked her.

"Yes I am. Why?"

"You look so different from the last time I saw you," I told her. I kept quiet before I started again. "Were you looking for something just then?" She stared at me. "I mean outside the flat."

"Oh, no, I dropped my keys and I was probably trying to retrieve them when you saw me." I did not believe her; I knew she must have been burying something.

She looked hard at me for a while before she talked. "I have been sick but I am okay now." I nodded my head. She looked at me for a long while before she told me quietly but painfully that she has cancer. She knew the news would shock me and she waited for it to sink down. I didn't say anything but only managed to stare at her.

"You can really run people with your eyes, aye," she tried joking perhaps to calm me.

"Don't work too hard. Try to take it easy," was all I could say to her.

"Here is different. One has to work hard in order to earn her keep."

"I know but work will be still here when we die," I said.

"Whatever," she said.

She kept quiet for some time before she started again. "It's not that bad. But one can never know the extent of cancer." Then she went quiet again. "I am receiving treatment but I hate it."

"It must be terrible for you."

"The pain is sporadic. When it gets me it is really bad."

"I am sorry to hear that."

"That's why I never came again to see you until now." She paused for a long time before she spoke again.

"Where is that bitch of yours?" I stared at her not knowing what she meant.

"What do you mean?"

"I am referring to that girl who shares the place with you. I hope she has not poisoned your heart." She sounded weird.

"She went out with Reimas. Is there something wrong?"

She looked me in the eyes. "I think I know who she is," she said and stopped abruptly. I looked at her intently. "Never mind," she dismissed me. "Listen, what are you doing today? If you are not too busy we can go to my place. I hope I can tell you everything that has happened to me before it is too late."

I looked at her not knowing where she was leading me. I felt very vulnerable and afraid. I didn't want to entangle myself in a feud that was between her and Uwegu. At the same time I did not want to be a pawn.

She stood up. "Shall we go then?" I hesitated but somehow I managed to get up and follow her.

We left and throughout the ride I stared at the passing landscape at the same time feeling ambivalent about Kate. There was both pity and dislike in my mind.

I pitied her because she was young and already she was destined for a terrible fate. I disliked her because she seemed to have some hatred towards Uwegu. Somehow I had a feeling that Kate and Uwegu knew each other and that they had an old score to settle. We continued on and as usual the traffic this afternoon was busy which slowed us down. We didn't talk much on our way. She tried to make conversation with me now and again. I found the ride boring. She kept on looking at me as she drove.

I kept quiet as I kept thinking about Uwegu accusing Kate of trying to kill her. I tried to take a good look at her. She was almost a skeleton. Perhaps Uwegu was right that she wasn't a pure *dimdim*. I wanted to laugh about how the two women were trying to destroy each other. *How could she be jealous when there was nothing between Uwegu and me, or was there*? Then I thought about the brief encounter I had with Uwegu and the thought excited me. It seems that brief fling has died its natural death. I regretted not falling into Kate's seduction earlier. Now that she was ill the attraction that I had for her earlier had gone.

"Oh, before I forget there is this *dimdim* guy who is an anthropologist and taught for some years at the university back home. I may have told you about Wilmot. He is old now. I think he is in his early 60s. He is a lovely man. He speaks fluent Tok Pisin too."

I didn't know why Kate wanted me to meet him except that she said he is an interesting character.

"Today you will meet him. He is at my place."

"I think you have mentioned his name to me before."

"Yes, he's been in the thick of things when he was in PNG. He is one of the first *dimdims* who I came to know who loved PNG."

"What does he do nowadays?"

"He has retired but I think he is working on another book about the Tolai people."

"I hope he won't bore me with all those *kiap* talk," I said jokingly.

"You'll find out when you meet him." She paused. "So how were your first few months here?"

"Been good actually. We have visited some of the interesting places in the city. Uwegu sometimes goes with her friends. Oh I didn't tell you, Desimoni the other guy had left us."

"So where did Desimoni go?"

"He went home back to PNG."

"Is he coming back though?"

"I don't think so." Kate shook her head. "Stupid boy."

We arrived at her place and there was a car parked beside her house. I got out of the car and she winked at me. As we entered I could hear soft music coming from inside. When I walked into the lounge there was this weird looking old man sitting drinking beer. His hair was wild and out of place and he also had a long white beard. He wore thick lenses that made him looked even stranger. His face was wrinkled and when our eyes finally met he stared at me so hard that I had to step back. He was smoking and the tray beside him was almost full of cigarette butts. He looked in his 60s. I stood back and waited for Kate.

As soon as Kate closed the door behind her, she called to Wilmot and introduced me.

"Wilmot, this is Perez the guy I told you about." He looked me up and down before he greeted me. *Another weird dimdim* I thought to myself.

"Hello Perez, *yu orait*?" the guy greeted me in his fading American accent, as he struggled to stand up. "My name is Wilmot; Wilmot Cox." As we shook hands I felt his fingers softly scratch the palm of my hand and when I looked at him he gave that funny smile. I withdrew my hand quickly and after a few more exchanges of greetings I sat down. I didn't feel at home with this guy. There was something strange about our meeting. Or perhaps I was just feeling paranoid because it was my first time to meet him. He had a look that was ambivalent and mysterious and my initial feeling was that he was gay.

"Take a seat," Wilmot told me. I sank into the sofa away from him and rested my head on the headrest. I stayed that way for a long time until Kate brought some cookies to me. In fact I was hungry.

"*Bipo mi wok long ples blong yu*," Dr. Cox began again. His eyebrows were white as snow and they were long and bushy too.

Kate offered me a beer but I refused. "Don't be so uptight." Kate got herself an orange juice and came and sat beside me. I know she just wanted to please me. I could see the dividing mark of her now saggy breasts. She caught me staring at her and she gave me that smile which sent waves of electric current in me.

"I worked in New Britain among the Tolais for a long time. I was in Rabaul when they killed Jack Emmanuel."

"Who is Jack Emmanuel?" I asked.

"He was the District Commissioner in New Britain. Anyway, they never really found the killers although they jailed a number of people for the murder. The fact of the matter was that the colonial administration didn't know how to deal with the people." Kate looked at him perhaps for more details.

"Well, these people were different from us for one thing. The *dimdims* didn't really get to know the people they were ruling. When Jack was murdered, the administration dealt with the suspects as they would with *dimdim* suspects. This is why the murder had never really been solved."

He stopped to drink his beer before starting again. "The murder of Jack was done in the traditional way. It was not a clean, straight-out murder. This is why they imprisoned the wrong people while the actual murderers were laughing at them."

"Sometimes you make me scared Wilmot," Kate told him. "You come up with bizarre ideas."

"I am an anthropologist; always remember that," and he laughed.

"Why didn't you advise the government that they had the wrong people?" I asked curiously.

"It was police business not mine."

"Surely they would have valued your advice," Kate commented.

"I was seeing by the government as a *kanaka* lover because I sided with the local people on many issues."

"You mean the Mataugan thing?" (A political group) Kate continued.

"That and other issues."

I sat there listening to them talking, the talk of two *dimdims*. Wilmot was somehow edging closer to the secret world where excitement and danger run side by side. At least that's what I thought.

"Jack was hated by many Tolais because he mistreated them. He jailed many locals for minor misdemeanors. He thought lowly of the people. He even murdered a couple of them." He paused for a long time before he spoke again. "I left the place because one young Tolai accused me of trying to steal their traditional knowledge. If I didn't leave the place quickly I would have been murdered just like Jack Emmanuel. I used to have a lot of kids coming to my place and they were really the ones who brought village gossip to me. They allowed me into their secrets and that's how I came to know what their fathers and mothers were saying and thinking."

"When I went to PNG to work, Wilmot was in his last semester of teaching before he came back. That's where I knew him," Kate told me.

"Why didn't you want to stay longer in PNG?" I asked him.

"There were rumours about kicking the *dimdims* out when the country gained independence. I mean I wasn't scared about anything. I have worked in many African countries before and I knew what it was like." He paused and drank his beer. I realised he was thinking about something.

"Is that what made you leave the place and come back here?" I asked.

"No, my contract wasn't renewed," Wilmot told me. "There was this young local anthropologist who replaced me."

"My case was different," Kate cut in. "Just because I didn't give in to this guy who wanted a screw, my contract wasn't renewed. I was going around with this other guy who was studying politics and others thought I was easy prey."

"Was it that young guy from Rabaul?" Wilmot asked.

"Oh you devil! How did you know that?"

"He took one of my courses and I heard rumours that he was going around with you."

"Oh damn, I didn't know that people knew."

"It's a small world Kate," Wilmot said.

"Oh he was damn good, that guy."

"By the way, where is that Milne Bay mother of yours who came and stayed with you at Uni?" Kate kept quiet for a long time. I knew there was something that wasn't right. "I mean your parents' former house girl."

"I have not heard from her for a very long time now. She is back home."

"Did you like the place though?" I asked Wilmot.

"Oh yes. PNG is a beautiful country."

"He's been to Africa," Kate told me.

"Africa must have prepared me well for PNG," Wilmot said smiling.

"The African experience would be quite different from what you experienced in PNG."

"Oh, yes but there were also many similarities."

"Such as?"

"Don't ask me that. You know very well what I am talking about," Wilmot got back at me.

"I suppose colonial experience is one," Kate came in.

"You could say that. What I was thinking of is that the people I was dealing with in Africa were similar to those in PNG." I kept quiet.

"A good place to exchange ideas is the ex-PNG Association which has a good network. I'll take you there and you can meet some of them. A number of them were lecturers at the University of PNG," Kate told me.

"That would be nice," I said.

"You have a mixture of *dimdims*, former *kiaps*, teachers, business people, flotsams and what have you," Kate continued.

"We also have a Wantok Association here," I told them.

"Yes, I have heard of that. I went once when I just got back from PNG. But it was boring. People don't mix around too much and if you are new you feel out of place."

"So, no one came and talked with you?"

"No, people came around to greet me. But then again you could sense that apprehension that you find with some PNG guys." She paused. " There aren't many *dimdims* of course."

"What about your ex-PNG Association one?" I asked her.

"What about it?"

"Do you have that many PNG nationals coming to your meetings?"

"No. It's mostly the *dimdims*. What you would call the ex-colonials," she concluded smiling.

"I know those types," I said. "All they want to do is brag about their encounters with the natives."

"It's not all that bad Perez. Most of them regret the way they had treated the locals," Wilmot contributed. "But you will meet some interesting people there, I tell you." "Some of these people have worked in the Solomons as well and they'll try their pidgin on you."

"Many of them were so high up there that they never tried learning Tok Pisin. It's only after their tour of duty there that they try to speak it because here they are nobodies," I argued.

"How could you say that? Many of these people developed your country," Kate said almost losing her control. If it wasn't for them you wouldn't be here."

I didn't say anything after that, as I didn't want to upset the two *dimdims*. Inside me I wanted to laugh. Here was this *dimdim* telling me about how they have developed PNG, that without them, PNG would still be backward.

"So what is your thesis on?" Wilmot asked changing the topic.

"I am not sure yet," I replied.

"At least you must have some ideas what you want to write about?"

"I was thinking more in line with the role of NGOs in community development in Papua New Guinea."

"Gees, you have it all worked out. That's a good topic.

We continued making small talk. Kate talked about when she was in PNG teaching at the university, about her life, and her experiences. We sat there listening to her. She was revealing some of her emotions and feelings. I wanted her to reveal more, about the mystery about her life but she had a tight grip on it. She told us how another *dimdim* lecturer tried to rape her when she was drunk at his house in PNG and how she didn't report the matter to the police because she didn't want to create problems. She also told us how she used to have a crush on another student from Madang. But mostly she talked about this student from Rabaul and how she once seduced him and how this guy was so good at it that she had a feeling that for PNG sex is a natural part of life.

"I wanted to marry that guy from Rabaul."

"Why didn't you?" I asked.

"Because he was a double-crosser that's why. A two-timing bastard!" she almost shouted.

"How did you find out?" Wilmot asked her.

"I found out at one of the parties when a drunken female *dimdim* colleague told how she was sleeping with this guy and from there I knew the asshole was a two-timer. When he tried to come to me I told him to 'f' off and go root with the other *dimdim* woman. He was cool about it and he smiled and said thanks and he was gone for good. I went home and cried my heart out. It was as if I was thrown in a pit; my stomach turned into a thousand somersaults and my nerves were giving way. Would you believe that? The bloody guy didn't worry one bit about losing me."

"It must be that Tolai magic at work," Wilmot teased her.

"Damn if I care about it," she said in an almost angry tone.

I had a feeling that she had something about PNG that she would always carry with her. She seemed to carry an oasis of memories. I also had a feeling that there was more to her attachment to PNG than she was telling us. I knew her father was a missionary in my country many years back but she never told us much about that part of her life.

She could have carried on, letting the memories surface until there was nothing left, I thought. But then again all that would be left would be a blank space. I felt sorry for her even though it was many years ago that these events took place. Every time she drinks, the memory would be retrieved from the recesses of her inside.

Chapter 17

Since visiting Kate's place, I kept on thinking about what Uwegu had said about her, the fact that she didn't think she was a pure *dimdim*, and that she blamed her for trying to strangle her sometime back. Although I tried to check Kate out, it was never conclusive. I kept on thinking about what she might have buried next to Uwegu's bedroom. At the same time, I was afraid to dig up whatever she had buried. Maybe I was just being superstitious. What Uwegu said about her clouded my mind. I even blamed myself for not asking Kate about her origins so we could lay the matter to rest once and for all. The more I thought about it, the more I got curious. When I got back from Kate's place, I did not tell them about it.

"Something had happened to me again. Someone had tried to strangle me again," Uwegu told me. She showed me the marks around her neck. "It's that same woman. Did she come here lately?" I shook my head in the negative, lying to her. "I know she was here." *How could she possibly tell that Kate has been here*, I thought to myself.

"Honestly Perez, it's getting on my nerves. What is she up to? What does she want with me?" I didn't say anything. Then I asked her whether there was something she wasn't telling me about Kate. She looked at me for some time before looking away again. "Does she have another name? The face is familiar but the name does not match," she told me.

"All I know is that her name is Kate and the surname is Nolan," I replied.

"Then I may be barking up a wrong tree," Uwegu said rather quietly.

Not long after, Reimas came and joined us. Excitedly he began to tell us a story that diverted the topic Uwegu and I were discussing.

I went to Paddy's Market last Saturday and met up with Rawiri and his two friends. In fact it was Rawiri who emailed me and told him to meet him at Paddy'sMarket.

"Where were his friends from?" Uwegu asked Reimas.

"They are Africans, sis. I think Rawiri must have conned them about getting them women from the Pacific Islands."

"How do you know that?" Uwegu asked.

"Because I overheard him telling them that I was the guy who would bring along the two women, sis. He told the two Africans that I didn't know English. I can only speak Spanish. "Which one of you can speak Spanish?" Rawiri had asked them.

"Come on man, you know we don't speak that lingo," one of the African guys told him. "Why you asking, man?" the other asked.

"Because this guy can only speak Spanish and our lingo. So I will be speaking to him in our lingo about the two women," Rawiri told them.

"Aah good, go ahead and speak with him," one of the Africans said.

"*Mi giamanim tupela olsem yu bai pulim ol meri kam long ol. Taim mi toktok long ol yu tok yes tasol. Oli askim long ol meri Pacific na mi giaman olsem bai mi pulim kam tupela na givim long ol*," Rawiri told me in Tok Pisin.

"*Na oli save haus yu stap long em?*" I asked him just to make sure.

"*Nogat mi no tokim ol tu. Mi giamanim ol olsem mi save stap long Wollongong. Bai mi toktok long ol nau.*"

"*Bai mi stap isi tasol*," I told Rawiri.

"This mate of mine tells me that the two ladies are willing to come and meet you. Give me the time and place you want to meet them so we will bring them there," Rawiri conned the two Africans.

The two Africans looked at each other and discussed quietly where they were going to meet. Then the tall one told Rawiri that the best time for them to meet was tomorrow, Sunday at 10.00 am at Circular Quay.

"That's exactly the place the two women had suggested," Rawiri lied to them. "Hey you won't regret it. They are the most beautiful women you'll ever meet or spend the night with. Tall, big and sexy! I just hope you two guys won't fail them. Can you go the whole night?" Rawiri sweet-talked the two Africans.

"Hey man, we are Africans. We can go the whole night," one of them told Rawiri.

"That's good. Alright, tomorrow at 10.00 am at Circular Quay then."

"You have our word," and they shook our hands and went their way.

"Oh my gosh!" Uwegu said laughing. "Is that what you guys do?"

"No, not all the guys do that," I said. "I mean I don't do that."

"They must have been very desperate to fall into Rawiri's charm and trick," Uwegu added.

"Sis, some of these guys are dogs. That's why HIV/AIDS is spreading so fast."

"You guys must be careful. You never know, you could be dealing with criminals," Uwegu warned. "You only come to know the face of a criminal when he is caught."

"They must have paid Rawiri some money," Reimas continued. "Luckily they met at the pub and they didn't know where Rawiri lived. After they left us, we laughed at their foolishness.

"See how stupid some people can be," Rawiri told me.

"You shouldn't have conned them," Uwegu told him.

"That's the price for their insistence, sis," Rawiri said.

"Bro, Rawiri later told me what he told them. He said they have been pestering him about Pacific Island women and he got tired and conned them."

"Why did Rawiri ask you to go and see him?" Uwegu asked Reimas.

"He told me that he was meeting this *dimdim* woman and he wanted me to accompany him to give him support."

"That's what some PNG guys do. How do you think the woman will feel seeing a group of guys waiting?" said Uwegu. "She will feel intimidated."

"Yeah, if you are man enough, have a one-on-one meeting," I supported Uwegu.

"Well, it wasn't me, bro. I went along because Rawiri asked me," Reimas tried to defend himself. "He also told me that he will buy us some drinks," Reimas continued. "After the two Africans left us we went to one of the pubs at

KX and had some drinks. Two guys who looked like they were from PNG came in and we just nodded our heads and continued with our drinks. Then Rawiri told me that he met this woman in one of the chat sites in the Internet and they planned to meet today. I was very surprised.

"I asked Rawiri whether he had given her his real name and other details and he told me that he gave her a false name and told her that he was from South America."

"What name did he give her?" "Fuentes," Rawiri said. She wanted him to send her a photo and he sent someone else's photograph. I told him that she is bound to find out and he dismissed my concern.

"Don't worry. I don't know what she looks like but she told me that she will be wearing black long pants and a blue sweater," Rawiri told Reimas.

"How long has he been communicating with her on the Internet?" Uwegu asked.

"About three weeks. Not long after, Rawiri told me to hurry up with my drink," Reimas continued. "The two PNG guys who came in must have been tourists. We could tell by the way they were carrying on. One had a potbelly. We drank another lot and then Rawiri led me out and we walked towards the meeting place. I started calling him Fuentes and he stopped me because he didn't want the woman to ambush us.

"Are you gonna really go up and meet her, bro?"

"We'll see," was all Rawiri said to Reimas.

"Have you done this before, bro?"

"I am playing this game for the first time. Kilroy does it often," Rawiri told him.

After walking another three blocks Rawiri and myself came to the place where they were supposed to meet. We were 7 minutes early, which according to Rawiri was good timing. He asked me to look around for a woman wearing long black pants and a blue sweater.

"I told her I will be wearing blue jeans and a black T-shirt," Rawiri said to Reimas. I laughed when I noticed he wasn't in blue jeans or black T-shirt.

"She's not here yet," Rawiri said. "Let's sit down there and wait."

"Did you tell her you will be coming with a friend bro?"

"I told her I was coming alone."

"Did she give you her name, bro?" "She told me her name was Faith."

"She must have given you a false name, bro."

"We'll see," was what Rawiri told me.

All this time we were talking his eyes were everywhere, searching the place. Somehow he stopped searching and we were talking about the two African guys. He told me they gave him $100.00 and would give him another $100.00 when they meet up with the women.

"Where is the $100.00 then, bro?"

"Damn, I bought drinks with it."

We must have lost our concentration for about 5 minutes because when he looked up he almost fell off the bench.

"What is it, bro?" I asked him at the same time trying to help him up.

"Let's get out of here," Rawiri said, getting up.

"Aren't we going to wait for this Faith woman, bro?"

I followed him and to a corner where we stood,and he pulled me closer.

"See, that's Faith." "Which one, bro?" "That huge one."

I looked closer following his eyes. Indeed there was this woman who was wearing black long pants with a blue sweater standing looking around. She was very huge and out of proportion.

"My goodness, how are you going to do it, bro?"

"Was she really big?" Uwegu asked.

"Man sis, she was so huge and she found it difficult to walk."

"Poor woman, Rawiri should have at least gone up to her and said hello," said Uwegu.

"What did you do next?" I asked Reimas.

"We stood there, watching her. Rawiri kept on telling me that she could be a different one and all that. But after 20 minutes no woman of the description Rawiri gave turned up, so we presumed that was her."

"You get all sorts of people in the Internet chat rooms," I told them.

"Yeah man, you have crooks, criminals, paedophiles and all sorts," Uwegu added.

"What did you do then?" I asked Reimas.

"Finally we left and went to another pub and had a few more drinks. We were laughing about it all. I mean I was poking fun at Rawiri. He gave me the chat site address and told me to try it out. He told me that he goes in there as 'Pluto' so if I come across a person using the name 'Pluto' that's him. All through this time he was looking for excuses to tell the woman.

"Are you going to try the chat site?" I asked him.

"I'll try it out on Monday, bro."

"What name are you gonna use?"

"Rawiri told me to use Uranus."

Uwegu shook her head. "I hope you don't get into trouble."

"What trouble?" I asked. "Just any trouble," said Uwegu.

"Sis, nobody knows you in the Internet," Reimas said, smiling. "And in any case, this is the way to get rid of homesick."

"Conning women you mean?" came in Uwegu.

"Sis, that's Rawiri's idea of fun. I am working on my idea of fun," Reimas said smiling.

"I hope it won't be that tasteless," Uwegu said.

"How do you mean, sis?"

"I mean it's not good to go on playing with people's vulnerability."

"No sis, my sense of fun will be similar to Elvis Presley's," said Reimas laughing.

"Whatever," was all Uwegu could say.

"The story isn't finished yet sis," Reimas told her.

"Continue then."

"The two Africans waited for almost the whole morning at Circular Quay. Rawiri gave the two Africans Kilroy's cell phone number and they rang it, and when Kilroy answered they got angry with him. Kilroy was all confused and it was only after a while when they called him Fuentes that Kilroy knew that it was Rawiri who gave them his number. The two Africans only stopped when Kilroy threatened to report them to the cops.

"Why did Rawiri give them Kilroy's number?" Uwegu asked.

"Kilroy must have left his cell phone with Rawiri. Kilroy uses Rawiri's place sometimes. But Kilroy promised the two guys that he would pass on the message to Fuentes (this is the name the Africans knew Rawiri by). Kilroy cooked up another story saying that Fuentes was actually away in Perth on some research trip. The bloody Africans believed him."

"*Plis yupela tu ya!*" was all Uwegu could say. "There are good ways to do that," Uwegu continued.

"How sis?" "I don't know but there are better ways to survive here," she said. "Talking about survival, you know some of Suniya's friends are part-time prostitutes."

"What? You mean Uni students?" I asked.

"Yeah. When they need money they just put up an advertisement or go to one of the brothels and sign up."

"Do you know any of them?" I asked her. "Suniya showed me one of them. She is from Thailand. Having difficulties with money," Uwegu said.

"That is sad."

"Well, what do you expect?" Uwegu came in.

"Can't they do something else sis?" Reimas chipped in.

"This is a quick way of earning big money," Uwegu said. "It's a secret but close friends know.'

"I haven't seen any of our wantoks do it, bro."

"You never know. This is a big city. This city is a monster," I said.

"If this city is a monster, Kilroy is the slayer of this monster, bro." We all laughed.

Chapter 18

The next time I met Kate was in the hospital. She was very sick and her hair was shaved off. This time I did not feel too afraid of her, perhaps my feeling was more sympathetic. She was undergoing chemotherapy but it seemed she would not come out of it. I felt sorry for her, such a vibrant and carefree woman and now she was reduced to a pack of bones. When our eyes met, I didn't recognise her immediately although she tried to smile. She was like a stranger adrift in a strange ocean. She seemed to have shut herself inside a tight membrane, which contained her pain. She sat up slowly but every effort she made was difficult and painful. It was so absurd to see her in this condition.

The thought about Deuba resurfaced and I wondered how she was doing with her new husband. I had not heard from her after that call in which the man threatened to kill me. A cousin of mine rang and told me that Deuba was going around with her colleague who was a married man, and that she has been involved in a number of confrontations with the man's wife. I wondered if she would look like Kate if she got the same sickness.

"Something mysterious and dark has been happening to me," Kate told me in a painful voice. "I don't think this is an ordinary sickness." I looked at her alarmed because for the first time it was coming out of a *dimdim*'s mouth.

"What are you talking about?" I asked her almost shaking with trepidation.

"It's true Perez. Since I got sick someone has been visiting me, a woman, sometimes she would appear like that woman you are staying with and sometimes she would appear like our former house girl. They all appear wanting to harm me."

"It must be the medication that is making you hallucinate," Wilmot tried to reassure her.

"I don't think so. This is something different; it could be something to do with my past. I have had two upbringings, one is the PNG side and the other is the *dimdim* side."

"You'll be alright," Wilmot reassured her at the same time looking at me.

I could see that she was in big pain. The words struggled to come out of her mouth. "No, this is something weird, something that you have not experienced. Someone is trying to get rid of me. Having lived in PNG, I have an indigenous side. It is something that *dimdims* like you, Wilmot, cannot understand."

I thought about Uwegu and I shuddered with fear. What if Uwegu was trying to payback? After sometime Kate turned to me. "What is that woman's name again?"

"Uwegu." "Is that the only name she uses?"

"No, she has another name, let me think." I thought long and hard but the name refused to surface. "I'll let you know when I remember it."

"Not Dodo," she asked.

"No," I replied. She looked away. Then she asked; "when are you leaving Perez?"

"I don't have that long to go now."

"Hopefully, I will be well enough to celebrate with you and see you go. I'll be out of the hospital next week."

I let Wilmot talk to her while I kept quiet. She just sat there and listened. I could see the nurses and doctors walking up and down. Next to Kate, a man slept and at his side stood his wife in a solemn mood. He looked terrible. What came back to my mind was my boyhood memory of the hospital as a terrible place, a place only for the sick and the dying. When I was a kid my mother used to threaten me that if I got into mischief she would take me and leave me in the hospital. So for me hospitals were associated with something bad.

"Let's go," Wilmot whispered to me after some time, at the same time giving a wink. I squeezed Kate's hand as I said goodbye. "She will be okay. It's just that she needs the chemotherapy every now and again. This will try to kill the cancer and stop it from spreading."

I didn't say anything, as I didn't feel comfortable with him. Now and again he would brush against me, unnecessarily touching me when he talked.

We came out of the building and I could breath freely again. It is a strange feeling when you enter the hospital. It's like entering the passageway that leads to the dead. We proceeded to where Wilmot parked his car and before we could get into the car Wilmot stopped. He opened a packet of cigarettes and lit one. "I really need it now."

"You know something?" Wilmot started as we got into the car sometime later. I looked at him. "Kate loves PNG because she grew up there. Kate's father was a missionary in New Guinea a long time ago. This is why she still has a strong attachment to the country. The parents were in the country for a long time. When Kate reached school age, she was sent to Australia to attend school. But during holidays she went back to her parents."

"That's interesting. She has never really told me about that," I answered with renewed interest.

"Perhaps she forgot or maybe she didn't want to be reminded of it. Perhaps she never trusted you enough," Wilmot continued.

"But why would she not trust me?" I questioned Wilmot. "Did something happen when she was in PNG?"

"Maybe she just has not come to telling you that part of her life yet." Wilmot stopped talking for a while, perhaps thinking. Then he started again. "I think Kate started her primary education in PNG but attended high school and university here in Australia. When she went back to work at the university in PNG her parents were already back here. By that time she had married but her husband eloped with her best friend. It was also here that something terrible happened to her parents and they divorced. When I was still in PNG they used to come and stay at my place from the mission station on their way to Australia or on their way back to PNG."

"Why did they divorce at such an old age?"

"I don't know. And in any case divorce happens to couples at any age."

"Where are her parents now? I mean how come no one is visiting her."

"The mother died several years ago and the dad is in a nursing home in Brisbane. He is now an invalid. Kate is the only child."

"That is very sad," I said as Wilmot negotiated a difficult corner.

"Kate's parents worked side-by-side with another missionary couple, the Hardings. The Hardings adopted two local boys and one of them may have something to do with the bitter feud that they had, and made them bitter enemies. This is what made the Nolans leave PNG early."

"What happened to the Hardings?" I asked curiously.

"They also returned, but some years later. They live somewhere here in Sydney, I think," Wilmot told me.

"What happened to the local boys they adopted?"

"They brought them here but one of the boys left for PNG not long after that because his natural mother was dying. I don't know about the other boy. He could have gone back to PNG too." Wilmot paused as he waited for the traffic lights to turn green. The road wasn't busy. "We are almost there now," he said as we entered our street.

"Just call the house anytime; I am looking after it for Kate."

"Alright," was all I said after he stopped and I got out. He tried to touch me but I was out of reach.

"That's alright young man. I'll see you again soon," at the same time winking at me.

I was still thinking of what Wilmot has jut told me, when I entered the flat. I found Uwegu and Reimas sitting close to each other reading a letter. They did not bother to greet me.

"What are you guys reading?" I asked, disturbing them.

"It's a letter from Desi," Uwegu told me.

"Really?" What did he say?"

"Bro, he is in for a big time, this Desimoni," Reimas said smiling. "How do you mean?" "Well, his father got him a cute little girl, bro. I know he won't sleep the first few weeks," Reimas continued.

"Cut it out Reimas," Uwegu scolded him. I went and sat beside them.

After they had finished, Reimas gave me the letter. In the letter Desimoni told us the reason why he decided against coming back. His father has arranged for him to marry. The woman that he was going to marry was from another island. She is a *hapkas*, a half *dimdim*. She just completed her secondary education but because the chief has asked for her to marry his son, the woman did not go on to further education. *"I have not personally met the girl but I have a photograph of her which was given to me by my father. Uwegu knows the girl and she may be able to fill you in with other details,"* he wrote. Then he asked how we were and asked if we could take his bag home when we go for our holidays. I gave the letter back. It was addressed to Reimas.

"Tell us about this girl that Desimoni is engaged to," I said to Uwegu in my attempt to get Kate out of my mind.

"I don't really know her well. She comes from another island but we went to school together. I was three years ahead of her."

"Is it true that she is half *dimdim*?"

"Yes, she is. The mother is a *dimdim*. I think she is from here."

"Where did they meet, sis?" Reimas asked.

"I don't really know that. I heard that the mother's parents were working in the area and the *dimdim* woman grew up there. So they had a relationship with this guy and that's how the girl was conceived."

"Why didn't the two get married sis?"

"The parents of the *dimdim* woman did not approve of it. That is why they left the place and came back here. The *dimdim* woman stayed back on the island until the child was about 12 months; she left because the man had impregnated another local woman."

"How come the mother just left the child like that?" I asked.

"She must have a crooked heart, bro."

"Another gossip was that, she wanted to take the child with her but the chief threatened her. And her parents didn't want to have anything to do with the baby. She also knew that we had very powerful sorcerers."

"Our medicine men are very powerful. Even Malinowski knew about the power our sorcerers wielded."

"Stop boasting, sis."

"I am not," Uwegu came back.

"I wonder where her mother would be," I said almost in a whisper. I had a funny feeling that the answer was with us but we weren't searching hard enough. I thought about Kate and what Wilmot had told me and my eyes blinked a couple of times, which meant that Kate could be the missing puzzle. I mean if your eyes blink when you are thinking about something, it means that soon something will happen.

As we talked about this *hapkas* woman I kept on thinking about Kate. I wondered whether she was going to be okay.

"So you will be the one taking his bag home then, bro?" Reimas disturbed me.

"Why me?"

"Because the two of us aren't going home, bro."

"Really?" I looked at Uwegu and she nodded her head. "Oh well, at least I am doing the chief's son a favour," I teased.

"You will be in the chief's good books, bro," Reimas said.

"Hey stop. The chief has big ears," Uwegu said. Reimas walked off without saying anything more.

We sat quietly again for sometime before Uwegu said. "Where did that *dimdim* take you to?"

"Oh, he took me to the hospital. We went to see Kate, she is in the hospital."

"Oh that one, bitch!" I looked at her hard. She was never like this before, but it was that nightmare she had that has made Uwegu a foe of Kate.

I stood up, disgusted by what Uwegu has just said. As I was about to go away from her, she apologised. After awhile she asked quietly, "what happened to her?"

"She has cancer. She goes in and out of hospital to get treatment."

"Just as well you didn't fall in love with her, bro." I didn't say anything.

"That Kate woman would probably know something about Desi's wife-to-be," Uwegu intoned. "You could ask her couldn't you?"

"But Desimoni never asked us to do that," I replied.

"But you never know, this information could be vital," Uwegu came in. "What I know is that this girl had lost contact with her natural mother when she was about 12 months."

"Gees, that's a long time," I said. "That's a cruel thing to do, don't you think?"

"What?"

"I mean leaving the child and not contacting her again. This *dimdim* woman must be a whore then," Uwegu came in.

"Something terrible must have happened. She wouldn't just walk off like that," I tried to reason with Uwegu.

She shook her head. "Some *dimdims* are stupid, they can't think straight."

"What's that suppose to mean?"

"I can't tell you straight Perez," Uwegu said almost irritated. "You know how it is with people back home. They don't talk straight; they talk in a crooked fashion." Uwegu kept quiet waiting for me to continue. I didn't say anything further. "We could try to find her mother here couldn't we?" I shrugged my shoulders.

"Can't we find out?" Uwegu said in a soft voice.

"We could. It's not hard to locate the mother."

"Then why don't we?"

"Because it is none of our business."

"Man, you are another brick wall," she said.

"I am not. I just feel that way."

"Whatever," was all she said. She stood up and walked to the kitchen.

Chapter 19

No matter how much we tried, we didn't succeed in locating Desimoni's bride's mother. The only person we did not ask was Kate, simply because she was ill. I mean, I did not have the opportunity to see her after the last visit to her. When I saw Kate again she hadn't changed much. Although she tried to be cheerful and positive, I could tell her pain was lurking just behind her cheerfulness, just waiting to pounce on her again like a dog waiting for its prey. To me, she looked like a walking corpse and I knew that she wasn't going to make it.

I was at home when Wilmot called to pick me up. By then I had dismissed his touches as accidental. When we arrived she was sitting outside on the patio.

"Hello Kate, how are you," I greeted her nervously.

"I am good. Well, at least I am trying to rise beyond the pain."

I gently hugged her and it was like hugging a pack of bones.

We sat around chatting. I thought this would be the good opportunity to ask her about the girl Desimoni was going to marry.

"We will miss you though," Wilmot said. "You have provided the link that was broken when Kate finally left PNG. Now it will be broken again."

"I hope not. I mean Reimas and Uwegu will still be here."

"Of course," was all Wilmot could say. Then Wilmot told us something about him almost marrying a local girl when he was doing fieldwork in New Britain.

"Why didn't you?" Kate asked him.

"She was very young, about 16 and I was in my thirties."

"I hope you are not gay," Kate teased him. Now my attention was captured.

"Bloody hell no, I am not! I mean anyone can be gay or lesbian and at the same time spend equal time with the opposite sex."

"What's that suppose to mean?" Kate questioned him. He kept quiet, pretending to light another smoke. "And what were those tapes doing in your cupboard?"

He quickly put off the match. "I was just curious. Oh well, I can't do anything. I am dead," he said laughing.

"Curious? How come you have lots of sex tapes at your place? To me that's not a sign of curiosity but a sign of an avid addicted watcher," Kate told him.

"Oh well, you won't believe me," he said with some nervousness. But I am not gay."

"If it's dead they have Viagra now," Kate told him.

"So I heard about it."

"What's Viagra for?" I asked. They both looked at each other and laughed.

"It temporarily cures impotency," Kate told me.

"I don't need it."

"I know you don't, but some people do," said Kate looking at Wilmot.

"I don't think Viagra would wake up a dead log," Wilmot said laughing.

"You never know Wilmot," Kate cut in. "They say the drug does wonders!"

"I mean why would men wanna wake up something that has gone through its natural process. It's just like trying to get the dead to live again."

"These *dimdims* are crazy aye," Wilmot said looking at me for support.

"That doesn't mean the feeling is not there anymore," Kate insisted.

"These *dimdims* try to defy God," I said trying to be philosophical.

"That is true," Wilmot came in.

"Oh come on, you two just wanna spoil the *dimdims*." She paused then started again. "Sorry I didn't take you to that other gathering."

"Which one?" Wilmot asked.

"The ex-PNG Association second gathering. It would have been good for him, Wilmot," Kate argued.

"He is not gonna learn anything. All they do is sing their own praises. Or brag about which woman they went out with and all that stuff."

"Come on Wilmot, they also talk politics, history and all that."

"They talk a lot of *mauswara* too," Wilmot continued.

"At least he could judge for himself Wilmot," said Kate. "You can be stubborn sometimes."

"In those days you have to have a tough skin in order to live and survive in PNG," said Wilmot. "I am glad I wasn't a *kiap*."

"They also committed atrocities as well in those days," Kate cut in.

"It was difficult; many *kiaps* did not know the people they were serving," Wilmot countered at the same time going into the house to get his cigarettes. Not long after, he came out with a strange carving that I had never seen before.

"Hey I never realised you had this?" Wilmot said holding the carving.

"That's a Trobriand yam house," Kate told him. "I had it with me all this time. I got it a long time ago. It's pregnant with a lot of memories."

"Where did you get it from?" Wilmot asked turning the carving over.

"A friend gave it to me when I was in Milne Bay."

"Really?"

"This was before I went to teach at the university in PNG," Kate told him.

"Must be a long time back then," I said.

"Oh yes, it was long time ago now. But it is still in a very good condition," Kate said. "This is one of the few artifacts I have from my other home," she said sadly. "Here take it back inside," and she handed the carving back to Wilmot. "It has a long story attached to it."

"Tell us the story then," Wilmot insisted after he had replaced the carving.

She didn't speak quickly. I saw her look into the distance and I knew she was debating whether to tell us or keep it to herself. I could feel my heartbeat increasing. Wilmot was looking directly at her. We waited in anticipation.

"It was given to me by my first boyfriend. We were very much in love. But in the 1960s cross-cultural love was forbidden. It was shunned by *dimdims*. It was a parting gift. He gave it to me the day before we left for here."

"Were your parents aware of it?" Wilmot asked.

"He passed it to his cousin who gave it to me," said Kate. "So my parents thought it was this girl's present to me. It has meant a lot to me. It was the expression of his love for me. I've always treasured it." She was quiet again perhaps thinking what to say next. "It wasn't his fault or mine. It was my parents' fault. I wish I had married him. I wonder how it would have been with him and our kids? I don't blame his adopted parents so much. I think they were okay, not so conservative as my parents. We occasionally visited them until my parents stopped suddenly. I didn't know why we stopped visiting them. It was only in later years that I came to know the reason." She paused again. "I was the same age as their son, Sean used to play together a lot with us. I guess my parents wouldn't have minded had I had a relationship with him. But it was because of my friendship with one of the two boys they had adopted that started the feud between my parents and them. It must have been so bitter that it was like we had been excommunicated from each other. I wonder where Sean is now. He went to Uni and left to do his graduate studies in England."

"We could find out from the ex-PNG Association gathering. Someone is sure to know where Sean is," said Wilmot.

"I don't want to do anything with a past that still haunts me,' Kate said emphatically.

We all kept quiet.

"The other *dimdim* missionaries didn't stay much longer," Kate started again. "They left PNG a couple of years after us. There was also some talk about Sean impregnating a local girl."

"Really?" How old was Sean?" Wilmot asked.

"He was 18 or 19. Both of us used to go back and forth to PNG because we were attending schools here in Australia then." She said. "We really enjoyed our time there."

"Did the other *dimdim* couple bring the two boys they adopted?" I asked.

"I am not too sure," Kate said.

"Who is this?" Wilmot asked.

"The two local boys the other *dimdim* missionary couple adopted."

"Yes, they brought the boys with them and I don't know whether they are still here or had gone back to PNG. There was talk that one of the boys returned to PNG soon after because his natural mother was dying."

All of sudden I noticed Kate's face changed as if she has seen a ghost or something. She almost dropped her glass of juice. Her reaction made the outlines of her veins stand out on her face making her look ugly.

"I didn't know they brought the guys here to Sydney," Kate said softly trying to hide her initial reaction. "Who told you that?"

"I saw the guys with them when I met them after they just returned."

"Man, look how out of touch I have been," Kate said. "But honestly I loved that place. It is my second home."

"Milne Bay is beautiful," Wilmot continued.

"It's sex haven for Malinowski," laughed Kate. "Where they practice free love!"

"I remember reading his book at Uni during my undergraduate years. We used his books as texts," said Wilmot.

"Yeah, his word was the Bible. There were many *dimdims* in the islands in Milne Bay when we were there. Some were running their own businesses, others worked for the government and many more were flotsams and castaways. Many of them married local women."

"Kate you know one of the guys who was sharing the house with us, Desimoni?" I asked.

"Oh, the little fellow?"

"Yes. He is actually the son of one of the chiefs in the Trobriands. He went home for holidays and he didn't come back. We heard that his father has arranged a wife for him." I told her.

"Silly boy. He should have completed his studies first," said Wilmot.

"It was his father who stopped him. He is heir to the throne," I said.

"I know but times are changing and he should finish his studies so he can be a negotiator of the two worlds,' said Wilmot.

"Who is he marrying?" Kate asked.

"Some half-*dimdim* girl."

I could see that she was again interested in the case. There was a sense of vulnerability too. I thought she had fear in her eyes. She told us that she knew most of the islands that consist of Milne Bay Province, and that was why she was asking.

"Although I had spent time in Milne Bay I am more intimate with the Tolais," said Wilmot. "These guys are much more aggressive than other groups."

"Where were you when they killed that *dimdim* kiap?"

"They killed him on the day I left Rabaul back for Port Moresby. The Tolais were beginning to resist the colonial government then."

"Did you know him personally though?" Kate asked him.

"Oh yes, I did. At that time there were not many Europeans."

"That is sad," Kate said.

"They wanted to use me to support their cause. One or two people wrote to the new District Commissioner telling him that I was behind them. So they almost kicked me out of New Britain. I mean in the course of my discussion with some locals I may have said one or two things which they interpreted as my support for their cause."

"Typical isn't it?" Kate stated.

"At that time yes. Now things have changed."

Then Kate burst out laughing and we looked at her. "I can't stop thinking about my brief affair with that Tolai guy. We used to meet at odd places. They almost caught us once in my office because I forgot to lock the door."

"You sure were a game," Wilmot told her.

"Oh well, what can I say." Then all of a sudden I could see pain wrapping itself around her. It made her breathing difficult.

After awhile Kate left for her room slowly dragging her skeleton frame with much labour.

"I'll be okay,' she tried to downplay the pain. "There are some drinks in the fridge if you like," she came back to us in a weak voice.

Wilmot looked at me and I nodded my head in the affirmative so he went and got two beers for us. I was happy that I had submitted my thesis. I had already written some letters home to potential employers and one or two have responded positively. I ceased talking and sat there listening to this *dimdim* telling me about his experiences. It was interesting to hear a white person come up with stories that you don't expect a *dimdim* to tell you. I mean about spirits killing another *dimdim* because he desecrated them and all that. I sat there quietly pondering upon the story about the haunted place until we retired for the night.

Chapter 20

I paid another visit to Wilmot when Kate was in hospital because my curiosity about him was becoming unbearable. I thought having sex tapes suggested other things. I was increasingly becoming suspicious of him and the story about him having sex tapes fueled my inquisitiveness. One of the first things I did when I got there was to check out his study room. I was surprised to discover that he had a lot of photographs of both *dimdim* and PNG children. The age range of these kids was from seven to 13 years. Although the photographs were not nude or dirty I was surprised that he kept so many pictures of children.

"Most of the photos that you keep are of kids," I said to him.

He looked at me for a long time. "I don't know it just happened that kids were around when I had my camera," he told me.

"You must be fond of kids then," I continued.

"Having not married, the next best thing is children. They bring life and happiness to you."

Inside me something was telling me that this was only a tip of an iceberg. I was very curious and I wanted to find out more about this man. How could he possibly capture only children? I promised myself to do more checking the next time I came to his place. I could see him perspiring as I looked at the photographs. We did not say anything. Then I noticed a photograph of 2 Kennedy Lane.

"Isn't this 2 Kennedy Lane?" I asked him.

"Yes, that's where I used to live before I moved here."

"Did you know that this block of apartments is haunted?" I asked him. It was then that I found out from him that the story about 2 Kennedy Lane as being haunted was a mixture of hoax and reality.

"The story about the place being haunted was started by some residents when I came from your country and lived there," Wilmot began. I looked at him not knowing whether to believe him or not. "Just listen," he told me. I kept quiet.

"It was because of me that the rumour spread about the place being haunted. I mean it could definitely be haunted. When I first came from PNG, I brought with me a large collection of things, from human skulls and bones to artifacts, carvings and other curios. I first stayed at 2 Kennedy Lane in a two bedroom flat. I didn't have many visitors. Now and again a couple of young guys came around for drinks and sometimes I would bring kids from the nearby primary school to see the collection I had. Their teacher was a close friend of mine and it was through him that we arranged for his pupils to come and study the collection. But mostly I lived alone and I liked it that way. Then strange things started to happen, what you would call paranormal occurrences. I've never witnessed them though but the other people who lived there did see strange things or hear strange noises."

"What strange things?" I asked curiously.

"People walking up the stairs, opening doors, trying to suffocate people in their sleep and all that stuff. A particular resident who tried to spread the rumour that I was sleeping with young boys got mysteriously ill one day. The doctors couldn't diagnose the cause and he left. He almost died. But I didn't think it was the spirits that were making him sick. I never thought about that. In fact I spread the same rumour when other residents were gossiping about me sleeping with young boys. The rumour helped divert their attention," he said laughing.

"But was it true that you did sleep with young boys?" I asked.

"Not at all, I was a father figure to many of the young boys."

I sat there listening to the *dimdim* anthropologist talking. There was a tint of doubt that coated what he was telling me. I let him talk while I tried to analyse what he was telling me.

"It was sometime later that I realised that perhaps it's to do with the things that I brought with me from your place," Wilmot continued. "I mean most of the things I brought with me were not from the museum but were given to me by people who trusted me. For some of these artifacts I had to go through elaborate rituals. Most *dimdims* don't believe it, but these things have powers."

"When I first lived there alone, things started to happen to me," I told Wilmot. "One morning when I woke up, the door to my flat was open but nothing had been stolen or disturbed. The other time I was reading in the middle of the night when suddenly a strange smell inundated my flat. I searched everywhere but to no avail."

"I lived there for three years until I bought the place that I am at now. I hope those strange things have stopped," Wilmot told me.

"So what happened to that *dimdim* who spread the rumour that you were sleeping with kids?"

"He left but not before the police came to investigate me. They found me innocent," he replied. "After he left, the stories began to spread like bushfire about the place as haunted and tenants started to leave. Some nights you would see curious people standing quietly trying to witness the paranormal activities. Even the police would come around to check the place out. I was glad that the story of the haunted place diverted the attention from the earlier rumour about me." *This is something,* I thought to myself. He made me more curious than ever. "You know something?" I asked him after a while.

"What?" he replied with inquisitive eyes. "Back home when people move they also tell the spirits to follow them. Spirits are just like us and they share the same space as human beings," I told him.

"That could be it. I don't think I told them to leave with me."

"But now they are happy at their new home," I said trying not to be too bleak.

"I hope they are," Wilmot said.

"They could be feeling homesick just like us," I tried to joke.

"They have not bothered me so far. There is one more thing why that rumour about 2 Kennedy Lane persisted. Another guy who didn't like me, tried to use the rumours to turn the other residents against me. He told a number of the residents that the collection of artifacts including the human bones was the cause of the place been haunted.

"Is he still around?"

"He left the university some years before I retired. The last I heard of him was that he was in New Zealand. He used to disparage the natives calling them untamed monkeys and all that. A number of times, the students complained about him because he was always demeaning the natives. He argued with me many times and even called me a *kanaka lover*."

"How could you have academics who are supposed to have broader minds on issues be so narrow-minded?"

"Well, you have all kinds of human beings in this world Perez. It's like you asking why God created Hitler at all. But it is no good struggling with memories that are not your own. Let's not be obsessed with that bloody guy. I wish he went to hell."

Wilmot's comments caught me unawares. How could he simply dismiss something that was real in this world, something that has crucified non-*dimdims* for a long time? I couldn't let go the images that Wilmot's story conjured up in my mind. But then again it was better to stop the images rather than get hurt.

"You must have left the place before one of the residents was allegedly murdered there," I told Wilmot. "That was some years after I left the place. So what? People die all the time here." "But they said his death was strange and the cops didn't find the murderer. Something else killed him."

He sat there and looked intently at me for a long time.

"What did you say about the murder?"

"I just told you. The cops weren't able to solve it. The guy was allegedly killed by something that was a mystery to the cops."

"Who told you this?" "The other residents told me. I moved into that place when I first arrived here. The alleged murder took placed in flat 22. "Are you sure it was flat 22?"

"Of course I am sure. Which flat were you living in?"

"I am not sure now. I lived there a long time back." He stopped talking for a while and looked outside towards the street.

"So what do you think killed that guy?"

"That's why I was asking you whether you stayed in flat 22. If I knew for certain that you had stayed there, I would tell you that it was the spirits you brought with you from PNG."

"I might have lived at flat 22 actually. Let me go and find one or two of the old letters that were sent to me when I was in 2 Kennedy Lane."

He left me outside and went into his study, which was full of books and artifacts. He was away for a long time. I could hear him opening boxes and moving things here and there. After a long while he emerged with two letters. He got his glasses and had a closer look at the address. Then he handed them to me. "Here, have a look. Indeed I had lived in flat 22."

As I peeked closer to the address on the envelope I read "flat 22." My hands started to shake a little as I gave him back the two letters.

"Yes, you sure lived in flat 22."

"So what do you think Perez?"

"I really don't know, sir. But if you ask me as someone from PNG, I would tell you that I suspect your Niugini spirits."

"Are you sure of that?"

"Then how come the cops didn't find the murderer? Almost all the murders committed here in Sydney have been solved. At least since I have been here," I told him.

"I have taken these artifacts for granted for a long time. I mean, I know that you people believe in their powers and I was even told about the powers by those who had given me some of these things back in PNG. I mean, I am not what you could call a full skeptic about spiritual powers. I have always maintained an open mind about these things."

"That's what is wrong with you *dimdims*. You don't believe in other cultures."

"The thing is I don't know which of these things are the most potent. I mean some of these may be just carvings, while some are imbued with power and are therefore powerful," Wilmot said.

He was quiet for some time before he began again.

"I do believe in some things Perez. Perhaps having left PNG for a long time now may have diminished my belief. You know how it is when you leave a certain place you also gradually forget some of the experiences you have had there."

"But if you have brought with you these artifacts which are believed to have spirits in them, you have to respect that."

"That is true, Perez," Wilmot said quietly. "Well, I think this murder in flat 22 was committed by the spirits, come to think of it."

"What should I do then?"

"I am not sure. I mean, they have not done you any harm, have they? Perhaps you could talk to them, tell them that they are not to harm anyone who comes to your place," I suggested.

"Yes, I could do that. I don't want something terrible to happen," Wilmot told me. "If it is true that the spirits from Niugini committed the murder in flat 22, I must go tell them not to cause harm to other people."

"I hope you have not inherited something that you can't control."

"Oh gosh, don't tell me that," he said covering his face with his two hands.

"I am just saying it. I mean they have not hurt you or something."

"What if I die, what will happen to my collection?"

"There you go. You have to plan now. You don't want the spirits to harm other people. The spirits must not stray. They must have a place to live when you are gone."

"I have never given much thought to these things. I mean many times I just saw them as carvings."

"They are spirits, they are alive," I told him. "So you must treat them as if they are people. You are an anthropologist Wilmot and you know PNG culture and how people relate to the spirits and their ancestors and all that. If you just pretend to the people you study then you are not a true anthropologist."

"What do you mean?"

"I mean studying people means being part of them, sharing their beliefs and all that. I don't know how best to put it."

"Oh yes, that is what an anthropologist is supposed to do. Perhaps my problem is when I transplanted these artifacts from PNG I lost belief in the spiritual side of them. I felt that once these things are in a foreign landscape they will lose their powers."

"No they don't Wilmot. It's just like people, us for instance coming here to study and we still have a strong bond with our homeland."

We talked some more about the artefacts and all that before we switched on to other topics. I could see that Wilmot was worried about something. He wasn't concentrating. Every now and again he would lose me and ask again what I was saying. So I had to repeat. As much as I tried to forget about the rumour of Wilmot sleeping with kids I couldn't get rid of it.

"You are not yourself Wilmot," I told him. "What's bothering you?"

"You know there was a time when Kate came to my house drunk. She became nostalgic thinking about the past and all that. I asked her to go into my study to fetch my cigarettes and somehow she stumbled over one of the carvings and fell. She swore at the carving and said nasty things to my collection. A week later she fell ill. I mean very sick. She was taken to the hospital and that's when they diagnosed her cancer." He stopped. "I am just thinking whether her sickness has anything to do with her desecrating the artifacts."

"She was never sick before?" I was shocked by this revelation.

"She would be down now and again with flu and cold but she was a very healthy woman."

"Gees you have got yourself into something big, sir," I told him.

"I am just guessing the case of Kate. I have never told her my suspicions," Wilmot said.

"Never mind, but try to keep an open mind about your collection. So what are you doing these days?" I asked Wilmot changing the topic.

"I am working on a book about the Tolai people. It has taken me about 4 years to complete the second draft."

"That's interesting. I hope to read it one day. Did you write a chapter about their women? They have pretty women too," I tried to bring humour into our conversation. "Don't talk about it. I admire their women," Wilmot said smiling. "They are very resourceful too."

We heard something fall inside the house and I shuddered. We were at his place in Glebe and one of his rooms was full of the stuff he brought from PNG.

"What was that?" he asked me. "I don't know. Go and check," I told him. He got up and went into the room where we heard the noise. It was like something had fallen down. When he came out he told me that one of the carvings fell from the hook on the wall.

"Let's not talk about them then. They have ears and they can listen to our conversation."

"Say something to them," Wilmot urged me. "I know you are their *wantok* and they will listen to you." I knew this was an opportunity to check for other pictures that he might have.

"Alright. Let me go inside. It's better that you go outside while I talk to them," I told him as I stood up to go inside.

As soon as he went out I went in and quickly opened the drawers. The room was in a mess and papers were everywhere. Then as I was about to give up I saw a box at the corner. I went and saw that it was packed with old albums. As I went through them quickly, I was uttering words in my language so he would know that I was talking to the carvings. Then I saw them— pictures of kids in various sexual positions. They were with older men and one of the men was none other then Wilmot. I was shocked beyond belief! My whole body was shaking and I threw the pictures back. HORROR was the word that captured my feelings. I felt nauseated and I wanted to vomit there and then. However as I didn't want Wilmot to know that I knew about the truth, I quickly spoke to the carvings in Pidgin telling them that I am a *wantok* and that I am visiting their guardian who is my friend. I also told them not to harm anybody except perhaps their guardian to stop him from abusing the kids. When I came out, Wilmot was smiling knowing that I had spoken to them.

"I have spoken to them," I told him at the same time sweating. Gradually my whole body became relaxed. Perhaps it was due to me speaking to the artifacts. It was as if they heard me and were aware that I was their *wantok*. That tense feeling I had was no longer there. However my mind was more confused and unsettled. I realised that under the façade of being a teacher and anthropologist Wilmot was a dangerous predator.

✳✳✳

I still had strong feeling that it was Kate who did something to our flat and that was why we were continuously encountering unexplained experiences. I mean, the whole place may have been haunted prior to our taking up residence but for us, it may have been the case of someone deliberately making sorcery because the person wanted to harm one of us. At the same time, I suspected that Desimoni or Uwegu might have brought something from home. You know how it is with us Papua New Guineans wherever we go, we take traditional protection with us. This is to protect us against sorcery, magic, illness and so on. At other times we use it to harm other people. I had a strange feeling that it is the combination of these forces that was affecting the residents of 2 Kennedy Lane.

Chapter 21

How time flies, and finally only a couple of weeks remained before I left for home. I had mixed feelings about returning home. It was time to say farewell some of my friends so during the day I went out to say good-bye to a couple of them who had studied with me, and I didn't get back until about 3 in the afternoon. The other day Kilroy rang and told Reimas that they might drop in to say goodbye to me and perhaps have a few beers. We didn't think they would be coming and that's why I took my time on campus. When they arrived, Uwegu rang me at the office and told me to come home quickly as the two guys were already waiting. I told her to tell them to go ahead.

"Please make it fast Perez. I feel awkward with these people," Uwegu begged me over the phone.

"Where is Reimas?" I asked.

"He is here, but you know how he is. He is so full of himself and he is boasting about his rugby club, Roosters." I laughed.

"That's alright. Don't worry I will be there," I reassured her.

I picked up my bag and went home. When I arrived the three guys were on their first bottles. Kilroy was talking to them about some fast money scheme and they were all-ears, including Uwegu. As soon as I entered they turned and Kilroy quickly invited me to listen.

"Hey Perez, I am talking to these guys about how to make fast money. I have all the literature here." He gave me one and I read through it. It said that one can contribute any amount starting with $100.00 and after four weeks your investment doubles to $200.00 and so on.

"Is this real Kilroy?" I asked him. "Even the banks cannot pay this kind of interests."

"Perez, don't be a doubting Thomas. This is an investment secret that very few people know about. You know where it started from? Bulgaria my friend."

He distributed some forms to us. "Complete the forms and when you guys are ready return it to me with the money."

Kilroy stood up and came to where I was sitting. "Mate we will miss you," he said touching me on my shoulder. I nodded my head.

"You have been our big bro," Reimas added. They talked as if I was leaving for eternity that day. But then again a wantok's departure was something attached with deep feelings especially in a strange place like Sydney. My leaving was like breaking off a branch of a tree.

"What are you going to do at home when you return?" Kilroy asked me.

"I am not sure yet. I have applied for a number of jobs," I told him. "But I hope I can get back my old teaching job at the university."

"I hope you can get a job right away," Kilroy continued.

"There is a lot of nepotism, bro," came in Reimas.

"It's who you know that matters," Uwegu added.

All this talk began to unnerve me in a strange way. I knew that I had some friends in influential positions back home that I could turn to but then again I was reluctant about doing it. I wanted to prove that my qualifications were as good as anyone else's or maybe slightly better.

"It's a sleazy world in PNG," Kilroy started again.

"What do you mean?" I asked him.

"I mean people don't care much about your qualifications. All they care about mostly is how you would help them climb up the ladder or how you would help them steal from the national coffers."

"You can try to avoid these criminals," I said.

"How?" Kilroy asked.

"I suppose by being clean and not associating with corrupt people."

"You would have to have a thick skin."

"You guys are scaring me already," I told them. "Let's talk about something else."

"You can make lots of money if you join this scheme," Kilroy started again. "Many people are now millionaires because of this scheme. Read some of their testimonies; they are all here."

I could see Uwegu and Reimas whispering and at the same time reading the literature that Kilroy brought with him.

"Bro, Uwegu will give you some money before you go," Reimas told him.

"That's the way to go, sister. It's investment for your future."

I wondered whether Uwegu was making a right decision. But then again it was her money not mine. I remembered Kilroy advertising a bogus product to cure impotence in which he made a lot of money before they almost caught him and I felt sorry for Uwegu and Reimas and all the vulnerable *wantoks* who would succumb easily to Kilroy's schemes.

"How much will you be investing Uwegu?" I asked her.

"About $200.00."

"Sis after this you won't complain about your relatives asking you to buy them presents," Reimas came in. Uwegu gave a faint smile.

"This will make you rich overnight," Kilroy added. He looked around. "What about you guys? Invest for your future. When you start young you will be a millionaire by the time you are 30."

I saw Reimas put his hand into the back pocket. His application form was already completed.

"Here's my application form with $100.00," Reimas called.

"That's the way, young man," Kilroy said to him at the same time tapping him.

"I'll give you $200.00 later," Rawiri told Kilroy.

"Good man."

We continued chatting. Most of the conversation was being dominated by Kilroy. We only spoke occasionally.

"I haven't been into any of the chat rooms for ages now," said Kilroy changing the topic of our discussion. "I used to go in regularly when I was on that other job. I had a computer of my own and it had Internet access. I used to download all these pornographic materials and all that stuff."

"What did you do with the pictures bro?" Reimas asked.

"Sold them to some *dimdim* bastards."

"They could have bought them easily from the adult shops," I said.

"But I was selling them cheap."

"Jack of all trades, this guy," said Rawiri.

"And a player too, bro," Reimas said, laughing.

"Player or not, I am for real," said Kirori. "They all have crooked eyes, that's all."

"And crooked heads too, bro," added Reimas.

"Plus crooked hearts!" came in Rawiri.

I could see Uwegu feeling uneasy. She got up and gave Kilroy her money and left us. She told us quietly that she was going to the library.

"In four weeks time I will bring your money together with the interest," Kilroy called to her as she was closing the door behind her.

"Thanks," was all she said.

"Did you hear about Desimoni spying on her while she was in the shower, bro?" Reimas began as soon as Uwegu was out of sight.

"Go on," said Rawiri becoming very interested.

"Both of them were alone in the house that day and then she went into the shower and Desimoni pretended to go outside; he came from the courtyard and was looking at her through the window. He told me that Uwegu was really rubbing herself and touching her boobs. It was when he stood on a can and it made a noise that Uwegu realised someone was watching her and when she looked out, she saw Desimoni running away."

"Well, at least he has seen it for himself," Kilroy said laughing.

"Kilroy, tell me which *dimdim* family adopted you?" I asked him.

"The Hardings," Kilroy said. "So I am known as Kilroy Harding."

"The local name Kilori doesn't rhyme with the *dimdim* name, bro," Reimas told him.

"That's why I changed it to Kilroy; it's my ticket to move around here."

"Bro, do you have any kids with any of these *dimdim* women that you've gone out with?" Reimas asked.

"Why are you so interested in Kilroy's private life?" I asked.

"How do you learn the ropes if you don't ask, bro?" Reimas replied. "You never know we could have our *wantoks* who are half *dimdims* here."

"I have a child back in PNG who is half *dimdim*," Kilroy told us. "I had an affair with a *dimdim* girl. We were madly in love with each other but her *dimdim* parents did not like the relationship so as soon as their daughter gave birth, they secretly gave away the child for adoption and they returned here. My adopted parents wanted to keep the child but they refused."

We sat quietly listening to this tale that was almost unreal, yet it was true. Kilroy told the tale in a subdued and poignant way, in a manner that made you feel for him. His story came in bits and pieces but when you joined these together you had a complete story.

He was quiet for a while before he spoke in an unsure way. "The child should be about 21 or 22 now. Perhaps she has married or is out there somewhere." He paused again. "I have not been home since I came here."

"That is sad, bro, Reimas said.

"As you grow older, you begin to reflect back on your life and you wish you could start a new life," Kilroy said. "I suppose that is how it is for me."

"Try to make an attempt to find your daughter and perhaps the mother of the girl, bro," Reimas continued.

"I have been thinking of doing that recently."

The atmosphere in the house turned somber after Kilroy finished his story. You could only hear small talk being made like the occasional cooing of birds. "How about you Perez? Do you have a woman?" Kilroy asked breaking the monotony. I wasn't expecting this question but it was already hanging over me, waiting. I sat there thinking of how I would tackle this one. I should have known that this question was coming. I was wondering how to deal with the question.

"I used to have a girlfriend back in PNG but we broke up just before I came here," I started slowly. "I mean, I wasn't serious with her. Perhaps it was my fault. I should have been more patient."

"Did that hurt you bad?" Kilroy asked.

"I guess it did. I guess deep down I really wanted her but I was pretending."

They all fell silent as they followed my story. "We didn't go out that long when we broke up."

"What was the problem, bro?" Reimas asked.

"She accused me of going around with her best friend, a much younger woman."

"Is that true bro?"

"I only flirted with her. I didn't actually sleep with her."

"Some of these women are downright dangerous, bro!" Reimas said.

"I hate those kind of women," Kilroy said. "They are bloody losers! All they do is leach on you, suck off you, and before you know it they are bloody gone."

"That's not the case with me. My girlfriend was actually good but it's the jealously thing that spoiled our relationship."

We relaxed and continued to chat about the money scheme that Kilroy was marketing. Kilroy continued to give us statistics and figures. It seemed he knew what he was talking about and we marveled at him. Suddenly his cell phone rang. He talked to the caller for a while.

"I'll be right back," Kilroy told us at the same time going out. We didn't have time to ask where he was going.

Not long after Kilroy had left, Uwegu came back. 'You guys are still here?" she asked.

"Don't worry Uwegu, we are almost done now," Rawiri told her. "I don't think Kilroy is gonna come back."

We drank the last few bottles and then Rawiri shook hands with me. "Don't forget to give Kilroy a buzz when you guys have got more money. Remember it's an investment for your future," Rawiri imitated.

194

Chapter 22

A couple of days after Kilroy and Rawiri paid me a farewell visit, I was packing up my personal belongings when Uwegu and Suniya came in. This was about 11.00 o'clock in the morning and they surprised me because Uwegu has a class at around this time. They were also surprised to see me still in the flat. Reimas has told me once or twice before that he had seen Uwegu and Suniya around this time returning to the flat. There are two bus stops adjacent to 2 Kennedy Lane. One goes straight to Uni and the other is for buses going the other direction to the city. Once Reimas was standing at the bus stop that goes to the city when he saw Uwegu and Suniya going into the flat from Uni. The other time, he was chatting with a classmate just down the other street when he saw them again about the same time. I didn't take it seriously when he told me that the two girls must be up to something. I could see that he was kind of suspicious.

"You are still here?" Uwegu asked me as we eyed each other.

"Oh well, I am packing my things. I have only a short time left before I go home."

"Oh, that's right." It would be rather sad when you finally leave."

"Aren't you having classes this morning?" I asked them.

"No, we thought we would work on our major papers here. It's too much disturbance out there."

I managed to lock my suitcase after struggling with it for sometime. "There you are bastard," I said quietly. "Well, go ahead and work on your papers then. I won't be long with this and then I'll go off."

"Have you submitted your thesis yet?" Uwegu asked.

"Already," I told her.

"Congratulations then," said Suniya. "You have done very well for yourself. I wish I was you."

I shut the other two boxes, which were full of books, and pushed them to the side, then I went into my room to get my bag. Uwegu and Suniya were already inside Uwegu's room. The window to my bedroom was open and as I was about to shut it, I saw Reimas who quickly made a sign to me to keep quiet. I didn't know what he was up to; Desimoni had hid himself among the shrubs where he had spied on Uwegu before. In fact, I wouldn't have seen Reimas had he hidden but he made himself known to me. I wondered why he was doing this. Then he came to my window and whispered to me that he was spying on Uwegu and Suniya because he wanted to put to rest once and for all what Desimoni had said about Uwegu — that she was a lesbo. I almost laughed and I tried to dissuade him but he wouldn't listen. So I left him and said bye to the women and left for Uni. I made sure I took the path Uwegu and Suniya could see so they would know for sure that I was truly gone. In a way I was indirectly aiding Reimas with his plan. I couldn't stop thinking about what Reimas was about to do, so halfway to Uni I turned back and came to the flat via another route.

As soon as I was closer to the flat I walked slowly but anxious at the same time to find out what Reimas was up to or what he has seen already. The place was quiet and at first I thought Reimas must have given up on his plan and left. I didn't tell Reimas that I saw a bite mark once on Uwegu's neck. As I got closer and closer my feet and breathing became heavy. It was difficult for anyone to see me from the street because of the thick shrubs. I walked cautiously, searching for Reimas. As I turned the corner I saw him looking busy outside. Apparently Uwegu had not shut the window and Reimas was looking through it. I tried to attract his attention but to no avail. I looked around and found a small stone, which I picked up and threw at him. He almost screamed but fortunately he didn't. He saw me and signaled to me to go over but I asked him to come to me. It took him sometime before he came to me. I could see that he was sweating and his body was almost trembling.

"What did you see?"

"Oh man, they are at each other," he said amid heavy breathing. "As soon as they knew you were gone, they started holding each other and went for it, bro."

"What are they doing now?" I asked more curiously than ever.

"Bro, they are almost there. Man, that Suniya is good at it."

"How do you know that?"

"Bro, she is the one initiating everything. Now I know, what Desimoni told us is true."

"When you were away I saw some marks on Uwegu's neck. I didn't tell you."

"Really, bro? She is wasting it. Oh, you could have seen how they were going at each other like hungry dogs!"

After sometime he turned to me and asked, "why did you come back, bro?"

"I wanted to watch too," I said smiling.

"You are a pretender, bro."

"How do you mean?" "I mean you should have asked her long time ago. I know she would have said yes to you."

Then I pulled his shirt and we left the place. We went to the street and sat down.

"So the secret is out, bro."

"Don't tell anyone. Keep it to yourself. At least we know about Uwegu now."

"Cross my heart, bro."

"Alright I believe you. If I hear anything you will be in trouble. It's against the law to spy on people."

"Why is she doing that, bro?"

"Perhaps she is lonely."

"Or perhaps she has discovered that she is a lesbo, bro."

"Living in a strange place can lead people to do strange things," I told him. "Or people just want to experiment things."

We kept quiet for a while as people went past us. I was thinking about what Reimas had told me. It was good that I did not see the two women with my own eyes. I was happy that I heard it from someone else. It made me realise that the reason why my brief encounter with her never blossomed was because she didn't like men.

"Man, they are wasting it. The thing has a purpose, bro," Reimas persisted.

"Well, we humans are complex beings. But I hope you don't get into this habit of spying on Uwegu every time she comes home with someone. It can lead you to doing silly things."

"Bro, I won't do it again. I just wanted to put to rest what Desimoni has said about her." "That's good."

"That's right, you are leaving us shortly."

"Not long to go now. I wonder what it will be like going back home."

"It will be strange for you, bro. Uwegu and I have planned to move out of this place when you leave. We will move into a small flat."

"I could help you look for a flat before I go."

"That's a good idea. You know the nitty-gritty of looking for places here, bro. I mean, I am a little shy sometimes."

"When I leave, you will be on your own so try not to be shy." I looked at my watch. "Shall we go to the flat now?"

"Come, I'll show you how to do a trick, bro."

I got up and followed Reimas to the telephone booth. There were two *dimdim* guys at the booth but they were not using the phone. They were just standing there chatting to each other. When they saw us they did not give way but continued chatting and laughing. After awhile Reimas told them that he wanted to use the phone but they continued to ignore him.

"If you are not using the phone get your bloody ass out!" he almost shouted, his body language showed that he was ready for a fight. I also moved in closer, cycing them. Reimas pushed his hand into his bag and as soon as the two *dimdims* saw that they took off, every now and again looking over their backs as they disappeared into the corner. "Bloody morons!" he shouted after them.

"Man you have changed a lot," I told him. "You are no longer that timid islander but an intimidating one."

"They have made me into a brave man, bro. This is the way to survive in this racist environment." Did you see how scared they were? *Ha, ol pipia lain; nogat bol blong ol!*"

We laughed and Reimas went in and I watched him dial a number. It was our flat number. He winked at me.

"Hello sis!"

"Hello Reimas what's up?" Uwegu replied.

"Is Perez home yet, sis?"

"Not yet. Why?"

"I want him to help me with my essay. I'll go look for him in his office and we'll come home, sis."

"He has already returned the key to the office. Check for him in the library where the newspapers are located."

"Okay, I'll find him and we'll come home, sis."

"Alright then."

"See you then, sis."

"Bye." And the phone went dead.

Reimas came out of the phone booth laughing.

"Is that how you do it?"

"At least you have to play it this way so she is not suspicious. I learnt it from Rawiri. Let's give them 20 minutes before we go bro."

"Man you are fast learning the sleazy trade," I teased him.

"Bro, you have to outsmart people. Always try to be one step ahead of people."

"I think this is why the *dimdims* are smarter."

"Bro, they are smarter because they are always one step ahead of us."

We walked to a shop and bought ourselves ice creams and slowly made our way back to the flat. As soon as we got closer to the flat we made a lot of noise so they would know we were arriving. When we opened the door they were sitting down drinking tea. They greeted us and I didn't notice anything that would give them away.

"Hello! Did Reimas manage to locate you?" Uwegu asked beaming with a smile.

"Yes, I was in the library when he caught up with me," I lied. "How about you guys? Did you do some work on your papers?"

"We have started on them but Suniya forgot the reference book so today we can't go any further. Suniya will be going soon; she has two classes this afternoon."

We did not say anything. She stood there fumbling with her books.

"See you guys," said Suniya as she collected her stuff and left.

"So soon?" I asked.

"Well, we have done a bit today."

"I have asked Perez if he could help us find a small flat before he leaves, sis."

"Yes, we have talked about it with Reimas."

"That's alright. I'll help you look for a flat this week."

"Good we can always count on you. I'll take a little nap."

"Okay, sis," said Reimas as he followed me into my room.

"Did you see the way they looked at us when we came in, bro?" Reimas asked as soon as we shut the door.

"I didn't notice anything. What did you notice?"

"Some kind of guilt from Uwegu's eyes, bro."

"In your wildest dreams," I teased him.

My room was bare, as I had packed my things already. I was both happy and sad to leave. I have been here for a long time and I felt that I was about to uproot myself again for another chapter of my life. I thought about Kate and wondered whether she has come out of hospital for good. The doctors had told her that her cancer was in remission and now she put herself into her work, which she almost lost.

Wilmot had moved back to his place, which he referred to as his hut. It was a nice little cottage, which was located in the leafy suburb of Glebe. His place was surrounded by trees and bushes and it was almost like a natural habitat. The trees and palms gave the house a kind of cover from the outside world. It was a three-bedroom house; one room, which apparently was his study, was full of books and artifacts. There were carvings from PNG that gave the house an eerie and a spooky atmosphere. The carvings lay there as if they were untouched for years. This is what made them spooky. Wilmot told me that his neighbours look at him as if he was weird. This was because he hardly had any visitors. I thought about the pictures I saw at his place and I felt disgusted. I wanted the cops to raid his house, find those pictures and prosecute him and the others who were involved in this activity. I did not tell the two about what I found in Wilmot's house. Despite this bad side of him, he was a wonderful person.

Later when I got out, I saw Uwegu reading outside in the lounge. She looked at me and smiled.

"What are you reading?" She showed me the cover of *New Idea* magazine.

I went and sat beside her. She offered me an apple and I got it from her. The closeness of our bodies made me crave for her. I wanted her. She had been alone for a long time now and so had I. My whole body was almost quivering as she moved closer and closer to me. We looked each other in the eyes and as I was about to pull her towards me, I heard Reimas opening the door and I moved away from her. You could tell in her eyes that she wanted me too. She gave me a seductive smile.

"How's your daughter and folks at home?" I asked her after a while.

"She is okay. She was sick a few weeks ago. That's what gives me strength, Perez. Knowing that I have my daughter back home. I do call once every two weeks."

"Are you still in touch with the girl's father?"

"No, we have moved on with our lives. He moved to Lae."

"I am sorry."

"It's alright. He is a humbug that guy."

"How old are you again?" I saw Reimas smiling from the kitchen.

"27," she said. "Why are you asking?" she asked softly.

"I just wanted to know. You have a long way to go."

"What do you mean?"

"I mean you are young and have many years ahead of you."

"What about you?"

"Hey, age is catching up with me."

"Bull!" she said smiling. "You know, you are a wonderful person to be with. You have helped us a lot and you are like a big brother to us." She stopped and then continued. "We will miss you when you go. I hope we can still remain in contact."

"You guys have been good to me too," was all I managed to say.

"Do you have a girlfriend?"

I looked at her and shook my head in the negative. "I used to but not anymore."

"Are you gay?"

I laughed and then told her I wasn't.

"Then get yourself a woman."

"I'll try to when I get home."

"What about you? Do you have a boyfriend?"

She was quiet for a while. "After we broke up with my boyfriend, my daughter's father, my folks chose someone back in the village. It was traditionally arranged." I saw sadness in her eyes. "Why do they have to tie me down like that? I mean, can't they let me go for a while. I will always go back," she said almost sadly.

"But you agreed to it didn't you?' I asked.

"I was practically forced to agree. The guy isn't bad but he has never gone further in his education."

"They must be expecting you home this summer?" I asked.

"Yes of course. I had to find an excuse that I have to do summer school in order to shorten my years here."

"Do you have a relationship with him? I mean a real one."

"No," she said. "We have talked once or twice but we were never alone. I only pretended to like him because of my folks. We are like two strangers who have found ourselves on each bank of a flooded creek on a desert island and trying to cross over to each other."

"Man, you shock me. Can't you write and tell them it is all over for you?"

"I just can't yet. I am in school and they are supporting me."

"You are a coward!"

"I am not. At least I have my future planned," she got back at me.

"The poor guy thinks that you are genuine and truthful."

"Shit, I don't want to talk about it. I don't want to be reminded of these traditional ties," Uwegu said very emotionally.

Reimas must have overheard us talking and he came to the lounge.

"What's that smile for?" Uwegu asked him.

"Was that why you didn't want Desimoni, sis?"

"Oh cut the crap! Desimoni is a chicken who in real life won't marry a commoner like me. I feel sorry for the woman who will marry him though."

"What's wrong with playing around a bit? It's good for your ego," I said.

"Just because he is the son of a chief, he thinks he is it! I bet he boasts about all the women he sleeps with," Uwegu said.

"What type of a man are you after then, sis?" Reimas challenged her. I had a feeling where Reimas was heading. I wanted to get out before the water boiled. Reimas had his own way of approaching things.

"It's none of your business."

"I hope you are not a lesbo, sis."

As soon as Uwegu heard that she stormed into her room. You should have seen the way she got up and left. She was furious.

"What made you say such a thing?" I asked Reimas. "Don't spoil your relationship with her. I will be leaving you guys shortly."

"I didn't think about that, bro."

"Go and apologise to her. You have hurt her feelings."

Reimas went and knocked on her door. She didn't respond. "It's me, Reimas. I am sorry."

I looked at Reimas. "She didn't respond. I am going back in."

"She will cool off. It's nothing really," I tried to convince Reimas.

We chatted some more before Reimas went into his room. I thought about what Reimas had told me about Uwegu and Suniya and I regretted not having a peek at them. Now I didn't know whether Reimas had told me the truth or not.

Chapter 23

A few nights before I departed I had a bad dream. I dreamt that I was at the funeral of a *dimdim* woman but I couldn't recognise her. She was young and was covered in a white sheet, her face contoured with pain that gave it a ghostly look. In the dream, I never shed any tears but just stood there eyeing the dead woman. There were very few people at the funeral, people I couldn't recognise. All of a sudden the *dimdim* woman changed into a brown-skinned woman so beautiful that I wanted her. I stretched out my hand to pull her up and that was when I woke up. I was scared and immediately after, my mind focused on Kate. That day the news came of her death.

I was at home idling away, impatient, switching the television from channel to channel when I heard a knock on the door. I knew Uwegu and Reimas had their keys and they wouldn't be knocking unless one of them has left his key at home. I switched off the television and sat quietly, listening. The knock came again and after sometime I got up and went to the door.

"Who is it?" I called.

"It's Wilmot, I have some bad news." Quickly I opened the door and there was Wilmot standing with a solemn face. "I am sorry to tell you that Kate died yesterday."

I was so shocked that I forgot all about the fact that he was a paedophile. I couldn't say anything but stood there, blank, lost for words. I stared into the open space as I thought about Kate. For a long time, I did not speak to Wilmot, nor did he speak. My heart was pregnant with sadness and loss. When I had regained my composure I asked Wilmot how she died.

"It was awful. She lost all her hair and weight and she was all skeleton. Somehow the cancer suddenly returned from its remission and spread quickly. All this time, it had that ghostly presence over Kate."

"Why didn't you come and get me? I was here all the time."

"When she knew she wouldn't recover she asked me not to tell you or come and get you, nor anyone else for that matter. I guess she didn't want you to see how terrible she looked. She couldn't help herself in the last couple of weeks that she was alive. I was the one who did most of her chores. She was like a child again, almost without independence."

"Have you told her family?"

"She has no siblings or close relatives. She told me to handle her personal assets with her lawyers myself. I mean, she already has her will."

"How about her former husband?"

"You mean Mr. Powell?" Wilmot intoned.

"Yes, is that his name?" Something was trying to register in my mind but not for long; I lost it.

"Yes. He has nothing to do with Kate." I nodded my head.

"To die without a family is very sad," I said.

"Oh well what can I say. I only need your help." I looked at him confused.

"Then her death is a non-event."

"You could say that." Wilmot stopped for a little while. Then he started again. "In her will she left some money for her daughter whom she had never seen or known since the girl was 12-months old."

"A daughter?" I asked surprised.

"Yes. She had a daughter from her relationship with a PNG guy."

"How come she never told me about it?"

"Perhaps she didn't want to talk about her past. Perhaps she didn't want to upset herself."

"But that is cruel isn't it? It's like she disowned her child."

"I don't know," Wilmot answered. "Did you know about this?" I asked him.

"No." Wilmot paused as he threw away the butt of his cigarette. "She is in the morgue until next week, Friday."

"But I am leaving in a couple of days' time."

"It doesn't matter. You have said your goodbye already. I only want you to come with me to her place and you can help me with her will."

"Let me get a decent shirt then," I told him.

When I came out of my room Wilmot was staring at Uwegu's portrait that hung outside her bedroom door. "I think I know this girl. I met her at Kate's house in PNG once or twice. Let me remember her name." He thought for a while. "I can't remember the name now. They used to frequent Kate's house at the university."

"Are you sure about this? You could be mistaken."

"Well there was this set of twins who looked very much alike. One of them was Kate's closest friend."

I laughed before I told him that the woman in the photo is Uwegu.

"She looks very much like someone I met at Kate's place. Oh well, it was a long time ago." Then I realised that Wilmot had never met Uwegu or Reimas.

This time the drive to Kate's place was the longest drive I had ever experienced here in Sydney.

For some reason, my mind was blank with occasional reminiscences of Kate. Now I knew that Kate's married name was Powell and I also remembered Uwegu telling me about her former tutor, a Mrs. Powell. Was this the missing link? We didn't talk throughout the drive until we arrived and I got out and waited for Wilmot to open the door.

I could feel the presence of Kate as we entered the house. It's that sixth sense that tells you that someone else was watching you. As soon as I sat down in the lounge, which was now bare, I put my head down and cried. Wilmot did not disturb me and let me pour my tears out. I remembered that when I first saw her at the airport, she was beautiful and attractive. We could have started a relationship, but a relationship that would have been doomed from the beginning. When I stopped crying, Wilmot brought out the will and showed it to me. I read the section about her daughter and how she wanted to leave her about two-thirds of her money. I must have gone through that section twice before I gave it back to Wilmot.

"Now, what I need to know is the name of this girl, her contact details and if she has any accounts with any banks in PNG," Wilmot told me.

"How come she never told us about this child until after her death?"

"How would I know Perez? I guess every person is different," Wilmot tried to explain to me.

"How can we confirm that she ever had a child?" It could be that her illness drove her to write crazy things," I said.

"I had made a few phone calls and two people have confirmed that she did have a daughter in PNG. That was one of the reasons why her parents left the country and one of the reasons for their bitter divorce. Another reason was that there were rumours about her father having a relationship with their house girl. You see Kate didn't really look like a *dimdim* because her mother was not a *dimdim*."

I was shocked beyond belief and I didn't talk for a while. Realising my reaction, Wilmot proceeded to explain.

"Mr. Nolan had a relationship with their house girl who was a local girl. When the Nolans arrived in Milne Bay they got the girl to work for them. She had just married with a child when her husband left her and she moved in with them at their house. It was there that Mr. Nolan impregnated her. Mrs. Nolan was barren and could not conceive. When the house girl gave birth to Kate they kept it a secret. They took the baby away from her and pretended that she was their child and brought her up."

"Are you sure of this?"

"Of course I am," looking at me with a strong glare.

"No wonder she looked different, more Polynesian. You know the guys were continually telling me that Kate was not a true *dimdim*."

"I should have told you guys earlier about her being part-PNG. For some reason Kate never wanted to talk about it and she never wanted to identify herself as part-PNG."

"She may have had bad memories."

"The fact that she is illegitimate maybe one reason," Wilmot told me.

I kept quiet, listening to Wilmot. It was indeed an interesting revelation.

"She went with a lot of secrets to the grave," I finally said. Wilmot only shrugged his shoulders.

"Try to find her as soon as possible. The sooner the better."

"Alright I'll try my best."

"Good one," Wilmot told me as he tried to touch me. I looked at him hard.

I told Wilmot how strange and bizarre this was. For Kate not to mention anything about her daughter whom she had left behind with the father in PNG many years back. While Wilmot agreed, he said sometimes it was the best way for a person to block out of her memory about something she loved so much. I knew that was a *dimdim* way of doing things.

"Tell me something about her ex-husband," I asked Wilmot.

"Well his name is Powell and they got married some years after Kate returned from her research in PNG. He was a nice chap and he was a teacher. After about 4 years of marriage, he ran away with Kate's best friend and a year later they divorced and Kate went to teach in PNG. She was known then as Mrs. Powell. She got into all sorts of trouble whilst there. She was having sexual relationships with her students, both men and women. Just before she came back, she was involved in a car accident in which two students died. I guess it was the bitter divorce that drove her to do those stupid things."

"Why do you think she hated Uwegu?"

"Who is Uwegu?" Wilmot asked.

"The girl who shares the flat with us?"

"I really don't know. It could be to do with a relationship. What is her other name?"

"They call her Daisy," I told him.

"No the girl Kate had a relationship with was Dodo. She had a twin sister. It was the other sister that caught them and reported Kate to the authorities who refused to renew her contract." I sat there kind of dumbfounded. Uwegu would be very keen to hear this story.

"What is gonna happen to this house and her personal effects?" I asked him after a while.

"It will be sold and the money will be given to the daughter."

"Gees, the daughter is going to be rich overnight."

"That is something she owed her, what you would call overdue love!"

"The girl is going to be very lucky indeed," I said.

"You know I told you about Kate becoming ill after she stumbled over one of my artifacts and she swore at it?" Wilmot told me. He stopped for sometime before he continued. "I think it is the spirits that caused her death. I have read some more about the powers imbued in some of these artifacts and I have a strong feeling that they had caused her death."

For the first time, I was listening to a *dimdim* guy who believed in spirits and the power of the artifacts that he had with him. It was kind of strange but it told me something else, that there are *dimdims* who shared our beliefs and traditions. Wilmot was one of them.

"Why are you so adamant about this?" I asked him.

"I am being myself," Wilmot told me.

"Something must have changed your mind."

"The doctors told Kate that they had gotten rid of the cancer and she would be okay, but all of a sudden the doctors were baffled that the cancer has rapidly sprung from nowhere and spread. So I believe it must be the work of the spirits."

Oh well, we'll never know for certain if her illness has to do with spirits or something else," I said.

"There is something else I wanted you to see. She left behind her diary. I'll get it and you can read the notes she wrote in the last remaining weeks of her life."

One of the few first entries reads: *"I am sorry for abandoning you my child. Please forgive me. I know you have wondered many times why I have abandoned you. I wish I could answer you truthfully. I also ask myself the same question."*

"Did she die in the hospital?" I asked Wilmot.

"She died here at home and we brought her to the hospital."

I wondered if her death was a result of suicide but I didn't suggest it to Wilmot.

The diary continued with the talk about the daughter she had left behind: *"I really loved the guy, it was a different kind of love but my parents wouldn't have anything to do with it. It was painful having to abandon my flesh; it was like cutting a part of me and discarding it on the wayside. It was hurtful to be told that I couldn't have the baby that I couldn't raise her up as my child. I hope my parents go to hell for all I care!"*

"This is very interesting," I told Wilmot. "It's mostly about her daughter."

"The good thing about it is that it tells us something new we didn't know," Wilmot told me.

"I wonder who this PNG guy is. She never mentioned him here. Are you sure she doesn't have any next of kin at all?" I asked again.

"Her parents both died and she is the only girl. The father died a few months ago,"

"That is sad," I said almost choking again with tears. "What about her PNG connection?"

"It's difficult to pursue that and in any case it would take a long time."

Wilmot got the diary and turned to another page and gave it to me. I read the content with disbelief. *"Daisy (or whatever your name is now) I hate you and I'll make sure you will suffer for what you did to me back in PNG. You dragged my name in the mud. You may not know but I also have roots in PNG. I have already locked you in, now your fate is in my hands.* "What is this supposed to mean?" I asked Wilmot.

"I really don't know. But it could be to do with her sexual intimacy with a girl in PNG."

We heard a noise in her bedroom and my goose bumps stood up. I looked at Wilmot and he looked at me.

"She must be around," I told Wilmot. But Wilmot didn't say anything.

I looked at my watch and Wilmot saw that I was anxious.

"I'll go and drop you off now. Please check with the girl and get back to me so we can settle everything regarding the child she left behind."

I stood up and told Wilmot that I want to have a few quiet moments in Kate's bedroom just to say goodbye to her. So he left me alone and I went to her bedroom and whispered my farewell to her. As soon as I closed the door to her bedroom I heard the bed click and I knew she was there.

"Goodbye Kate," I managed to say as Wilmot locked the house behind us.

When I arrived back home, Uwegu and Reimas were there, waiting for me. For some reason they suspected that something wasn't right. As soon as I entered, they all looked at me and saw that my eyes were red. They stood up and walked towards me at the same time. Reimas was the first one to hold me.

"Bro, what's the matter?"

I didn't talk for a while, as my tears were ready to come down again. Uwegu came and also held me. I wiped away my tears and then told them that Kate had died.

"Oh, poor woman," said Uwegu.

Reimas gave me that puzzled look.

"She was the one who took us around looking for our accommodation."

"Sorry," Reimas said.

Uwegu pulled my hand towards the couch and asked me to sit down.

"So she is no longer alive?"

"She died yesterday," I told them.

Madi, my love for her," Uwegu said. She was quiet before she spoke again. "Although I hated her, in death that hate turns into sadness and love. This is how it is with me. I feel sad. I don't hate her anymore because she is gone forever."

I held her. "Now you are at peace with her. Did you know that her married name was Mrs. Powell and that she was part-PNG?" They all stared at me.

"You're joking right?" Uwegu said at the same time covering her face with both hands. I shook my head.

"I knew that the face was familiar except the name eluded me—yes, she was that Mrs. Powell who was my tutor at the university." She laughed as if she was going insane. Then talking almost to herself she said, "Mrs. Powell did you know I am Daisy and you sexually abused my twin sister? Yes Mrs. Powell, Dodo had died in a car accident. Now you can meet together again and continue your relationship in the spirit world." We kept quiet and didn't know what to say. She calmed down a little later and we continued.

"So what's gonna happen, bro?" Reimas asked.

"Her body is in the morgue and Wilmot, the other *dimdim* guy is taking care of her business. He has asked me to take care of another thing though." Reimas looked at me. "To find the name and details of Kate's daughter."

"Did she have a daughter?" Uwegu asked, surprised.

"Yes, back in PNG. Apparently she had a relationship with a local boy and she gave birth to a girl."

"When was this?" Uwegu asked.

"I think when the father was working as a missionary."

"There are many *hapkas* children in Milne Bay. I wonder which one would be this."

"She did not mention anything about the name of the guy."

"Bro, why would they want to find the daughter when she is already dead?" Reimas asked.

"Because, apparently Kate left her some money in her will."

"Man, she is gonna be lucky, that girl," Reimas said.

"Could you give me Desimoni's address again so I can contact him?" Uwegu went into her room and got the letter that Desimoni has written and gave it to me. I opened it and saw the address on the right-hand corner of the page.

"I have a feeling that girl could be the one that Desi is going to marry," Uwegu said quietly. I looked at her.

"What makes you think that way?" "I just remembered that people were saying that she was a daughter of a *dimdim* girl whose father was a missionary there. In the end, they had a falling out with another *dimdim* couple. The girl was adopted by a childless couple. I could be wrong. It's better that you contact Desimoni as soon as you are able to."

"We could ask Kilroy. He was adopted by a missionary couple. He should know something, bro," Reimas told me.

"That is a possibility. I never thought of him. Give me his number and I will call him straight away."

When Reimas gave me Kilroy's number I rang him. I couldn't get through to him so I left a couple of messages in his voice mail.

"We'll just wait and see whether he calls back, bro."

In the meantime Uwegu made some coffee and gave it to me. They must have realised that I was now vulnerable and it was their turn to protect me. "I found something," she told me as I was drinking coffee.

"What did you find?" I asked.

She showed me some sort of a bottle wrapped with a black cloth. Inside the bottle there was some form of liquid with a mixture of herbs. "It was buried right beside my room. This is what was affecting me. Now I have neutralised it and its power has gone."

"It could be nothing; someone may have thrown it out a long time ago."

"No Perez, when I dug it out, my right hand went numb so I had to get my traditional oil and rub it. Then it was okay."

"Who could have buried it and for what reason?" I asked no one in particular. Uwegu did not say anything further.

We waited but Kilroy never returned my call that day.

In the evening I wrote a letter to Desimoni. I made sure that what I said was clear and without any ambiguity. I wanted him to locate a *hapkas* girl, who should be around 22, the daughter of a *dimdim* girl and a local boy. The grandfather was a missionary, I wrote in the letter. I asked him to give me the name and the contact details of the girl and if she has any bank accounts. I told him that I will be in Port Moresby very soon and I gave him my Port Moresby address. I also told him that I was bringing with me his bag that he had left behind. I sent the letter via express mail.

"I don't think it will be difficult to find the girl," Uwegu told me as we sat around.

"What makes you think that?"

"People are bound to know about her."

"But you said there are many *hapkas* kids there."

"Each *hapkas* child has its own story of conception." I smiled at the way she had constructed the wording of her sentence.

"You have put it very well."

"I wonder where Kilroy could be. He has not returned the calls, bro. I have not met Rawiri for a few weeks now."

"They must have been swallowed by the city," Uwegu joked.

"No kidding, this city has a strange way of ingesting its victims," I said.

"I know Kilroy would know something about this girl."

"Try and remember Uwegu," I prompted her. "It's important that I locate this girl before her money falls into wrong hands."

"Bro, if Kilroy doesn't come back to you, you will just have to wait for Desimoni to write," Reimas told me.

"I suppose so." We talked some more about this mystery daughter of Kate before Reimas told me that they have found a flat, which they will move into after I leave.

"It's closer to the university," Uwegu told me. "How did you manage to find it?"

"My girlfriend told me about it and all we will do is repay her the bond fee."

"Who owns the place?" "Another Italian guy, bro," Reimas said. "He is happy with the arrangement."

"That's good."

"We will miss you, bro," Reimas said.

"At least we have learnt a lot from you," Uwegu added.

"You guys can always look me up in Port Moresby when you are in town," I told them. Although they heard me, no one said anything. They just sat there looking into space. I knew we were going to miss each other when I finally leave. But it didn't matter. We are always on a journey going places.

"How could she just waste away like that? She was so vibrant and active," Uwegu broke the short silence. Reimas and I directed our focus on her. "I mean that Kate. She was young and so full of life."

"Life is strange and we can't fully understand it," I said.

"True Perez. Like the Kula Ring, we live our lives in different stages, different ways and different places but ultimately we return to where we have begun," Uwegu said almost with finality. Then she stood up and left.

Chapter 24

Finally it was time to leave Sydney. That morning I caught a cab with Uwegu and we rode to the airport. Reimas spent the night with his *dimdim* mates but called to say he would catch up at the airport. I had an ambivalent feeling; it was a mixture of sadness, anxiety and joy. No one said anything in the cab. Not long after, I was once again at one of the busiest airports in the world. All around us there was this continuum of arrivals and departures. On the screen monitors the flight arrivals and departures flashed almost every 10 seconds. All these were punctuated by announcements in several different languages — announcements of delayed flights, missing passengers and safety messages. The place was bustling with activity. Finally Reimas appeared and joined us.

Now and again I looked up from my coffee, expecting Uwegu or Reimas to say something, anything to cool my nerves. I was again on transit, on a journey, a catalogue of my professional life, going places. I studied the map of the city; not that I wanted to have a look around. I didn't have much time now. Uwegu pretended to read the newspaper while Reimas quietly fiddled with his camera. The map pinpointed the landmarks of the city and other tourist attractions. I became preoccupied with the map, the routes — bus routes, train routes and all the other routes available to visitors. It reminded me of the many paths back in my small island, which I walked many times. These were similar routes. Mobility is inextricably part of modern day life, I thought. These travels were nothing new; my ancestors also traveled in much the same way as I do; from village to village, from island to island, and so on. Even today there still exists this crisscrossing of routes and pathways. Everyone is a traveler. We are always involved in some kind of travel.

I wanted to get up and just walk around but then again I might miss Uwegu and Reimas. It would be difficult to find them at this airport because of the smorgasbord of passengers in global transit — people, men, women and children. Every now and again I was disturbed by the announcements, bringing me back to reality. I thought about the numerous journeys I had made in this part of the world. They were not only physical journeys; they were at the same time journeys of the mind and of the spirit.

The Air Pacific flight from Fiji has just landed and I could see the passengers coming out of the gate. Islanders in colourful shirts were making trips here either to visit relatives or as emigrants. Most of the emigrants were displaced people moving to other places, new homelands, new life. I thought about Gupta, whose applications for permanent residency has been rejected many times and I felt sorry for him.

I don't know how many times I shook hands with Reimas and Uwegu after the first boarding announcement was made. (Reimas managed to get a couple of pictures of us all). As they finally waved goodbye to me, Reimas and Uwegu told me how I would find the place different from what I am used to.

"Bro, I hope you will quickly adapt to the place."

"It will be strange," Uwegu added.

"I hope not," I said. "I have been there before. It's where I had started out from."

"But you have been away from it for too long," Uwegu said.

"Two years is not a long time."

"I hope not," Uwegu said.

"Bro, kiss the soil for us when you land."

"I am not your pope!"

"Don't be silly Reimas. Kiss it for what?" Uwegu scolded him.

"Like how the Pope does it every time he lands at a new place, bro."

"Cut that crap, will you?" Uwegu told him.

"You know what I will do?" I said. "As soon as I land I will pick a piece of soil and throw it towards the plane."

"Oh bro, you are funny."

"Pass our greetings to Desi," said Uwegu.

"Bro, tell him to take it easy." "I will do that. Do look me up when you guys are in town."

"We will, don't worry," Uwegu told me.

It's kind of funny how after sometime, coming back to a place one is familiar with, all of a sudden, it becomes strange. I boarded the plane with a kind of trepidation and an uncertain hope of what was waiting for me at the other end of my journey. You know how when you travel to other places you are unsure of yourself, what to expect and how sometimes that uncertainty is a disaster in itself, or that rude awakening that you get when your expectations lead you to the unexpected. That's the kind of feeling that I had as I was leaving Sydney that day.

The flight to Port Moresby was rather uneventful except for two bumps as we encountered a couple of mild turbulences about one hour out of Sydney. I sat quietly in my seat, contemplating my arrival and what the future held for me. The plane wasn't full and there were no familiar faces that could cheer me up. I refused the food offered to me by the air steward but only asked for water.

The further we flew away from Sydney the more I thought about Kate and Wilmot, and the place I had left behind. I thought about Reimas and Uwegu and their piece of PNG, which has been transplanted yet to another flat. I had helped them move to this new flat and Uwegu had to dismantle her piece of PNG (the artifacts and souvenirs) and reconstruct it again at the new flat. I knew I was yet on another journey, which will be broken temporarily. I wasn't really looking forward to my arrival but then again I didn't have much choice. Throughout the flight I had butterflies in my stomach. Perhaps it had to do with the dread of arriving at a destination, which has become alien after a long absence.

Indeed as soon as I got off the flight from Sydney, the atmosphere and every thing else around me felt alien and smelled different; the barrenness of the landscape was uninviting and detestable. It was as if I had landed on another planet. This place, which was always familiar to me, has suddenly become unfamiliar. I found it hard to accustom myself to the place. It was like how I felt the first time I arrived in Sydney, lost, disoriented and without a bearing.

Upon arrival, I walked slowly to the carousel to collect my luggage. I wondered if someone was waiting for me outside. I suddenly thought about Deuba and wondered if she knew I was arriving today. Perhaps not. Two years is a long time for someone to wait. I could hear people speaking in Pidgin but it sounded strange. I was all tensed up for some unknown reasons. As soon as I collected my bags, my first thought was to get in touch with Desimoni who upon receiving my letter was already in Port Moresby. It was important that I give priority to what Wilmot had asked me to do. I owed it to Kate and to Wilmot too. When I came out, the university bus was waiting for me. Once I had my luggage in the bus we took off for the university. I was allocated a room at Tuloan Lodge. I got off, got my things out and waved goodbye to the driver. I stared at the room and it didn't look appealing. Perhaps it was my nerves. I tried my best to arrange the room again so that it was comfortable. All I was really doing was disturbing a pattern, a composition (already designed for me by someone) for the sake of my unsettled self.

Inside the room I found a note from the head of my department and a set of keys to my office. The note said that I was to begin the following week and if I could go in and see him any time I was ready. So someone had already beaten me to this room, I thought. I waited for something to happen, anything. I didn't really know what! Somehow I managed to get myself together and I went to the public phone and rang the number Desimoni had given me. It rang for a while before a female voice answered it. I asked for Desimoni and not long after, he was on the line.

"Hello Desimoni!" I greeted him as soon as I recognised his voice.

"Oi, it's you Perez. When did you arrive?" Desimoni asked in his high-pitched voice.

"An hour ago."

"Welcome home then. You will find it hard to adapt but gradually you will find your anchor again."

"Thanks. Are you able to come over and see me?"

"Where are you now?" "I am at Tuloan Lodge, room three." I gave him the direction and he asked me to wait for him.

After replacing the phone I returned to my room, locked my door and waited for him outside. Many of the people who walked past were unfamiliar. The thing about these people was the looks and stares they gave me. A few greeted me. I returned their greetings absentmindedly. The place was barren and dry. It was the dry season and the temperature had risen dramatically today. Not long after, I heard a car blast its horn and I knew it was Desimoni. He got out and waved to me and I returned his wave at the same time walking towards the car. He came with his in-laws and they took me back to where they were staying, at a house owned by Desimoni's brother-in-law.

"Your letter arrived when I was already here in Port Moresby. We came to buy some stuff for our house," Desimoni told me.

"Just as well otherwise I wouldn't have gotten to you quickly," I said.

When we arrived Desimoni motioned his bride to come over. Desimoni did the introductions. She was soft-spoken. Naibusi (that's her name) was indeed pretty and she had features of her *dimdim* mother Kate. She isn't really what you would call petite though. She was about five feet, five inches tall, (a little taller than Desimoni) slim in build, with straight hair. She had blue eyes and this is what made her outstanding and beautiful. Blue eyes she inherited from her *dimdim* mother. Naibusi had this habit of smiling all the time, that's what perhaps makes her all seductive and sexy and what hides her facial expression even when she is not in a good mood or angry. That's perhaps where her fatal (not in the bad sense) attraction comes from. She was about 21-years old and I thought that they matched each other quite well. Indeed she had this unusual sway when she was walking that Kate didn't have. (If she had, I had never noticed it).

As soon as the introductions and the first chewing of *buai* were over and I felt comfortable, I finally broke the news about Kate's death to her daughter. As I was still focused on her I saw Naibusi quietly bow her head and she began to weep softly. Her weeping was no ordinary one. It was that wailing that is so moving and emotive that it can bring pity and grief to everyone around. I felt sorry for her because she was mourning for a mother who would always remain a stranger to her. It was indeed a sad and moving scene to see an abandoned child weep for a mother she had never known except through stories. I don't know whether she had ever wanted to go and see her mother or whether her heart was trained to cherish another mother. As soon as I saw her cry, my eyes began to moisten and I tried to hold back my tears but I couldn't. Not long after, everyone else was crying quietly. Desimoni quietly got up from where he was sitting, came to his bride and held her. He was the only one who didn't cry. Then I heard him speak to her in their language, perhaps words of endearment and comfort. It was a community mourning a distant loss, a loss of a life that was almost like a fairytale to them. I knew that they were crying not so much for the *dimdim* woman but for Naibusi. Whereas I was weeping for both Kate and Naibusi. The scene was almost surreal. Indeed it was like in a dream: we were people mourning for the death in a dream. After we all stopped crying, we chewed *buai* again and we were all merry again. It was Desimoni's father-in-law, Tokwepota who disturbed the temporary silence.

"*Tambu* (in-law) told us all about you," Tokwepota, his father-in-law (adopted father of Naibusi), told me. "He told us how you looked after them and how you were always there for them." Then he lowered his voice as if he didn't want others to hear. "His father should not have stopped him from going back to school. I was angry but what is a small fish against a mighty eagle. The chief (Desimoni's father) asked for my daughter for his son. It was an honour for my family and I told the chief that we would wait for Desimoni to complete his studies and come home. That is why I stopped Naibusi from school."

"So what happened Desimoni?" I asked him.

"When I came home for my holidays my father stopped me from returning to Sydney because he told me that I must take my place in the family."

"At least he could have allowed you to complete your studies."

"Sometimes his father is very stubborn," came in Tokwepota, his father-in-law.

"You should have tried to convince your father," I said. "If you complete your studies you would be in a better position to help your people to understand the many peculiar ways of the *dimdims*."

"Or he could become a *dimdim* himself," Naibusi's elderly uncle said laughing.

"Bah, then he wouldn't be one of us and he would rubbish us like the *dimdims*," Tokwepota argued.

"*Tambu* told us about the crooked ways of the *dimdims*," Naibusi's mother (adopted mother) joined in, making the conversation light again.

"Yeah, sometimes they are amusing, these *dimdims*. You wouldn't understand them," I told her. "At other times they are plain stupid." They all laughed.

"When they come here all they are hungry for is to do it with our women and once the woman is expecting, they don't wanna know," Desimoni's *tambu* continued.

"They are not all like that, *tambu*," Desimoni chipped in.

"What do you mean? How come we have lots of *hapkas dimdims* all over the place?" Naibusi's father continued.

"Maybe our women have something special that *dimdim* women don't have," I said laughing.

"Blame our women as well," came in Naibusi's mother. "They can't keep their legs shut for a moment." This was followed by more laughter. "They pretend to shut it when the poor brown snake approaches but when they see the *dimdim* snake slowly making its way to them, they open their legs for it to enter." Another burst of laughter. "We only learn about it when the belly is swollen and by that time, the *dimdim* has long gone.

Then we all commented sadly and quietly, "Poor girl, she has swallowed the *dimdim*'s seeds again."

I sat there listening to all the teasing and joking that was going on around me. After another round of jokes I got to the point of my coming to them. I told them about how Naibusi's natural mother hasd left her some money and how it was important for me to get Naibusi's details so I could send this information quickly to the lawyers acting for Kate. I could see the faces and looks turning serious once they heard that Naibusi has some money coming. I hope I did the right thing by telling the whole lot of them. I wondered if I had done the right thing. Perhaps I should have told Desimoni and Naibusi alone.

"Desimoni must have already told you about this matter. I wrote to him earlier."

"Indeed *tambu* Desimoni told us about it," Tokwepota spoke after a short time. "As soon as he got your letter he came to me and told me about it. I confirmed that Naibusi was indeed Kate's daughter," Tokwepota told me. "Here, see this birth certificate," and he pushed the worn out piece of paper and indeed the mother's name was Kate Nolan.

"Tell the *dimdims* that we brought her up and made her into a woman. Tell them that we are the parents," said Tokwepota's wife.

"That is not necessary at that moment," I told her. "Maybe later it will become necessary."

"But they need to know that. Her mother threw her away like rubbish and I was the one who picked her up, cleaned her and fed her," Tokwepota's wife continued.

"*Tambu*, those things will be recorded later," Desimoni told her.

"At least I am reminding you young ones who know how to read and write. I don't want the *dimdims* to trick us. They are very cunning."

"Her *bubus* (grandparents) were useless. They called themselves people of God but inside their hearts they stank," Desimoni's father-in-law said. "Every Sunday Pastor Nolan preached to us about love, kindness and forgiveness yet he himself didn't practice it. He called himself a man of God, my foot! *Em giaman lotu man!*" Did you know that Pastor Nolan impregnated their own house girl and that was how Kate came to be? She was a pretty girl who had just married with a 6-month-old baby when they got her to be their house girl. When rumours started spreading about Pastor Nolan and her having an affair the husband left her. We thought that Kate was the *dimdim*s' own child but it was only later that we learnt that she was the result of a union between the pastor and the house girl." For the first time, the birth story of Kate was being confirmed to me.

"Kate's mother's people, especially women, are well known for flying in the night," Naibusi's mother told me. "The pastor was lucky that they did not harm him."

"Do you think Kate might have learnt to be a flying witch?" I asked.

"I don't know but she spent her childhood here. Why are you asking?"

"Just asking," I answered, not wanting to reveal Uwegu's experience.

"These *dimdims* truly have crooked eyes. While our eyes can read through impassable paths, theirs seem only good for straight roads. See how stupid and careless that *dimdim* girl and her missionary parents had been, abandoning a human being as if it was an animal," Naibusi's mother said.

"Perhaps there was something bad that made her to forsake the child," Naibusi's cousin said.

"The Chief asked the *dimdim* girl's parents to let her marry the boyfriend but they didn't want anything to do with the baby," Desimoni's father-in-law said. "In fact they had a big argument about it and Pastor Nolan threatened to take the Chief to the dark house."

"Why is that?" I asked.

"Because the baby was *hapkas*, that's why. Their daughter's relationship with a non-*dimdim* guy was unacceptable. It's against the *dimdims'* way. It's polluting the *dimdims'* blood," Tokwepota said. "They truly have crooked heads. How can they represent God when they had such dislike of other people, people not of their kind? How can they teach us about love and forgiveness when they are the opposite?" another relative commented.

"The Chief was right. He asked the *dimdim*, pastor to allow the daughter to marry the boy for the sake of the child but he refused bluntly. It shows we care and value human life more than these *dimdims*," Naibusi's uncle came in.

"These *dimdims* too are stupid ya."

"Crooked thinkers!" said Naibusi's cousin.

"Oh well, that was a long time ago now. Today *dimdims* are marrying our women and our guys are marrying their women. Life has changed for good," a young cousin of Naibusi said.

"But still many of these *dimdims* continue to be born with crooked eyes," Tokwepota said.

"People are not the same. We also have people with crooked eyes in our midst," Naibusi's young cousin argued.

"Yeah, but at least once we are taught not to judge the book by its cover, we listen. But these *dimdims*, they are stubborn. Once they make up their minds, that's it," Tokwepota came in. "This girl was thrown away by the *dimdims*. It was my wife and I that brought her up and made her somebody. Look at her, she is not a full brown-skinned girl; she is half *dimdim*." He stopped to spit out the betel nut in his mouth before he started again. "But if her *dimdim* mother had left her some money, then her heart towards Naibusi wasn't cold as we always thought. She must have loved her somehow. I mean the ways of the *dimdims* are sometimes strange."

"Where is Naibusi's natural father?" I asked.

"We are not quite sure. He was adopted by another missionary couple and they took him with them when they left. There was talk later that he was killed in a diving accident in Port Moresby.

"Some say he committed suicide," Naibusi's mother told me.

"Others say he is in Australia married to another *dimdim*," Tokwepota said.

"What was his name?" I asked.

"I can't remember his local name. He came from a different island. The missionary who adopted him banned us from calling him by his local name. He said the name was associated with the devil. He even cursed whichever person would call the boy by his local name so we were afraid of the curse. We only knew him as Harding," Naibusi's uncle said. "Oh, he was a very handsome guy."

I wanted to ask if his name was Kirori (Kilroy) but I suppressed it again." No wonder the *dimdim* girl fell for him," I said.

"You know Naibusi's *dimdim* mother well don't you?" Tokwepota asked me.

"Yes I did know her well."

"Was she good? Did you like her?" Tokwepota persisted.

"She was different from many of the *dimdims* I have met. She was kind. She tried her best to identify with us. But she never mentioned anything about Naibusi. Perhaps she didn't want to bring pain to herself," I said. "There was also another *dimdim* who previously worked here as an anthropologist."

"Oh that one whose house was always full of little boys," Naibusi's mother said.

"He was good with the kids; he would give them balloons and all the things that kids like. His house was like a kindergarten. Pity he never married."

"Later there was talk that the *dimdim* was sleeping with some of these kids. We did not believe it because a man cannot sleep with his own kids," Tokwepota told me. "When we asked the kids, they denied it." He kept quiet before he spoke again.

"Tell us one thing; how did you find out that she had a child back here?" Naibusi's mother asked me.

"We found out after she died. She wrote it in her diary and will."

"I have a feeling that it was her parents who drove her to abandon Naibusi," Naibusi's uncle said.

"We will never know the truth," Tokwepota said.

I sat there listening to Desimoni's in-laws talking away. After a while I told them that I was going and I asked Desimoni and Naibusi to come and see me the next day so we could talk more. After chewing another round of *buai*, I left.

That night I couldn't sleep well as if the darkness was like needles pricking parts of my body and mind. I tossed from side-to-side throughout the night. Strange, spooky sounds were audible and I wondered what was next to come. I stayed awake thinking about Uwegu and Reimas and other things. What bothered me most was Naibusi's father. I knew that Kilroy was adopted by the *dimdims*. I had a strong feeling that it could be him unless it was the other local boy they had adopted. But if it was Kilroy how come and Kate never met up with him again. Kilroy never mentioned anything about Kate either.

Then I thought about Deuba and wondered where she could be. Since I arrived I had not had time to ask around for her. I knew she was already married but then again for old time's sake I wanted to greet her and perhaps apologise for what I had done to her. Then for the first time I heard the roosters crow and I forced myself to sleep.

The next day, Desimoni and Naibusi arrived early. I was in the office when they entered and I was glad to see them although I didn't expect to see them that early.

"The news about Naibusi getting some money isn't going down well with some of her relatives," Desimoni told me.

"Oh dear," I said.

"You know how it is with relatives here," Naibusi told me quietly in her soft-spoken voice. "But I think we can handle the tide." For the first time when I heard her speak I knew she was intelligent and I pitied her for not continuing her studies.

"I should have told only the two of you, shouldn't I?"

"But news was bound to spread anyway," Desimoni said. "Don't worry you have done your part. It's just that people are going to come up with all sorts of excuses to try and have a portion of Naibusi's money."

"I hope you can deal with that," I said.

"We will handle it," Desimoni told me.

"How much money do you think I will get?" Naibusi asked me timidly.

"I am not sure of that. But Kate has left you two thirds of whatever money she had. Also once her lawyers sell the house and the contents, the money will come to you. This is why I needed to get all your details," I paused. "You are looking at many thousands." Naibusi quietly squeezed Desimoni's hand.

"I am not sure what Desimoni's father will say about this. He has not heard about it yet," Naibusi said.

"It's none of his business. It's your money, not mine or anyone else's," Desimoni told her.

"Here, I want you to double-check this before I send it," I said pushing Naibusi's details to them. Desimoni got it and they went through the details until they were satisfied with it.

"The details are correct," Desimoni told me returning the piece of paper back to me.

"I am going to send this via express mail. I want you to stay in Port Moresby until the money had been paid."

"We won't be going anywhere. We will wait for you here," Desimoni told me.

"That is good. Check with me every now and again in case something else comes up," I told them. "Or before I forget, Uwegu and Reimas sent you their greetings."

"How are they?" Desimoni asked.

"They are okay. They dropped me off at the airport."

"I hope they are behaving themselves," Desimoni said standing up.

"One more thing I want to ask you guys about." The two looked at me. "Are you sure that Naibusi's natural father is dead?"

"We aren't really sure," Desimoni replied. "Why are you asking?"

"Nothing really. I am just asking," I said dismissing them.

We shook hands and they left me.

Chapter 25

No matter how much I wanted to see Deuba, my pride prevented me from doing so. She called and left messages several times but I did not return her calls. She knew I was arriving that day and in fact she was at the airport but I did not see her. Maybe she wanted to see how much I had changed after two years away from home. I tried calling her best friend but I was told she had left her employment some 6 months ago. Coincidently, I met up with my cousin who told me things about Deuba. "You should call her up and apologise," the cousin told me.

"Apologise for what?" I snapped back.

"For the pain you've caused her, abruptly breaking the relationship without giving it second thoughts."

"What about me? What about the pain she caused me, accusing me of something that I never did? It's too late for apologies we all have our lives to live."

"If you don't apologise to each other, the wounds of that relationship will remain unhealed. She has been asking for you."

"But she is now married and I don't want to cut in between them. How would her husband react when he finds out that we have been talking?"

"It's not really a true relationship. The guy is a married man."

"So what they are living together and I don't want to create problems for myself," I told him.

"Oh well I was just trying to bring you two to apologise and let the matter finally rest." Then he went away.

The next day, I had two threatening phone calls from someone who claimed to be Deuba's husband. The person told me that he would get me no matter how long it would take him to do that. I was confused and didn't know how to react. I wanted to report the matter to the police but upon second thoughts I decided against it. I didn't know what to do. I went home early that day and went straight to sleep. I didn't want to tell people about it. I tried calling my cousin but his phone went unanswered so I gave up. I reassured myself that it was really nothing and that someone could be playing a prank on me. But in the middle of the night I heard noises like someone trying to cut through the wire fence that surrounded the lodge. This was followed by the barking of the neighbours' dogs. I sat up and as I was about to peek, I heard the security guards and I regained my composure.

I made up my mind to go to the village with the idea that perhaps when I returned things would have cooled down. It was also an opportune time to see my folks and in particular to pay my last respect to my favourite uncle who had died when I had just arrived in Sydney. Before I left, I tried calling Deuba but I was told she was out of town. Next, I tried calling my cousin but he wasn't at work so I gave up. As I came out of my office I saw two guys standing in the corridor talking quietly. Now and again they looked my way. I was suspicious and I went back in pretending that I had left something. When I came out they were gone so I hurried away to the bus stop to catch the bus to the airport. I arrived just in time to check in and board the flight.

✳✳✳

The threatening phone calls that I received and the conversation that I had with my cousin about Deuba affected me deeply as I stared for a long while at the sea as the PMV bus came into view of the coast. I knew that here people can almost do anything, even murder. The police here were almost useless and could not be trusted, unlike in Sydney. This thought made me more fearful and vulnerable. It was as if my escape from Deuba was only temporary and now I was back in that web and it would start all over again. After we landed, I walked over to the bus stop. I was surprised to see the two guys I saw in Port Moresby again but they did not say anything to me. I wondered who they were. For all I knew they could be students also going home for the break. They did not get into the bus I was in and I dismissed the thought and tried to enjoy the ride. Deuba and I used to travel this route on our way to town when we were in secondary school. Most of the road was inland but this stretch of road ran adjacent to the coastline with a full and magnificent view of the Pacific Ocean. We always looked forward to this tract of road. At times when I was depressed the sea brought back a rejuvenated soul.

My eagerness and excitement about the sea is unlike that of others. I mean I know the craze that the average *dimdim* person has for the sea. Mine is different from theirs. I don't know how different but I just know. I am an islander and the sea has always been an indispensable part of my life. My confinement within the cityscape gave me that powerful inclination and longing for the sea. Sydney (and now Port Moresby) with their threatening structures, hostility and their impersonalness caged me in. Sometimes the sea felt strange, unfriendly and distant. But most times it was inviting and friendly.

As we drove towards the last bridge, another bus sped along from behind and as it was overtaking us, it almost collided with us. When I looked, I saw among the passengers the two guys I saw earlier. Obviously they were drunk.

"What's happening?" I asked the driver.

"They just tried to bump us," the driver said.

"Who are they?" I asked.

"Some idiots from the next village," someone replied. The next village was where Deuba came from. It was a small village about a kilometre from my village.

"*Ol sipak lain ya*," someone else commented.

"But they almost got us involved in an accident," I said.

"Let's catch up with them. Who do they think they are," someone suggested to the driver.

"Let them go, they are a bunch of criminals *ya*," another man said.

By the time we passed Deuba's village the bus was nowhere to be seen and I knew it had already arrived. There was something out of the ordinary that was bothering me. Something told me that this was no ordinary near miss. I gave up thinking about it, got off at the junction and walked to our house to the embrace of my mother and family. My homecoming was like the return of the prodigal son. My mother cried as if I was returning from the dead. In the end it was a happy reunion but a difficult one for me.

The village life was strange but I found some sense of freedom in the village. So much had changed and the village I used to know had been transformed almost beyond recognition. I caught up with family and friends and I tried to readjust to the daily routine. Going fishing and diving among the war relics gave me a certain degree of autonomy and freedom. It made me forget about the incidents that happened to me. In the evenings my mates would come and listen to me tell them stories about Sydney and all the *dimdim* places I had been to. In many instances when I ran out of stories to tell, I would make them up. They could not tell the difference because they had never been overseas. The village was their entire world. My mother had warned me several times not to wander in the night as there were many jealous people. So my mates came to our house where I told them stories.

One night a group of drunken youths came to our house and started an argument with my brother. I was inside the house eating when I heard the commotion. My brother was accused of stealing betel nut but he insisted that it was from our betel nut tree. Later we realised that it was only a pretext for other motives.

"What is happening?" I asked my mother.

"Those are only drunkards," she replied. "That's their usual routine."

Not long after, a fight broke out and that was when I realised that they were Deuba's relatives picking on our house. I ran outside but by the time I arrived the fight had stopped and the drunken youths had dispersed. I felt ashamed and blamed myself for bringing trouble to my family.

"It's not your fault. These are drunken youths who have nothing better to do but drink and cause trouble," my elder brother told me.

"But I heard them mention Deuba's name and my name," I insisted.

"You got it all wrong. These are stupid youths who were asking for money to buy more beer and when they were refused, they started to fight us," my brother told me. "It's nothing to do with you and Deuba."

Despite my brother's denial I did not believe him because I heard Deuba's name mentioned during the commotion. I hated myself for bringing trouble and shame to my family. I wanted to leave there and then but my sister pleaded with me.

"This village has changed since you were here last. The serenity and peace that you once knew of is no longer here," my sister told me. "Now you are witnessing a new village without a soul."

"But don't you have elders to maintain peace?" I asked.

"Do you think these young people will listen to them? The village elders have lost their voices and now they are only walking corpses," my brother replied.

"A lot of criminal activities are taking place here. Criminals from other places come to the village to hide and people here harbour them," my sister added.

I sat quietly listening to what they were telling me. Now I fear for my village, it was falling apart.

✳✳✳

I was into the beginning of my second week in the village when a message was relayed to me to return to Port Moresby. My elder brother who went to town in the morning to sell his garden produce brought back the message, which was given to him by the director of the university centre in town. I had a feeling that it had to do with my application for conference travel. I had applied to attend an international conference just before I came and I told my boss to take care of it.

"You have not even rested after all these years working and they want you back?" My mother said quietly when she heard about my recall to Port Moresby. "What type of people are they? I hope they are not lying to you."

"Mother, Perez is now a big man at the university. He is no longer ours alone. He also belongs to other people," my sister tried to explain to my mother.

"Bah, I was the one who gave birth to him."

"Of course, mother, but he is no longer your small kid," my sister continued. "He has work to do."

"I know that. But at least let him finish his two weeks here and he can go back to them."

I just sat there listening to them talking. My two brothers were smoking and chewing betel nut outside.

"*Mama, Perez bai kambek gen,*" my brother said in a reassuring tone.

"I hope so. I hope he will come back when my eyes are still open," mother said sadly. "He was away when his father's brother died and he was away when his father died and I know he will still be away when I die."

"Mother the good thing is that Perez is back in the country and you can always go and visit him," my sister told her.

"Do you think I can go and visit him? Look at my legs; they can't carry me far these days."

"Mama, nowadays people travel in planes. Who said you are going to walk?"

"Who would want to die flying in that big bird?"

"I'll come back soon mother. I am just going because an important message came through from Australia."

"And when are you going to settle down?" my mother came in again, slightly changing the direction of the talk.

"He will marry when he is ready mother," my sister said. "And in any case when he marries, I don't think you will have much time with your son."

"But I want to see and touch my grand children before I sleep the long sleep. I know I have your kids here with me but I also want to have Perez's kids. He is also my child." She stopped for a while before she started again.

"And what happened to that Deuba woman who you were going around with? She is a good woman who comes from a good family."

"Good woman, my foot!" my sister said.

"Enough mother, Perez has to go and catch the bus now," my brother said.

I went over to my mother and she hugged me and her tears wetted my face. I let her hold me for as long as she liked but my sister came and gently broke us apart. She held on to me as if she didn't want to lose me in this quagmire of never-ending travels. She was like an anchor whose chain is always letting go when the journey begins no matter how much she wants to strap me down.

I had wanted to begin the journey early but I guess my old mother didn't want me to go early, so she didn't wake me up until 5.00 am. Although my alarm went off at 4.30 am, I slept on until mum shook me gently and when I checked my watch it was 5.00 am My muscles were twitchy with pain and I was uneasy. Daylight was swimming in through the cracks of our house. I threw off my sheets and got up. It rained the whole night and the place was unusually cold. My other brothers and sisters and their families were already there chatting away when I had my breakfast of taro and smoked fish. The villagers were already up and about. Once again I was a traveler on an unending journey but with many temporary breaks along the way.

By 6.30 am we were all at the side of the main road waiting for the bus. (It's about 5 minutes walk from our village to the junction). The outside air was cold and chilly at this time of the morning but as soon as we made some distance, I started to get sweaty and hot. I got rid of my outer shirt, leaving only my T-shirt. When I heard the sound of the bus I started to run but one of my brothers told me it was a truck so I slowed down again. It wasn't long before we arrived at the junction. We chewed more *buai* until the right bus came to a halt and I got on, finding a seat at the back. The bus was full of mothers going to sell their produce at the town market.

It was relatively a quiet trip. Occasionally I was disturbed by a child crying and mothers chatting loudly. They distracted me from enjoying the view of the sea. As soon as the noise died down I would return my gaze and stare at the fleeting ocean. This sporadic distraction didn't threaten the tranquility I was feeling. But my thoughts were elsewhere — indeed anticipating the worse. It was calm today; several canoes were out early and there was also an ocean liner, which was visible on the horizon. It was one of those big cargo ships. I imagined myself swimming in the sea, the joyous shouts of village kids amidst angry mothers. An odd figure was walking on the beach. Further up, a truck was being driven out onto the main road. It was indeed beautiful. As soon as the sea was out of sight (as the road wound inland again), my mind began to refocus on the reason for my early morning journey to the airport. I didn't know why I should break my holiday and return to the city, but I had a feeling that there was some bad news.

As the bus finally came to stop at the airport terminal before it continued on to town, I felt something stir inside me. I waited for the other passengers who sat in front of me to disembark. I checked my watch. It was little past 7.30 am; I was way ahead of time. The Air Niugini flight was arriving at 8.30 am. I finally got out of the bus and stretched myself. The other passengers got back into the bus and left for town. I got a *buai* and chewed it as I waited outside the passenger terminal. Cars and buses were gradually arriving to drop off passengers and wait for inbound ones. I stood there looking around the place. Some things have changed while others were the same as I last saw them. The airport terminal was new but already there was graffiti on the walls. The public toilet was full of sexual comments and drawings of mostly naked women in different sexual positions. I almost laughed, as this was no different from the toilets in Sydney. Comments were scribbled both in *Tok Pisin* and English. There were a few names added, mainly names of women. After surveying the place, I went straight to the small kiosk that served coffee, cakes and soft drinks, and I bought myself coffee. I could sense that people were staring at me. As I was trying to sit down, I heard a familiar voice, "Hey, where are you off to this early?" I turned around, only to find arms wrapped around me and a breath smelling of alcohol. It was Kumalau a cousin of mine who worked at the airport terminal as a baggage handler or something. His eyes were bloodshot.

"I am off to Port Moresby," I managed a reply.

"So soon?"

"A message came through for me to go back."

"Please buy me a Coke," Kumalau requested. I gave him some coins. He went and bought himself a drink and came back.

"I drank with some friends until the wee hours of this morning," he told me.

"Are you working today?" I asked as I saw his boss eyeing him and trying to make contact.

"I am, but don't worry." I just smiled and waved him towards his boss.

"I'll catch up with you some other time."

"Come on tell me. Why the hurry?" he begged, drunkenly.

"Your boss is waiting."

"Oh, shit!" and he rushed toward his boss. I didn't wanna know what his boss did with him after that.

In between drinking my coffee I thought about what news awaited me. Once again I had mixed feelings. My entire mind was focused on what to expect. If the news about Naibusi's money isn't promising I wondered how she would respond and react when I meet and tell them so. I also wondered whether those threatening phone calls would continue and eventually materialise into something nasty. I was apprehensive and anxious. And the butterflies in my stomach were unsettled. Absentmindedly I went through the paper, which I bought together with my coffee. Nothing exciting in the paper today: it was the usual. I could sense eyes clandestinely watching my every move even in this small town. They are just like the *dimdims* in Sydney, I thought to myself. Then I remembered that having been away for a long time made me a stranger here. It was only the sound of the plane taxiing towards the terminal that brought me back to reality.

As soon as we were airborne, I felt a sense of estrangement and rebuff from the land that gave birth to me. The stares that people gave me at the airport were an act of unrecognition. Perhaps it was my fault for not spending much time in the village and renewing my connection. I thought about my mother and my family and I knew how my ephemeral sojourn gave them a false hope of my mooring and how it had also given me a glimpse of a recoiling society I am gradually estranging from.

I was surprised upon my arrival that my office was broken into and vandalised. On my table someone had left a headless rat and behind the bookshelf another person had defecated. It was a disgusting sight. The secretary had already rung the carpenter to fix the door and cleaners to clean the office. There was nothing valuable for them to steal except for my computer and a few Australian coins.

Two letters were waiting for me in my pigeonhole. It was delivered by a courier a couple of days ago. One letter told about the acceptance of my paper by the conference organisers. Deuba had also pushed a note under my door. The secretary told me that a Dr. Cox had been trying to contact me for the last few days.

The second letter was indeed from Wilmot and it told about a counter-claim lodged by a Kilroy Harding who claims to be the natural father of Naibusi. I stopped reading, shocked beyond belief.

"So Kilroy is the missing part of the puzzle," I whispered to myself.

Wilmot however assured me that even if the plaintiff wins, Naibusi won't lose her share. The only concern he had was the delay because of the pending court case. At the same time he asked for more information on Kilroy.

"I am presenting you with a layman's explanation of the case," Wilmot wrote. *"But be assured that Naibusi won't lose any of her share. That is guaranteed. It will only mean a delay in the payment."*

I was relieved but astounded that indeed Kilroy was the natural father of Naibusi. It was funny though how they have never mentioned each other or gotten back together. I wanted to laugh as the whole thing was like a farce to me. It wasn't real as if I was watching a movie or something. The more I thought about Kilroy the more I felt like laughing. I didn't think he would do something like this. Perhaps I was too quick to judge him that I didn't allow for the complexity of human beings. At least it wasn't all as bad as I had anticipated. There was also a note, which told of Desimoni's visit, but I wasn't in. He wrote that he would call again soon.

After a while I sat down amid the cleaning going on and thought about who could have done this to my office. I didn't have any clues and the security guards weren't helpful either. I shrugged my shoulders, got the phone and asked the switch lady to get me a number in Sydney. I waited but my phone didn't ring. When it finally rang it was the switch lady telling me that the number in Sydney wasn't responding. I began to read through Deuba's note. She wanted to see me when I got back from home. I was puzzled and I thought of calling my cousin. No, I told myself. I should write to Dr Cox first before anything else. I got a pen and started to draft my reply to Dr. Wilmot Cox's letter.

Chapter 26

Some months into the year (after Naibusi had finally received her money from Kate's lawyers), I received a surprise visit in my office. There was this strange knock (which I didn't recognise) and when I opened it, there was Reimas standing all smiles.

"What brings you here?" I asked him, surprised.

"Bro, I have received some bad news from home."

"What news?" I asked alarmed at the same time.

"My sis rang and told me that my uncle had died, my mother's brother."

"Oh, I am so sorry to hear that Reimas."

Reimas has that strange way of sensationalising things, making your heart jump despite the fact that the news may not be important.

"But how long ago was this?"

"A few weeks ago now but bro, he was my favourite uncle. I suppose that's how life is, aye?" Reimas tried to rise above his sadness.

"Sit down and relax. How is Uwegu?"

"Oh that one? She is bad news bro."

"What do you mean?" I asked.

"Bro, she is truly a lesbo now. I have caught her several times with this Asian girl in the living room kissing."

"Did she say anything to you?"

"What could she say bro? All she told me was, 'Times have changed; now it's girl power."

"What did you say to her?"

"You know me, bro; I am an easy going guy." I just smiled.

"What are you planning to do then?"

"I am on my way to the village then I will go back to Sydney. I managed to convince the AusAID guys to give me a ticket."

"Both ways?" I asked.

"Just one way, bro."

"How are you going to go back?" "Don't worry, bro, I'll find a way."

"Was your uncle sick or something?" I asked him.

"He just fell and died, bro."

"What do you mean?"

"Sorcery, bro. We have a lot of bad people at our place." He stopped for a while to gain his breath and then continued. "My uncle was the one who arranged for the first *dimdim t*o stay in our village, bro."

"What *dimdim* are you talking about?"

"Come on bro, you are pulling my legs again. Remember I told you about one *dimdim* anthropologist who wrote some books about our people. I was about 7 years old then."

I sat there trying to remember but I couldn't recall it.

"Perhaps you have forgotten, bro. Too many things in your mind."

"I am usually good at remembering things but I am afraid I have no recollection of this one."

"Bro, I am sure I told you about this anthropologist by the name of Koksi." I shook my head in the negative.

"Bro, the story is nothing. I was only reminded of it by the news of the death of my uncle. I don't know whether you would be familiar with the guy because he wrote a number of books about us."

"I am planning to write a book about how the *dimdims* saw us when they first came to our islands so if it is not too much for you, I would like you to tell me the story."

"Are you gonna write my story too, bro?"

"I'll just have a feel of it first."

"Okay bro. I'll tell you the story as it will help me to remember my uncle."

"Go ahead then."

"When I was a kid something strange happened, something that I will never forget. One day when we kids were playing, a ship arrived. It was one of those small ships that came about once a month to buy copra from the villages along the coast. Some of the children who were playing on the beach relayed the message that a *dimdim* was coming ashore to stay with us. We stopped playing and went to the beach to see this person. In fact he was the first person to be ferried down to the beach by the crew. He was a tall guy, with a long beard. He had a lot of things with him, camera, tape recorder and other stuff. When I arrived he was already on the beach talking to the other kids. Many of the kids couldn't understand what he was talking about and all they did was laugh at the way he was talking. Realising that no one was understanding him, he tried speaking in Pidgin, a broken one at that. Perhaps he saw that I looked intelligent and he directed the question at me, *"Where big man blong ples stap?"*

I spoke to the kids about my uncle who was the big man in the village. One of them told me that he was in his garden so I told the *dimdim* guy.

"Big man em long garden."

"Tokim em Masta Koksi laik lukim em," the *dimdim* said.

"Someone quick go get Luka," (my uncle's name), I told the other kids. When I turned around I saw my uncle's son. "Hey, go get your father. Tell him a *dimdim* is here and wants to see him."

He ran all the way to the garden.

The *dimdim* guy asked me; *"Yu tokim mi laik big man?"* I nodded my head in the affirmative. *"Gutpela boi tru,"* he said shaking my hand.

The other kids laughed imitating him at the same time. I stood there with him. I wanted to talk with him but I knew only a little Pidgin and virtually no English. I was only in Standard One and all we were learning was ABC and 123. I remembered that the mission station was nearby and I said to the *dimdim* fellow, *"Mission blong pastor klostu."*

"Take me there then," the *dimdim* said after awhile. "Big man em slow too much."

Some adults, together with the other kids helped with his bags and things, and we escorted him to the mission station, which was about half a kilometre from the village. When the pastor saw us, he walked towards us. Then he shook hands with the *dimdim* and they chatted for a while until he asked us to take his things to the mission guesthouse adjacent to the pastor's house. The *dimdim* gave us some lollies and we went our way, while the curious ones remained.

When I arrived back in the village my uncle was already in the village waiting. There were also other villagers with him. They must have heard about the arrival of the *dimdim* guy and they all came to gather here to hear what brought him to our village. My father wasn't with them though. He had gone to our coconut plantation early that morning and he hadn't come back yet. I walked slowly to where my uncle was.

"Where is the *dimdim* guy?" my uncle asked.

"He is with the pastor at the mission station."

"Is he coming back to the village?"

"Maybe," I said.

"What is he here for?" another villager asked.

"I don't know but it seems he will be here for a long time."

"Where is your father?" Uncle Luka asked. "He's gone to the plantation."

A while later, maybe one hour later some of the kids returned from the mission with the news that the *dimdim* was on his way to the village. My uncle told us to tidy the place, as he didn't want the *dimdim* to think we were untidy like pigs. So we got into cleaning the meetinghouse. News spread quickly that the *dimdim* was coming to the village and everyone was curious. Since the establishment of the village, no *dimdim* had ever lived long with us. We have had patrol officers, doctors and scientists come and go but they would stay for a few days only and move on. We also had a few *dimdim* crocodile hunters who passed through our village to other destinations. Now this would be different; a *dimdim* was going to stay in our village for a long time.

"They are here," someone announced and when we looked we saw the *dimdim* guy with the pastor coming towards the meetinghouse. My uncle stood up, dusted himself and walked towards them.

"*Ah pastor welkam long ples blong mipela,*" Uncle Luka greeted them.

"*Gutpela tru big man, mi bringim kam Masta Koksi*. He is an anthropologist and he will be based in your village. He studies indigenous cultures, *pasin blong yupela, sindaun blong yupela* and how you live," he tried to explain to us. "Koksi is from America. *America man em gutpela tru, em rausim Japan long war, ah*," the pastor continued.

We all smiled because we have heard stories about how the Americans had saved us from the Japanese during the Second World War. All this time Masta Koksi was smiling, shaking hands with Uncle Luka.

"He will be here for about three years and I want all of you to give him every assistance he needs," the pastor continued. "Look after him, soon your village will be famous and people will know about your village and you. Master Koksi will write a big book about you all and your village."

"*Pastor bai mipela lukautim em gut tru. Nau em bai stap long haus kiap pastaim. Tumora bai mipela wokim niupela haus blong Masta Koksi*," said Uncle Luka. Then my uncle called out to the women to clean the kiap's house so Masta Koksi could stay there.

"That is very good," came in the pastor. Then he spoke in English with Masta Koksi. It was funny how Masta Koksi had a different accent from the pastor.

One of the kids said to me, "That Masta Koksi is not talking straight; he is singing." I pinched him and whispered to him that now the other villages will be jealous because a *dimdim* will be living with us.

When the pastor left for his station we all escorted Masta Koksi to the *kiap*'s house and let him settle in. We kids hung around, curious about this white man. Uncle Luka had to chase us away. Masta Koksi had many things; there were three metal boxes plus other things. He also brought with him many types of equipment.

In the evening the women brought him food, local food and he sat down to eat while we kids stayed around in case he needed something. As he ate he tried to make conversation with us. I was the one who knew some Pidgin and broken English so I managed to reply to some of his questions.

"Why is he very curious about every thing here," asked Mikaele.

"He is going to write a big book about us and our village," I told him.

"What for?" someone else asked.

"So that the world will know about us."

"He is here to steal our spirits," came in Maire.

Then it dawned on us. He could have been sent by someone who wanted to kill us and steal our land. We have been hearing a lot about a big company, which was trying to steal land to dig the ground for some minerals. This company tricked the villagers into obliging.

I got the courage to ask Masta Koksi. "*Masta Koksi yu kampani boi?*"

He looked at me for a while perhaps trying to understand what I meant. Then he answered. "*No, mi no kampani boi. Mi kam long America. Mi laik save culture blong yupela.*"

"*Ah, yu no kampani boi,*" I said.

I conveyed to the others that he was not involved in the company that was stealing land from the people in order to dig for minerals.

"Are people thinking that I am from the company?" he asked.

"No," I managed to say.

Perhaps in his mind he didn't believe me. I could see that he looked worried. His face told a hundred pictures. When the elders came we kids left them alone. We didn't want to disturb their conversation with Masta Koksi. My father was also with them. They talked with Masta Koksi for a very long time. I didn't hear my father return because I was already sleeping. When I woke up the next morning I heard my dad talking to my mother about Masta Koksi.

"He is here to study our way of life, how we do things here, learn our language, our customs and everything."

"I am feeling shy already. In our custom a woman is not supposed to tell any man who isn't her husband about herself. A *dimdim* guy at that!" my mother said.

"Maybe he will ask you women about general things not about women's business," my father tried to reassure her.

"What will he do with all these things?" Don't tell me he is here to steal our spirits. If he does we will lose our powers," my mother continued.

"Bah, can't you be realistic, woman? He is here to do us good. What village will refuse a *dimdim* staying in it? I bet you, the other villages will envy us because we have a dimdim in our midst," my dad told her.

"I hope so," my mother came in. "I can see that he is young. The way he looked at the girls when he arrived."

"That's his job, to study us," my father told her.

The next day I got up early and went outside to see if Masta Koksi was up and about. I couldn't see him outside his house so I went to my cousin and asked him if he has seen Masta Koksi. He shook his head.

"Hurry up, we have to go to school," he told me.

The excitement about the *dimdim* guy has made me almost forget that I had to go to school at the mission station. I quickly went back to the house, washed my face, ate a big piece of taro and raced outside to walk to school. I wondered where Masta Koksi has gone. When I arrived at the mission station I saw Masta Koksi chatting with the pastor.

The bell rang and we all went in to the classrooms. We tried asking our teacher what Masta Koksi would be doing. He didn't know either. All he said was Masta Koksi will be studying us and he will write a big book about us. In fact we wanted the class to finish quickly so we could go and see Masta Koksi. The teacher was annoyed with our behaviour and lack of concentration that day.

"If you want to be like Masta Koksi, then you have to concentrate in your studies," he told us. We didn't believe him. As soon as the bell rang we rushed out of the classroom and ran to the village.

We found him chatting with three girls. He was writing something and the girls were giggling all the time. We quietly surrounded them and I tried to see what he was writing but with my very limited knowledge I couldn't even read what he was writing. Masta Koksi told us to go away as he was busy with the three girls. So I told the kids to leave them alone and so we reluctantly left.

The girls have been to high school so they could communicate with Masta Koksi very well. The prettiest one of the girls was betrothed to one of my cousins. But my cousin was away working in town and he hadn't been home for many months.

I went away disappointed at Masta Koksi not wanting us around. But I had other things to do. My father had asked me to collect some firewood so I had to go to the bush and collect some before he returned. The other kids went to their houses except for the stubborn ones who hovered around trying to eavesdrop on them. I couldn't care less.

Reimas stopped for a while to blow his nose. I sat there waiting for him to start. When he came back he told me that, that was the end of the story.

"So what happen to this Masta Koksi then?" I asked him.

"That's what I wanted to tell you about. That is the climax of the story. He is actually in Sydney. I met him," Reimas told me excitedly.

"Really?" How did you find out about him?"

"He found me, bro."

"How come?"

"He came looking for me and Uwegu and that's how I met him."

"What?" I asked confused.

Reimas put his hand into his bag and brought out a big brown envelope addressed to me. "Here, this is for you from Masta Koksi."

When I got to read the sender bit, I started laughing and Reimas joined me. The name Koksi was the indigenisation of the name Cox. The person that Reimas was talking about was none other than Dr. Wilmot Cox.

"That's from Masta Koksi," Reimas told me still laughing. "Bro, no wonder I had never found the books he wrote about us. When I finally got the name right I went to the library and found two books he wrote about my village. My uncle's name and almost all the villagers' names are mentioned."

"You guys are funny with *dimdim* names," I said.

I opened the envelope and started reading the content while Reimas continued talking.

"Uwegu and I didn't know that Kilroy was the guy who fathered Kate's baby. It was Wilmot who told us and since that news Kilroy has never again visited us. And that child is now betrothed to Desimoni."

"Yes, it's a strange story indeed. I mean the one about Kilroy and Kate."

"And a strange twist of fate too, bro."

I looked up after reading the letter. "At last everything has been settled," I told him.

"What's that supposed to mean, bro?"

"Naibusi finally got her share of the money," I told him.

"Damn, that's a lot of money. Desimoni will be happy bro."

So what's the story about Kilroy?"

"Wilmot told us that he tried to lodge a counter-claim but the court threw it out once they realised that he was an illegal immigrant in the country. He has gone into hiding."

"Poor guy, I feel sorry for him."

"There is more to the story of Kilroy. You know that fast money scheme that he got us involved in," I nodded my head. "He conned us, bro. We lost everything. Uwegu paid him $700.00 and I gave him $500.00. I don't know how much Rawiri and the others paid him. We should have known better."

"I knew he was conning you guys."

"Why didn't you advise us, bro?"

"Because it was none of my business." I paused before speaking again. "What about Rawiri?"

"He left college some months ago and is working on an overseas vessel that sails around the world. He sent me a postcard from Hamburg and another one from London," Reimas said.

"Why did he leave his studies?"

"I think he failed because he was too much into the Internet chat site, bro."

"How is Uwegu getting on with her studies?" I asked.

"Oh, she is okay. I spied her last semester's results. She got mostly Bs and only one C and one D."

"Man, she is doing excellent."

"Except that she has changed into a lesbo, bro."

"Perhaps that's how she has been all along, except that she never came out about it," I said.

"She is finishing at the end of June next year. That means leaving me on my own if I go back," Reimas said.

"What do you mean, if you go back?"

"I will have to find money for my return ticket bro."

"I am sure your folks will assist you."

"Well Wilmot said for me to contact him if I didn't find money to buy my return ticket."

"Well, I suppose you deserve it because you are the person who helped him when he first arrived in your village."

Reimas paused and then said something quite funny.

"No, bro. I suppose it is the exotic thing again that makes Masta Koksi want to help me out with my return fare."

I laughed for a while before I replied. "This exotic thing is like a fish bait for the *dimdims*."

Chapter 27

A couple of weeks later after Reimas visited me I had a strange visit from two cops. They were not in uniform but their identification cards showed that they were members of Interpol. They were courteous and they started off the conversation by chatting about the current events. Then the senior one coughed a couple of times, perhaps clearing his throat for the main reason for their visiting me.

"Mr. Perez," he began. "We are here to talk to you about Dr. Wilmot Cox who we understand is a close friend of yours." I nodded my head in agreement. "How well do you know Dr. Cox?"

"I came to know Dr. Cox through another person, Ms. Kate Nolan," I replied. "God bless her soul, she has already left us," I said rather to myself. They nodded their heads. "She introduced Dr. Cox to me at her place while I was a student in Sydney. I know him only as an anthropologist who worked here for many years before returning to Sydney."

"We know you have spent time at his house, did you ever notice anything strange, out of character perhaps?" the second officer asked.

"All I know is that he has a lot of carvings and artifacts from here. His study is full of them. They have even accused his collection to be the cause of many unexplained paranormal occurrences. You know what I mean, don't you?" They did not respond. "I mean spirits haunting houses, trying to kill people and all that stuff."

"Yes of course," the senior officer uttered. He looked at his colleague before he started again. "Would you say he was fond of children especially young boys?" I didn't answer for a while and I could feel their eyes watching me closely.

"I have not seen him with kids, the times I visited him. He was always alone."

"What would you say about his sexual preference?"

"I really wouldn't know about that but there was one time when Kate asked him whether he was gay and he denied it," I answered at the same time debating whether to tell them about the sex tapes and the pictures I once saw at his place.

"We want you to tell us the truth about Dr. Cox. You are an intelligent man and you have a moral conscience."

"What is this all about?" I asked them.

The junior cop looked at his senior. "There is an international investigation about the sexual abuse of children both here and overseas. He is one of the main suspects. We already have evidence about him sexually abusing young boys while he was here in this country. Some of the kids he and his mates abused here have been traumatized badly. A number of them are mentally affected." He ceased talking for a while and looked at me. "Mr. Perez, before Ms. Nolan died police interviewed her and she had given them incriminating evidence against Dr. Cox." *Are they telling me the truth or are they trying to corner me*? I thought.

"I really don't know him personally. I only know him as a friendly chap who had worked in this country. Kate would be in a better position."

"Thanks Mr. Perez, if there is anything more you want to tell us, here is my card," said the senior cop at the same time handing his card to me. "You can call us anytime."

As soon as they left I closed my door and sat nervously thinking what this was all about. I wondered whether they had also interviewed Reimas and Uwegu. But why all of a sudden do they want to investigate something that happened many years ago? I was baffled. I thought about Reimas and wondered whether he was back in Sydney? I knew he was staying with Wilmot and he would be one of the first to be interviewed.

As I was coming out of the office I saw the head of the Anthropology School, and I went over to him. He would know Wilmot because he was one of the oldest teaching members of the School. He was lighting his pipe when I finally caught up with him.

"Hey, I heard your office was vandalised some weeks ago," he said to me.

"Yes, I was away from home when they broke into the office. Well there was nothing for them to steal anyway."

"You are lucky nothing was stolen from your office." He tried lighting his pipe again but he didn't succeed. "So you are back teaching with the same School, aye?" I nodded my head.

After a while I asked him about Wilmot. "Hey would you know Dr. Cox? He used to teach here before."

"Of course we taught together here before he left. What about him?"

"I had a visit from the police awhile ago. They are carrying out an investigation about him and others."

"What for?"

"They say he is one of the prime suspects in a paedophile ring," I told him.

"Oh my God! I know him as a good bloke with an unblemished academic record."

"Apparently the crime was committed both here and in Australia. Has there been any gossip about this when he was here?"

"Not that I know of. Other people might know something about it."

"Why did they come to you?"

"Because when I was in Sydney I used to frequent his place a lot," I told him. "Interpol is investing the case. I feel for him but what can I do. Anyway nice chatting with you, I better go."

"Take care and welcome back," he said once again trying to light his pipe.

I left him and went to the cafeteria to have lunch. There were many people around, students rushing in and out of lecture rooms. Others loitering around, chatting to friends. I walked past the forum area, and as I was about to enter the cafeteria someone called me. When I turned around I realised it was Tokwepota, Desimoni's father-in-law. I walked over to him and we shook hands. "What are you doing here?" I asked him.

"I came to visit my cousin who works at the Botanical Garden."

"Did you catch up with him?"

"Yes, he just left and I was heading to the bus stop when I saw you."

"Come and I'll buy you lunch."

We walked to the cafeteria and after I bought our lunch, we walked outside to the lawn and sat down. It wasn't that hot and the shade of the trees protected us from the sun. He spat out the betel nut in his mouth and began to eat. We did not talk for a while.

"Some policemen came to see me this morning," I told him half-way through our lunch.

"Are you in some trouble?" he asked me with a worried look on his face.

"Not really. They want to find out about Masta Koksi." He looked intently at me. "You know that *dimdim* anthropologist who worked here before?"

"Yes, I know him. What about him? Has he killed someone?"

"No, they say he slept with young boys here and in Australia."

"Yes, he used to invite a lot of young boys to his house when he was here. They often slept at his house."

"But do you know if he had sex with them or took photographs of them without their clothes on?"

"People talked about him sleeping with some of the kids but I don't know whether that was true. But there were very strong gossips about him sleeping with these young boys." He ate some more before he started again. "Two of these boys are now *longlong*, you know they want to do it with other men only. People say they got the sickness from the white men."

A car blew its horn disturbing us. I waved back.

"I only saw one incident," he said finally. "One evening when Masta Koksi came to do his fieldwork, I went to his house. There were young boys as usual playing around in the moonlight. I tiptoed up the ladder and walked into the house. It was quiet and no one was in. I stood there quietly until I heard a noise in one of the rooms. When I peeked in, I saw Masta Koksi with a young boy on the bed. The boy was naked and Masta Koksi was touching his private parts. I left the house disgusted but I never told anyone."

"Did you recognise the boy?"

"Yes, he is one of them who have the sickness. It's a terrible sickness; he will never marry. All he is interested in is sleeping with men and not women." I shook my head. "It's a *dimdims'* sickness but now it has affected our people."

"I hope he doesn't go to jail. He is a nice chap though," I said. "Didn't the police hear about this when he was here?"

"I don't know." He kept quiet before he spoke almost to himself. "How can a man sleep with young boys? If it is to do with young girls, I will understand."

"There are crazy people out there. They can do anything and they can defy God too!"

"Then they are not people but monsters. I also heard rumours about Naibusi's *dimdim* mother sleeping with girls and boys when she was teaching here before, "Tokwepota told me. "These *dimdims* are different from us, aye? I mean look how Pastor Nolan slept with their house girl. It must be in their blood."

Anyway I will let you go it's getting late," I told him. "If you see Desimoni and his wife, pass my greetings to them."

He stood up, dusted his shorts and after chewing *buai* he left for the bus stop. I thought about what he told me and wondered whether to believe him or not.

I went home straight away. There were no longer threatening phone calls and just as I thought it was over, I saw a note pushed under my door. I got it and opened the one-page note. It was not signed. It only read: *"We are monitoring you. If you say anything to the police we will get you. Shut your mouth and you will live. Don't call the police."* I threw the note down and my body started to shiver. I didn't know what to do. I wondered who could have left the note. The handwriting was strange, one that I have not come across. I wondered what this was all about. I knew people were watching me and if I made the slightest of mistakes, I would definitely die. I closed all the windows and locked all the doors and lay down on the bed. *Who could these people be? Were they part of the paedophile ring? Or was someone just trying to intimidate me?* I wanted to go and call Wilmot but then I hesitated. I was only relieved when my cousin came and took me out to his place.

"Are you okay? He asked me, as we stood ready to get on his car.

"Yes, I am good."

"But you don't look cheerful to me," he continued.

"Too much work, I suppose."

"I hope it's nothing to do with Deuba," he said.

"No that is past."

"I know something is bothering you," he persisted. "Anyway when you are ready you can tell me. Let's go to my place and have some nice home-cooked food."

"That would be nice," I said as I bucked the seat belt.

✳✳✳

The next day as soon as I got to the office the secretary came to my office and told me about a strange call that she received in the morning.

"Some *dimdim* guy called for you but you weren't in. He told me to tell you to pay attention to the note he pushed under your door." I looked at her puzzled. "Did you find any note?" she asked.

"Nope," I lied to her. "Was the voice really a *dimdim*'s voice?"

"Yes, he was a *dimdim* alright."

"Could be a local talking like a *dimdim* for all we know," I told her.

"No, this one was a *dimdim*," she insisted. "I hope you are not in some kind of trouble Perez. If anything, just call the police," she advised me.

When I entered my office another note was pushed under the door. It was the same note written obviously by the same person. I picked it up and push it in my drawer. I could not work the whole day and at lunchtime I went out and caught a bus to find a mate of mine who is a lawyer. When I got to his office he wasn't there. I waited for sometime before I left. As I arrived at the gate I saw him chewing *buai* and I went over to him. We shook hands and I asked him if he could shout me a few drinks.

"What's the matter? You are not the drinking type," he said to me.

"I just need a drink."

We talked some more and then we left for his watering hole, which was close by. He bought me a drink and we started chatting. "So how have you been?" he asked me.

"I am good. Work is okay," I replied.

"How about that woman you were going around with?"

"We broke up. Now I am on my own."

"You could have brought home a *dimdim* woman," he said laughing.

"What would she do here? They go for guys with fat wallets."

"Come on there are those who are genuine," he continued.

"But they are hard to find. Those that are easy to find are the ones that swing from branch to branch." He laughed and got us another round of drinks. The place was empty as it was a weekday and many of the patrons were at work.

"You know, there is a major investigation going on. There is a major paedophile ring and some of the people involved are in this country." My mouth was open and I did not say anything for a long while.

"Are they locals or *dimdims*?" I asked.

"They are mostly *dimdims* but we'll never know until the investigation has been completed.

"Are you involved in anyway?" I asked him.

"Yes, our law firm has been hired to provide legal advice."

"I was interviewed by the cops a couple of days ago. It was to do with Dr. Wilmot a friend of mine whom I met in Sydney. He used to work here as an anthropologist."

"Don't get yourself into this matter, it is very messy and dirty," he told me. "There are powerful people involved," he advised me. "I know Dr. Cox. He is one of the suspects."

"But why would people threaten me about all this?"

"Have you been threatened?" he asked surprised.

"I have received two notes threatening me not to say anything. One was pushed under my door at the lodge and the other was pushed under my office door. The note was written by the same guy. There was also a call made to the office and the secretary told me that it was a *dimdim* guy who called."

"That's strange. Listen you keep your mouth shut about it and don't tell anyone about it. But keep those threatening notes in a safe place. We'll get the bastard and I will make sure he is punished. Keep out of trouble though."

"But why me?"

"I think because you are a close friend to Dr. Cox who is one of the main suspects. They think you will provide information to the cops."

I emptied the glass and told him I was leaving.

"Do you want me to drop you off?" he asked me with a concerned look.

"I don't want them to see me with you. Let me get home alone."

In the evening a couple of days later I was outside my flat when I saw a car driving slowly up and down the street. I couldn't see the person driving because the car was tinted. I wondered what the car was looking for. I alerted the security guards and by the time they came, the car was nowhere to be seen. I became afraid and went inside. It was becoming unbearable for me. It was like falling into a trap that was already set before my arrival. I did not sleep for a long time. I was on the alert, getting up at every noise. It was becoming miserable. I thought about the notes and the story Tokwepota told me and I felt sorry for the guys. At the same time I also sympathized with Wilmot.

A week later I was unlocking the door to my office when the head of the Anthropology School called out to me. I waited for him.

"Here, read this," he handed the newspaper to me. It was *The Australian*. The front-page news was about the busted paedophile ring in PNG with three *dimdims* who so far had been caught. One of them was an ugly, potbellied *dimdim* who owned a workshop in town. He was also the patron of the Disabled Children's Foundation. Next to him was none other than Wilmot Cox. I didn't recognise the other person. I was shocked beyond belief. I wondered which of the three *dimdims* wrote the threatening note to me. I returned the newspaper to the owner.

"Now there is some relief," he told me.

"This is just the tip of the iceberg," I said. "There are many more to be arrested here. But how come the papers here have not covered it?"

"Maybe because this investigation is being handled from Australia," he told me.

"There is no mention of Wilmot," I said.

"This is just the start. Wait and you'll see the giants fall down one by one," he said and left.

I kept on thinking which one of the three *dimdims* wrote the threatening note to me. It could be a collaborative effort, a desperate tactic to save themselves. The next day their pictures and the news were all over the local papers. Apart from the three there were two locals who were also involved. When the news broke they were nowhere to be seen. I felt sorry for Dr. Wilmot Cox, but then again it was his fault. I was so relieved and happy and I went about my normal business with ease.

Chapter 28

Uwegu spoke to me with tenderness, a solicitude that gave me pause. I loathed its air of peace. But as she continued her story, there was something in her tone that suggested a deep wound or regret. She kept on talking about herself. This was another passage back to the origin. She was retracing the path that she treaded on the last time she was here, this time with new vigour and enthusiasm. Her telling of the story was like rebuilding a place from old scaffolding on an ancestral ground. Each story was built on the previous memory and as she told it, she was weaving it with the present.

We were sitting on a sand dune at the far end of the stretch of beach. The sea was calm only sporadically broken by a fringe of small waves that broke and lost themselves again. From the distance the rock formation that towered above us resembled a grumpy ogre striding over the crest of the small hill. There was something different about the story that she was telling me, something secret, almost enchanted and yet haunting, and full of deep wounds. It was as if nothing had ever been different, something that was so hidden that it could never be found. As I listened, I felt my eyes twitching as if I was going into a spasm or something.

✳✳✳

I was at the office when the phone rang. I didn't want to answer it at first, thinking it might be one of those strange, threatening phone calls. When I finally answered it, there was a brief pause, as if the person on the other end wanted to confirm whether it was actually me. Although the voice sounded familiar, I couldn't recognise it. It was only when she introduced herself that I started laughing and getting all excited at the same time. Indeed it was Uwegu. I was relieved.

"What are you doing here?" I asked her excitedly.

"I have completed my studies and I am back here."

"Oh, congratulations. I am happy for you," I told her. "Where are you now?"

"I am calling from a public phone downtown." Then I heard her talking to someone. "Sorry that's my little girl."

"Oh really? How is she?"

"She is good. She is having a day off today because mum has finally arrived."

I laughed. "Kids are like that," I told her.

After we had talked some more she asked, "are you busy today?"

"I don't have classes today."

"How about us meeting today. Come down here, we'll be at Ela Beach."

"Okay, wait for me there. I'll just ask a colleague and borrow his car and come down."

"Alright, I'll be here then."

I couldn't handle myself well after Uwegu called. I was excited. It has been a long time since I had last seen her and I wanted to meet her and catch up on all the news. I rang my colleague to ask if I could use his car and he said it was fine by him. He knew this was the first time I had asked for his car and he wondered what I was up to. I told him a few lies and off I went to meet with Uwegu.

I couldn't contain myself as I drove towards Ela Beach. I wondered how our meeting would be, whether Uwegu had changed much and all that. The road was not busy at this time of the day and I managed to get there quickly. As I approached the beachfront I began to drive slowly as I embarked on my search for her. A car behind me blasted its horn and I had to drive faster. I started looking for her amongst the many people who were having lunch or just loitering around. Finally I located her and her girl at the far end of the beachfront where it was quiet and not many people were there. She was also looking out for me.

As soon as she saw me, she ran towards me leaving her daughter behind with another woman, perhaps her sister or aunt. I parked the car, got out and soon we were embracing each other and laughing at ourselves.

"Man you look different," I told her.

"What do you mean?" she said at the same time checking herself.

"You have become more beautiful."

"Oh, I am flattered," she said.

"You also look different. You have a more scholarly look," she told me. "Come let us go and you can meet my daughter."

Then we walked slowly back toward her daughter and the other woman. She introduced me to them. Her daughter was indeed pretty and her smile was captivating. She was little shy but her mother urged her to shake my hand and greet me. I could see she was wearing one of those shorts and T-shirts her mother had gotten from Sydney.

"That's my cousin," Uwegu introduced the other woman to me.

After a while Uwegu walked with me to the kiosk. After I bought lunch we all went back to where her daughter and the cousin were. I gave them their lunch while Uwegu and I had ours.

"My daughter is going with my cousin to the shop and from there they'll go home," Uwegu told me after a while.

"I can drop them off," I offered.

"It's alright. They'll catch a bus."

Not long after, Uwegu's daughter and her cousin left and we were alone again.

"Come, let's go to that end of the beach," Uwegu suggested. I got up and we walked over to the other side and sat on the sand dune. She was still eating her lunch, and now and again I glanced at her. I wondered whether she knew about Wilmot's arrest.

"Many things happened after you left us Perez," Uwegu began.

"You mean back in Sydney?"

"Yes."

"Tell me," I urged her. "What happened to Reimas?"

"That is a sad story. He tried to rape me. He was drunk and came home one evening while I was having a nap on the lounge, and he just came on top of me and started kissing me."

"You're joking," I said in alarm.

"I am not. I didn't feel him at first. He kissed me and I thought it was Suniya playing with me and then he was sucking on my breast when I finally opened my eyes and pushed him away. I wanted to call the cops on him but then again I felt sorry for him. He was drunk. When I asked him the next day he said he didn't know a thing."

"He could have been drunk too," I said.

"At least he should have asked me if he wanted a relationship with me."

"Would you have agreed?"

"Not necessarily, but I would have given it a good long thought."

"Where is he now?" I asked.

"Apparently, he moved out to stay with his *dimdim* mates just after you left. Last time I heard he was staying with that paedophile."

"What paedophile?" I asked very curiously.

"Well, not exactly a paedophile. It's that Wilmot guy; there are rumours that police have found incriminating evidence about Wilmot's sexual activities with young boys."

"Carry on," I told her becoming interested in the story. I didn't tell her that I had been interviewed by the police.

"Rumour has it that in the past he was involved in sleeping with children. Apparently one of the neighbours found a photograph of naked boys in the rubbish bin and reported him to the police. That's when they raided his home and found other things."

"Gees, so what's gonna happen next?" I asked her. I didn't tell her that he had already been arrested.

"I don't know but this happened some 30 years ago both in PNG and here."

"Poor man," was all I could say. I didn't tell her that I also saw some photographs at his house.

"I pity him; he is a nice old man," Uwegu said.

"A nice old fella with a terrible past. You know Desimoni's in-laws mentioned something about young boys staying with him when he was in PNG."

"Really? So he had preyed on our boys back home too aye? He is a dog then," Uwegu said in a surprised tone.

"Funny how we had befriended *dimdims* with crooked pasts. I mean, Mrs. Powell or Kate was sleeping with my sister and others, and now Wilmot had been exposed. We too have crooked eyes because we never scrutinised these *dimdims* except to fall into their charms and traps."

"I hope he can prove himself innocent. Funny you can't tell about these people. I mean you can tell about someone with a disease but not someone who is a paedophile."

"*Tru ya*. God shouldn't have created them in the first place," Uwegu replied.

"What about Kilroy?" I asked her.

"Poor guy. I felt sorry when I heard that he was the one who had a child with Kate. You see how these *dimdims* made him to be a pendulum. It was their doing that made him end up not settling down in Sydney. They should have left them alone, I mean him and Kate." Uwegu paused to drink her juice before she started again. "I wonder if Kate knew that Kilroy was in Sydney at the same time as she was. Or if Kilroy knew the same."

"That is a good question," I said. "But even though the *dimdims* may have made him to be like a yoyo, he was able to come on top of it. Would you know what happened to him?"

"You may have heard that the court threw out his claim because of his residency status. We have never heard from him again after that," Uwegu said.

"Don't worry he is a survivor, that fella."

"I know," Uwegu said. "He will surface again soon."

"Which lawyer did the case for him?"

"One *dimdim* lawyer."

"Had Kilroy won his case, that lawyer would have cut him down by one third," I said.

"Greedy pigs!" said Uwegu. "Anyway, Reimas might have told you that Kilroy conned us and we lost our money."

"Yes, he did mention it to me."

"Aah, you remember Carlos?" she asked laughing.

"You mean Rawiri?"

"Yes, that guy. He is a sailor working on one of those huge ships that sail all over the world."

"Damn, now he is gonna see those places I always wanted to go and see." I stopped for short time. "How did he find the job?"

"In the Internet," Uwegu told me.

"Blooming hell!" I said laughing.

Then Uwegu looked straight into my eyes and asked. "What about you? How have you been?"

"I guess I am good," I replied. "I am gradually settling in."

"You don't look like it," she insisted.

"I am trying to," I said.

"And what about you? Are you happy coming back here?"

She didn't answer me for a while. She sat there scooping sand with her hand and slowly pouring it out as her eyes surveyed the sea. Perhaps she was thinking about what she wants to tell me. Then she slowly stopped scooping up the sand and turned to me.

"I don't really know. I feel like a stranger here. Although I am physically here, my mind is elsewhere. To be honest with you, I feel insecure here."

"Why? When you were in Sydney you were always feeling homesick and dislocated."

"I know. Perhaps my feelings have changed. I dread coming back home. I don't know what awaits me here."

"There must be something that prevents you from feeling at home again," I said.

"Maybe, Sydney was more secure despite some of the unfriendly *dimdims*." She looked straight at me. "How did you find the place when you first returned?"

"I couldn't handle the change but gradually I told myself that whether I like it or not I have to make myself at home."

"I guess because you don't have an unpleasant past here."

"What do you mean?"

"When you go to a place where your life was crooked, wasn't normal, you won't like going again to that place. That's how it is with me here."

"Am I missing out on something here?"

"It's a long story Perez. I have never told anyone about it. I have always kept it to myself."

"If you don't mind, I want to hear it."

"Promise you will keep the story to yourself." "I promise."

"My father died in a plane crash when I was about 2 years old. I had a twin sister and another sister. When Dad died, my twin sister and young sister were adopted by an aunt. Then my mother remarried. My natural father is from another place that is why I look different from my siblings. When I was growing up I used to watch my stepfather abuse my mother. I don't know why my stepfather did that but it continued until he started to abuse me as well. He would punish me for little things. He would belt me and all that. My mother was very quiet about the abuse; that was why no one knew outside the family. If he saw me chatting with a boy he would belt me after I came home."

She stopped for a short while before she began again. "It was only me and mother that he abused. He didn't do this to his real kids."

"That's terrible. I guess you have never shared your story with anyone; that is why it still hurts."

"No, I have never. It's too painful to share with anyone. Anyway, one day when I was at secondary school I came home to an empty house. My mother and my other siblings ran away because my father had belted her. I stayed home because it was night and I had school the next day. I was sleeping when he came home drunk. Then he came to where I was and abused me." Uwegu stopped abruptly and cried. "I can't go on."

"It's alright," I tried to comfort her.

"Sorry Perez. You see why my coming home is painful. I only came home because of my daughter."

"But he won't do that you know, you are a big girl and you are educated," I tried to reassure her.

"But my past haunts me. I can't get it out of me. It's like a stain that you can't get rid of no matter how much you try. This awful past has driven me to do crazy things both here and in Sydney. You know I told you about Mrs. Powell. Well she used to sexually abuse my twin sister at Uni and I caught them on a number of occasions. That was why I developed a very strong hatred of her and it was me who reported her to the authorities and her contract was not renewed. I also cursed her and she was involved in a car accident."

"I bet he was just trying to take out his frustrations because someone had cheated him."

"There are other ways to do that, don't you think?"

"I suppose so," I said. "But I don't think he will do it again."

"Because he is no longer with us. He is dead."

"Try and get over it then," I said.

"How could I? That is why my daughter's father walked out on me because most of the time I kept to myself, I shut myself to him."

"Oh, I am sorry."

"It has affected me deeply Perez. Sometimes I want to kill myself. But later I told myself, that was too cheap. Now I know how the kids from abusive families feel. I guess this is what drove me to do those stupid things in Sydney. I was trying to find my bearings and my way out of a painful past."

"The more you talk about it with people you trust, the better you will feel. Talking is a therapy you know," I tried to advise her.

"I trust you, that was why I told you about it Perez," Uwegu told me quietly. "I see you as my confidante."

"I suggest that you go and see a professional counselor."

"Are there any here in PNG?"

"I think so," I said.

"I'd rather see a *dimdim* counselor than a local," she told me.

"Why?"

"*Dimdims* distinguish between what is confidential and what is not," was all she said.

"I see what you are trying to get at."

"It's difficult isn't it?" she said. "I mean it will never go away, it's like a scar left by a wound."

"If you try harder to forget, a new skin can gradually grow over the scar."

She sat there but didn't say anything more. Perhaps she was trying to make sense of what I just said. It was me who disturbed the short silence.

"Did you know it was her when you first saw her in Sydney?"

"You mean that *dimdim* woman, Kate?"

I nodded my head. "The face was familiar but you were calling her a different name. But somehow I knew it was her." She kept quiet for a while. "I suppose she knew it was me too. She did try to destroy me but I had my things too. When I found the bottle buried beside my room I knew it was her who did it."

"What are you planning to do now?" I asked her.

"I saw my former boss this morning and he asked me to go and see him next week."

"Now that you have your paper in Business and Accountancy you wouldn't have a problem getting a job anywhere," I reassured her.

"You reckon?"

"Hey, you have very good prospects here."

"I hope I won't be running into one of those males with crooked eyes again here."

"Oh, there are many of them around. You only have to play your cards right," I told her.

She kept quiet as she scooped a handful of sand and poured it out again. I stared at the rock formation, which looked like an ogre behind us and wondered about it. It looked as if it was protecting us from some enemies. Then I wondered what was on Uwegu's mind until she disturbed me from my thoughts.

"I hope I can also find a guy who will be understanding."

"What about the guy you told me about; the one your folks arranged?"

"He impregnated another woman so we broke up."

"You must also be willing to open up and be accommodating to him."

"I have been thinking a lot about it lately."

"Don't worry, things will be good for you."

She looked up at me. "Do you think so?"

"I believe so."

She smiled and held my hand. "I will always count on you, Perez."

"Trust me, Uwegu."

"I do," she said letting go my hand. "I hope you won't go somewhere again soon."

"I don't know but we are always traveling. Even when you are physically at the same place, your mind and spirit travel all the time." She laughed.

"You never really got to tell me about Deuba. What happened?"

"It didn't work out for both of us."

"But she is here. Did you try to contact her when you got back?"

"She did try but I have not yet responded." I did not tell her that I had received threatening phone calls from a man claiming to be her husband.

"Well, maybe you should."

"Thanks, I'll think about it," I replied. There was a prolonged silence as we watched the waves breaking softly onto the sand. The beach was almost deserted.

"I hope Desi had made up his mind to settle down," she said quietly. I looked at her not knowing how to respond.

"You were actually intimate friends at school weren't you?" She nodded her head.

"That was a long time ago now. We weren't intimate for that long though. Now we have grown out of it," she concluded with a cute smile.

We talked some more before I told her that it was getting late and that we should leave.

"Look how beautiful the sea is today," Uwegu said getting up.

"It was a witness to our meeting here today," I said smiling.

"You are always creative, Perez."

"It helps soothe the pains."

"Thank you Perez. At least I got to talk with you today. I feel much better now."

It was almost four when we walked back along the stretch of beach and got into the car. A number of people were sitting around the beach while some kids were swimming in the sea.

I slowly drove away following the back road, which was not busy. Uwegu was silent for a long while until I broke the silence again.

"How is your girlfriend Suniya?"

"She also left. We completed our studies at the same time."

"That's good."

"Have you come across Desimoni and his wife at all?"

"Not after Naibusi got her share of the money from Kate's lawyers."

"I hope they do something good with it."

"Let's hope so. They must have returned to the village. I have not bumped into them here lately."

"What did you think of her?" Uwegu asked me about Naibusi.

"She looks a bit like Kate and she is humble and friendly."

"She is a good girl. I know Desimoni won't have any problems with her."

"Reimas was here for sometime too," I told her.

"His uncle died and he came over. Wilmot paid for his return airfare to Sydney," Uwegu told me. "When you left, Wilmot came frequently and took us out once he realised who Reimas was. Then when Reimas got back from PNG, he began to frequent Wilmot's place."

"Did he see you off when you were coming?"

"He came to say goodbye the day before I left."

"Then he didn't mean what he tried to do to you then."

"I hope not," Uwegu told me.

"Hey, where do I drop you?" I asked her as we came to the junction.

"Just drop me off at the market. I need to buy some greens."

I smiled as I came to a stop.

"What's that supposed to mean?" she asked.

"Well, it's back to the local diet again," I said.

"Tru ya."

"Alright, check me out anytime if you need help or just for a chat."

"I will. Thanks," she said waving.

As I drove back to the varsity, I thought about what Uwegu had told me and I wondered what the future held for all of us, Reimas, Desimoni, Uwegu, Kilroy, Rawiri and myself. We were like actors in a movie, acting both our lives and other people's lives. Although some of the audiences would dismiss us as acting out a fantasy, there would be many more who would take us for granted. Life is a journey through both charted and uncharted passages. And we are all travelers on a journey through these passages. Along the way we encounter other people on other journeys. In the end what is different is that some of us travelers will reach our destinations, while others will perish along the way because of their crooked eyes.